Doves and silk h

DOVES AND
SILK HANDKERCHIEFS

G. H. Morris

Constable · London

To my father

First published in Great Britain 1987
by Constable and Company Limited
10 Orange Street London WC2H 7EG
Copyright © 1987 by G. H. Morris
Set in Linotron Palatino 10 pt by
Rowland Phototypesetting Limited
Bury St Edmunds, Suffolk
Printed in Great Britain by
St Edmundsbury Press Limited
Bury St Edmunds, Suffolk

British Library CIP data

Morris, G.H.
  Doves and silk handkerchiefs.
  I. Title
  823'.914[F]   PR6063.0748/

  ISBN 0 09 467940 1

My great-great-grandmother, Jane Brightside, and her first encounters with flying man

My great-great-grandmother, who had been born on the day of the battle of Waterloo, slowly climbed the slope of Hunger Hill. A body of immense durability; climbing the contour of the hill the old woman assumed the powerful posture of a quadruped. A slow engine, she lugged a string of invisible coal tubs, mooching through the incline. Despite the years of pulling below ground her frame had never naturally succumbed to tortuous perversion, but now on Hunger Hill geometry fixed her, bent into the dark and angular landscape. Gravity plotted her journey along the well worn path. She gazed beyond into the yawning sky where touches of salmon flashed from the east. Below and behind her the few terraced houses stood awake and small in the near dawn, and below them the telltale squeak of the winding machine cycled in the new century and still below that, imperceptible to all but those who have spent a lifetime hearing it, came the tap-tappings from those who hewed the coal.

It was nigh on sixty years since she had been down a pit. Sixty years since John Brightside, by the eerie gloom of his candle, had first seen her ample buttocks running the tubs and sworn there and then that she should be his wife. Sixty years since his mate had teased the young John unmercifully. 'She'll be too much for thee, young lad,' he grinned. 'Suck thee in, boots and all.' But young John had been struck with a passion for the older woman which none could comprehend and which only the marriage bed might fulfil. And so it did. Every night for thirty years his passion for Jane Brightside was fulfilled. And each day for nearly thirty years the passion was sustained by the image of Jane's buttocks under her grubby skirts running the tubs. 'She's ugly as the devil hisself,' his brothers had taunted, but it made little difference, for the engine of the fever which drove him came not from her face but from that part of her anatomy which lay hidden and wrapped in grimy sackcloth. 'She's an arse on her like an 'oss,' they then offered when they learned of the true centre of his passion; but John only smiled a knowing smile and from that night forbade the woman destined to be his wife ever to descend the pit again – never to bend her magnificent buttocks towards another man.

'Nivver, nivver, nivver,' snorted the youthful Brightside as he nestled between the woman's thighs and where he remained for nigh on thirty years until the day the roof fell and the pit prop split open his head like a ripe coconut. And for the sixty years, since the day of her marriage, during John's lifetime and since, Jane had, each dawn, collected plant material for her medicines and potions. Within easy reach of the village, on the hills, in the hedgerows and by the river bank, she was able to find biting stonecrop and woodvine, deadtongue and monkshood, always filling her basket with a colourful selection of flowers, leaves and roots. In the churchyard from among the gravestones, she could even find deadly nightshade with its purple bells, an extract of which she sold to the apothecaries in Leeds and Wakefield. She would collect sun-spurge for warts (the juice of which is said by Dr Livingstone to kill zebras) and buckthorn as a purgative, yarrow for nosebleeds and inflammation, and out of which she made a beer, which tasted most foul but was so strong in alcohol content that even the hard drinkers were rendered insensible by no more than a pint or two.

Now approaching the stone wall which encircled the summit of Hunger Hill, like a crown on the brow of a proud medieval king she could see the yellow blaze of stonecrop which grew from the gaps in the stone. It was said that the Romans had built the original wall but succeeding generations had refurbished and replaced it until now the dry sandstone wall with its outpourings of golden moss and yellow stars told only of all too few days of the present summer. She looked again to the east where the sun now rising shone through a coal dust haze casting blood-red shadows on the rock. The crevices, out of which grew the worm-killing plant, were intensely dark and secretive, hiding green stems which trailed from the narrow cold into sunlight. 'Birds bread,' her father had called it, but she had never once seen a bird of any description feed upon it. She could see now, as she prised specimens from the cracks in the stone, the sun rising above the river below. Down at Bottom Boat the red ball was kicked about

6

above the gently waving poplars which lined the banks. Jane let her eyes scan the sky around and upwards; she was looking for men. Flying men. Or machines perhaps. Flying machines. Ever since that morning during the summer of last year she had been searching the skies for flying men. She had been in Kettle Flat, a hollow piece of scrubby land, perhaps a crater sometime formed by a small meteorite, when out of the sky again fell an object. It fell right out of the sun along with the sparrows, the thrushes and the sedge warblers. It was then that she had met Duncan D'Arcy and Lady Annabelle Kerr; they too had tumbled drunk and downside up, together with the object, from the sky. Each clutched a bottle of champagne and they both fizzed and giggled. 'What is this place?' he'd asked. 'Ardsley,' she replied, stupefied by the glamorous finery – he in silk, she in chiffon and lace. 'Where you come from?' Jane finally had the courage to ask. 'Alexandra Palace, dear,' he'd replied. 'Air race you know.' Jane blinked uncomprehendingly. 'Never seen one of these before?' he enquired. 'No, don't suppose you have,' he answered himself, swigging from the bottle. 'Mark my words, madam, one day soon flying machines will fill the air.' His silk waistcoat glistened in a golden sun so that she had to shield her eyes from the explosive sheen. 'Common as the railway engine soon – you'll see,' he said and he offered his bottle of champagne. She gulped and spluttered her first and only ever swig of the fruity drink. The bubbles went up her nose, causing her to sneeze. She handed the bottle back after wiping the neck with a coarse dirty hand. He didn't seem to mind but went on, 'Perhaps you could direct us to a hostelry. We can have the airship collected later.' Jane looked at the broken basket and heap of crumpled material which billowed over the undulating ground. This she presumed to be the thing which the man referred to as an airship. Then, remembering her manners she offered a curtsey and withdrew a bottle of yarrow beer from among the blossoms in her basket. Duncan accepted her gift and much to her amazement drank almost the lot down without pausing for breath. 'Sorry Annie,' he said guiltily to his companion when he finally passed it. 'Saved you a little.' And he offered the lady the last drops of Jane's beer. The lady gulped the beer, belched and then all three laughed heartily. Since that day Jane's world had not been the same.

Literally, the world had changed. If machines could fly, then which was up and where was down. The sky sometimes appeared to be upside down. How strange, she thought. One could float all the way from Castleford to Leeds in a contraption. Travel in a medium without obstacles. What freedom, she rejoiced. Did it matter which way up the sky was if there were no obstacles? She scanned the expansive, now fully awake and very blue sky, again, looking for men, one way up or another.

Although we called it a village the few streets which constituted our settlement and housed our small community was by definition a hamlet. There was no church but we had an alehouse. It was, at the turn of the century, like any other of a hundred or so similar communities scattered like stardust across the West Yorkshire coalfield. The family house built from heavy grey stone sat in the middle of a terrace of identical dwellings, sombre even rough but never brooding. The house was too small to overpower a man. Men and women then were masters of the piles of stick and stone which made a home. People poured out of the matchwood doors, growing organically from the buildings. The terrace was ours, people exuded from the brick like the yellow starry stonecrop creeping from the Roman wall on Hunger Hill. Jane's son, James Brightside, and my paternal great-grandfather had been the first to live in the house. The coal owner who sank the shaft and built the houses for the colliers to live in, stood in the rain and said to him and his new wife 'Tha' rent's three shillin' a week. Choose an 'ouse; there's nowt between 'em. One's same as t'other. But tha' can choose. They're mostly empty yonder.'

So James Brightside, with his new wife, Aggie, chose the one with the fewest and the shallowest puddles outside the front door and settled into the dark inside to watch the bouncing rain. But soon the house began to fill, first with children, then with his mother after the death of John Brightside, then with lodgers as many as seven or eight at a time. The downstairs parlour and the upstairs two bedrooms began to creak with the weight of colliers black and grimy, but each a five-pointed star like the stonecrop flowers in the wall. Eventually into the house too, came the grandchildren, among them my father but more of them later. Suffice it to say that the smoky terrace and its occupants was like a train load of bright-eyed Indians hauled across continents and so

8

excited they were too at the prospect of their cramped and chattering journey.

Returning from her walk on Hunger Hill, great-great-grandmother entered the parlour through the door which led directly from the street. The uneven hollows in which the puddles had formed when James Brightside came to the house were long gone, replaced by a grassed lawn on which the youngsters played cricket (aspiring to be a Rhodes or Lord Hawke), a game peculiar in that the eleven was made up by dogs who fielded at the boundaries. Her granddaughter, my father's aunt Henrietta, stoked a roaring fire. Summer it was, but in the collier's home the boiling of water to wash the dirt from the menfolk was as constant as the sun in the heavens. All down the terrace, water was boiling atop the roaring coal fires. That selfsame coal which they had hewed perhaps a week before was now heating the water to bathe the soot from their bodies and the ache from their limbs, preparing them for another day on which they could limp to the pit. It was a constant passage of energy from the coal to the water to the collier to the pick and back to the coal. In most homes the colliers would bathe once or at most twice a week, the rest of the week a sort of strip wash would suffice, but in our house Jane's command was law. 'The mucky beggars get a full tin bath after each shift – medicated too,' she instructed all. And out would come the potions and the lotions, left on the mantelshelf, above the roaring fire for the men to administer to their tubsful of steaming water, while the women disappeared to the Lord knows where. It was a matter of endless debate amongst the men as to where on earth the women got to when they were left at home to bathe. The earth closets, the alehouse, a walk to the church in the next village, but no one knew for sure. They just disappeared and then quite magically reappeared as the last man was belting the trousers into which he'd just climbed, hair still wet and uncombed, but clean and smelling sweetly as the flowers in great-great-grandmother's basket.

At this time, at the turn of the century, our house breathed a little more easily as the population within contracted. As well as great-great-grandmother it had housed my grandfather, Ernest – it was his name that was scrawled into the blue rent book which stood upright upon the mantelshelf behind a ticking clock; his wife, Emily and his youngest sister, the Henrietta to whom I have

9

already referred. Then there was my father, now aged six, and his twin brothers, Albert and Lancaster, who were his juniors by a couple of years. The three children slept together with their parents in the larger bedroom while Henrietta and her grandmother slept next to them in the smaller room. Two lodgers, Mr Pettit and Mr Junkin, slept in wide winged chairs flying in the night-time parlour below, but always out of their cockpits and off to the colliery before the rest of the occupants had stirred and leaving behind them for the children to ponder the curious smell of sleep absorbed into the fabric of their makeshift beds.

Henrietta stoked the fire holding the long metal poker at such a distance from the heat to enrich only her air of absent-mindedness. The reality of her situation, twenty-two and un-married, ensured a vacancy filled inwardly with dreams of men. But not only that; there was something more. Henrietta was a poet, locked in like a bookworm, tight between pages she ate her own silence. Her grandmother startled her as she came in.

'Where's the children?' she asked.

'Playing cricket on the common,' Henrietta answered. 'Didn't you see them as you came in?'

'No.'

'They're out there somewhere,' she shrugged and turned her attention again to the boiling of water.

'Mr Pettit and Mr Junkin will be home soon, luv,' she heard her grandmother saying.

'I know, grandmother,' she said irritably. 'I can't hurry the water. It'll boil when it wants to.'

The old woman ignoring Henrietta's irritation asked, 'Did you see the stones today?'

At first she didn't answer, then she said, looking into the fire, 'Yes, I watched them awhile.'

The old woman waited for more, then, when it was apparent that nothing more would be added she spoke again, looking to the pen and ink which sat upon the mantelshelf above her granddaughter's stooped and long back.

'Did you write?'

'No, not yet.'

In the silence that followed Jane went into the back scullery, a tiny room beyond the parlour, where she stored her flowers and concocted her potions. She quietly unloaded her basket, twining stalks and hanging bundles from the low ceiling to dry. Some roots she placed directly into bottles and storage jars, replacing them carefully in their correct place among the tiers of shelving. She waited patiently for her granddaughter to talk, when she did Henrietta said, 'The river's in flood. The stones are covered again. I saw two small fishes playing hide among them. They were stickleback I think.' The old woman allowed the flesh about her face to creep into a smile while her eyes remained fixed on the task she was performing. 'Then you'll have much to write about,' she said at last with satisfaction.

'Yes, I suppose,' Henrietta answered poking absent-mindedly at the coals. She was preparing a journal, a kind of natural history of a group of stones down by Bottom Boat. She had for three years now been writing this history of the stones. Noting the imperceptible changes. The weathering of rock. The growth of lichen. An evolution Mr Darwin might have called it. Many would have chided her for even thinking of that name, but the idea of imperceptible change appealed to her. Not much to note in a lifetime perhaps, but just sufficient to make it all worthwhile. Nothing to disturb the living but enough to surprise the long, long dead. Her thoughts were broken by a tapping coming from the fire just above the glowing coals. The noise familiar to both women but more so to Jane because of her great advantage in years brought the latter quickly back into the parlour.

'It's Mrs Gill,' she said. 'Pass it on girl,' and immediately Henrietta went to the opposite wall and started to tap on it with the still hot poker. The tapping had been a signal from their nextdoor neighbour Mrs Gill to make them aware that a stranger had entered the village. She in turn would have heard it from the Hendersons and so it was that news travelled in the terrace, by way of Yorkshire range and interconnecting walls.

The two women together with all others who had received the warning draped their heads in black shawls and hurried to the front of the house. A chorus of curious, sometimes frightened women greeted the stranger as he walked to the common, herding unsure children before him. He was very tall and thin, wearing a faded frock coat and tight trousers which rode up at the ankles. On his head adding fearful height he wore a battered stove-pipe hat. His long white beard gave him a patriarchal look, although Henrietta was sure that he was a man of fewer years

11

than the beard might suggest, certainly no more than forty she guessed. To her grandmother, however, the stranger looked like an etching she had once seen of Noah. In each hand he gripped a large suitcase, the weight of which sagged his shoulders, seemingly lengthening his already long arms. The spring in the stride of his spidery legs confirmed to Henrietta that she had been correct. This was no Noah, here indeed was a young and handsome stranger. Disguised maybe, but definitely Adonis. The man bounced along, knees well ahead of shoulders held back by oppressive weights. Arms in their turn lagged some way behind the shoulders as they dragged the cases along. Staring at the line of waiting women, he made directly for Jane whose face probably offered the best of a welcome among a score of black looks.

'Robber,' he said from amid shining white teeth.

'Cell. Robber?' He seemed to ask.

'There's no jail here, luv,' Jane replied helpfully.

'Shail?' he repeated searching the sky for meaning and finding an answer in that place which somehow links our brains to a vast beyond. 'No. Robber goods.' He made the last word rhyme with moods.

'I think he's a salesman,' Henrietta advised her grandmother.

'Yes,' said the stranger, catching her words and raising a bony finger to point at my great-aunt. 'Sell. Robber.'

'You'd better come in,' Jane said moving aside, at which a great intake of breath could be heard from among the chorus.

'Witch,' they said. Only a witch, or something worse could speak to and befriend strangers in such a way.

Once inside the parlour the man deposited his cases on the pegged carpet, which the women were constantly making and replacing from old rags, and immediately flailed his arms windmill fashion.

'Leeds. Strong,'he said indicating that he had walked at least ten miles, and flexing his arms at the elbows.

'Robber?' He nodded to Jane.

'What is this robber, luv?' she asked, as if speaking to a child.

'What is?' asked the man and immediately went down on one long knee to open a case from which seemed to coil dozens of black snakes. Both women gave short piercing screams, which brought faces to the window and open door. The neighbours saw only an open case out of which had poured a few pneumatic bicycle tyres, the last of which was still cycling unaided about the parlour. The remainder languished against the various bits of furniture where they had come to rest. The stranger handed a card to Henrietta. A neat hand had written in ink an explanation for the stranger's visit. She read aloud, in a weak voice.

'My name is Elyahou. I am from Transylvania. I wish to sell you rubber goods. I have bands, stamps, mackintoshes, golf balls and cycle tyres. False limbs and doormats are my speciality. Also pneumatic playsuits for the children, these may be hired for one penny each per day. Ideal for birthday parties and other celebrations.'

Elyahou grinned, recognizing the concluding words.

'You wan'?' he enquired.

Henrietta shook her head, withdrawing from the man's thrusting face. 'Mackintosh?' said the man pulling a dirty grey waterproof from the case. She shook her head again. Anxious faces were pressed up to the door. Could these hussies succumb and hand over money to a stranger?

'What was that about stamps?' Jane asked her granddaughter.

'Stamps, yes,' said the man still on one knee and already rummaging in the second case. 'You wan'?' he asked with a trader's desperation and now banging a large rubber stamp soaked in ink onto clean paper held to the ruffling pegged carpet.

The two women and everyone outside too strained forward, trying to read what had appeared by magic on the virgin paper.

ELYAHOU TSIBLITZ
RUBBER GOODS
SHIPS YARD, LEEDS

The man looked round at all the black shawled heads.

'Elyahou Tsiblitz, robber goods,' he shouted from the floor, and reading from the paper, stressing again the double 'o' sound and grinning widely.

'Can I have one of those with my own words on't?' Jane asked.

Elyahou shrugged, not understanding.

'Write,' she instructed her granddaughter. Henrietta took her pen with the ink bottle from the mantelshelf, tugged the paper from the man's hand and seated herself at the table, pen poised.

13

'Henrietta Brightside,' the old woman dictated. Henrietta unsure, at first, eventually wrote in large, neat, capital letters, looking eagerly to her grandmother for the next line. 'Child of charm, poetry and love,' she continued, a small grin playing at her mouth. Then seeing Henrietta's reticence she added, 'C'mon, girl. Get it writ. This is my present to thee. So tha'll do as tha's telled.' Henrietta wrote obligingly, handing the paper to her grandmother after blotting it carefully.

'How much?' Jane asked, thrusting the paper back at Elyahou.

'Two pennies,' he said, understanding the universality of the old woman's request.

'There now,' she said poking her hand deep into her pinafore and producing two bright new pennies. 'You bring that to me next time you pass, and don't be long mind.' Elyahou nodded brightly. The chorus outside winced, as the shiny pennies were passed across from one hand to the other, and just as three breathless children pushed their way through the door. No, not more, the neighbours seemed to be daring them. Not now. Not in front of the children.

'You wan' suit?' Elyahou asked delving deeper within the second case. 'Here, for childs,' he added pulling out the pneumatic suits which on his card had been advocated for birthdays. My father and the twins were struck dumb as he pulled himself up to his full height, almost touching the ceiling, and his agile arms quickly dressed each child in a suit of smelly rubber. When finally all three stood before the whole mournful female content of the terrace, bedecked in their suits, which seemed to hang in tatters from their thin bodies, the stranger clapped his hands once like a prestidigitator would do before performing a wondrous piece of magic. 'Hi!' he shouted, and pulled a valve on Albert's suit. The inrushing air caused him to be transformed into a round ballooning chicken. 'Hi!' shouted the man again and hey presto, my father became an overfed sheep and with a final monosyllabic ejaculation and a great inrush of air Lancaster floated to the roof bedecked in the costume of a bee. The wondrous cries of 'Oh!' from his audience ensured once and for all that Elyahou would have a market, albeit a small one, in our village. Within moments he had sold out of pneumatic tyres and doormats. Even a false arm had been sold to Mrs Henderson but the Lord knows why. Mr Junkin returned home amidst the commotion to pur-

14

chase a new set of rubber teeth, and Elyahou himself freely admitted that he had never sold so much knicker elastic in a single session (albeit said in a strange tongue which none present could understand). Over a thousand yards of it had gone to the women of the terrace. Mr Pettit who had a way with numbers and who knew about such things worked out that if put together it would have wound four times round the whole terrace and when stretched at least six times. 'Some knickers,' my grandfather was heard to say, raising his brows when told of it.

Amidst those bizarre and joyous moments my father and his brother Albert danced and sang in their inflatable costumes and above it all Lancaster buzzed tearfully about the room. Great-great-grandmother, who was for ever, at that time, searching the sky for flying men, never would have dreamed even in her wildest fantasies that the first person she should see actually in flight would have been her great-grandson, Lancaster.

The *History of the Stones* and how my great-aunt Henrietta came to lose her virginity

It was more than a year before Elyahou Tsiblitz visited our village again. The neighbours had long scoffed that great-great-grandmother had seen the last of her twopence and even she, a most ardent believer in man's inherent goodness, was beginning to think that she had been cheated and that Henrietta's present would never arrive. So it was, with a mixture of anger and relief, that she greeted the news of the stranger's second coming. A minute before Mrs Gill had put her poker to use at the Yorkshire range my father and his twin brothers had rushed breathless into the house to inform those present that the rubber man (for so they had dubbed him) had entered the village. This gave both Henrietta and her grandmother valuable seconds in which to prepare their respective faces. The former, beneath her shawled head, assumed the disinterested gaze of one whose heart pounds the true nature of longing while the older woman, overcoming her initial feelings of anger, assumed an approving smile and air of relief. They both walked slowly to the already open door, to greet, in their different ways, the man who had first brought both a bizarre new technology and the wonder of flight to our home. The masks which each had assumed were quickly dispelled, however, when they caught sight of him. The frock coat and the stove pipe hat were unmistakably those of Elyahou but no more did he bounce his cases along at the ends of long rubbery arms. Instead the same cases were strapped to a cart which was towed behind a giant tricycle. The flapping shoes at the end of his long legs created great circles, driving the contraption with the three spoked wheels onto the common.

He looked as if he might have belonged to a travelling circus. Despite the fact that the long white beard no longer grew from his jowls and had now been replaced by a brown Wild Bill Hickock style moustache, Henrietta felt her Adonis looked older. Her heart ceased its racing, her face registered disappointment.

'Where's his beard?' her grandmother asked with a frown as the man cycled to their door.

'Don't know,' Henrietta replied, wondering if the question deserved an answer at all.

'Where's your beard, Elyahou?' the old woman piped as he dismounted, smiling, through his pearly white teeth.

'Beard. Gone,' he said, indicating the world beyond the village with a large hand.

'It makes you look younger,' she said, now smiling approvingly again as the neighbours began to close around the stranger and her front door. He shrugged, not having understood, and went to the cart at the back of the tricycle. He started to unfasten a suitcase. 'Robber!' he shouted to the village at large. 'Robber goods.' Rubber boots spilled out onto the ground.

'Oo, I'll have one of them,' said Mrs Henderson, who it seemed would buy anything from the rubber man.

'You'll need a pair, luv,' a neighbour reminded her.

'What, two?' she asked.

'Yes, they're boots, luv. For't feet.'

'Oh. Are they?' she replied, pulling a face as if deciding she wouldn't have one after all.

Elyahou removed a card from the case and gave it to Henrietta, prompting, with his eyes and a gentle movement with his hand at her arm, for her to read it. It bore the same neat writing which the first card had shown. She cleared her throat and read aloud, with some embarrassment.

'My name is Elyahou. I'm sorry I didn't come sooner, but I have been travelling in Europe. I apologize for keeping you waiting. God bless you all when wearing my rubber boots.'

When she had finished reading he took back the card from between her limp fingers and replaced it with the long awaited present from her grandmother.

'Indelible,' he said. 'No go,' he then added, shaking both his head and his raised index finger. The latter was moved back and forth in very small motions as if he were trying to warn her of the permanence of some imaginary markings. Henrietta nodded understandingly and with excitement turned back into the house, eager to try out her new present. Throughout the next

17

hour or so during which the second bazaar was held with just as much enthusiasm as for the first, great stampings were heard to come from the parlour indicating to all that it had certainly been a twopence well spent. My great-great-grandmother spent most of the rest of the day carrying her justified smile between neighbours and loudly clanking the loose change which often accumulated in the depth of her pinafore pocket.

Before the sale got under way the children pestered both their parents and the rubber man to try out the inflatable suits. To show no favouritism Elyahou asked the children to draw the costumes from a sack. There were a dozen in all, one for each child who craved the excitement of dressing up and very soon, using the same dexterity he had shown on the previous occasion Elyahou had dressed them all, inflated their costumes and had them bouncing around the common in joyous mimicry of a well-stocked menagerie. All except Lancaster, that is, who had again got the bee. Tearfully, the twin ascended heavenwards, my great-great-grandmother wondering if perhaps he might never come down, particularly when, after a while he sailed right over the houses. He came eventually to land much to her relief, but not his own, in the ash pits. It's a strange thing, but on each occasion that the costumes were donned in our village my Uncle Lancaster always had the bee. He was the only villager always to fly in a costume at the times of the Transylvanian's visits, and with one notable exception, the only one ever to fly for real. Eventually he joined the flying corps and later the Royal Air Force, and by some peculiar twist of fate, just a little creepy really, he died piloting the bomber which bore his name, but that's another story.

After the dressing up the boot sale got under way. I write boot sale for Elyahou had little else to sell. Nevertheless, within the hour his stock had been exhausted and every collier had a new pair of rubber boots purchased by some lady on his behalf. Even Mrs Henderson, changing her mind yet again, had bought an odd right boot for herself, sharing the expense of a pair with Mrs Colley whose husband had lost a leg in a pit accident the previous summer.

Before taking his leave, the rubber man shook my great-great-grandmother warmly by the hand and said, 'Present, yes?' Henrietta watched as he took from under his stove-pipe hat a cloth cap which he had been wearing beneath and handed it to the old lady. It was of a soft brown material and had an expensive satin lining. The old lady with rough but honest grace and insisting that exchange was no robbery, slipped the man an assortment of medicaments from her store in the scullery. When Elyahou had gone and the neighbours had returned to their own homes, Henrietta said, 'It's beautiful, grandmother. It's from America,' and she pointed to the silk label inside which read, 'Wizak Hatters, Paterson, New Jersey'.

After supper that evening and after each of the menfolk had bemoaned the fact that rubber boots would be of no use in a pit, where a dropped implement would almost certainly break the toes, the old woman handed the cap to Ernest explaining that it was a present from the strange Transylvanian.

'By, it's a grand cap is this, grandmother,' Ernest said, stroking the satin lining. 'Hello,' he then said, 'it's already got somebody's name on't' – bending the cap closer to the light at the window so that he could read out, 'Gaetano Bresci.'

'Give it 'ere, Ernest,' said Mr Pettit who knew about caps.

'Bresci,' he read finally. 'Isn't that t' bugger who murdered King of Italy?'

'Who? Humberto?' said my grandfather. 'Don't be daft, Bill.'

'Ay. Shot him stone dead last year,' said Bill who knew a thing or two. 'I'll not kid thee.'

'Give it back,' said my grandfather, grabbing it from his lodger's hands and fitting it to his head before it could be dispatched back to Milan. 'Fits a treat,' he said, and didn't remove the cap for a week. In fact nobody was quite sure how it came to be removed. He just came up out of that dark stinking hole in the ground one day minus cap, and with a pale ring around his hairline. 'Can't understand it,' he muttered ''Ad it on't 'ead this morning when I went down.'

When James and Aggie Brightside first went inside our house and closed the door on the teeming rain and over-filled puddles, a quiet descended upon the stone interior which James later described as darkness. Not the darkness of the pit, which heaven knows is dark enough, but a silence and darkness living in the very fabric of the house he had said. It was as if there was no air in the house, just dark and quiet stone. Now, I have already said

19

that the quiet was soon dispelled, that the insemination of children and others into the home brought a tumbling joy to the house and so it did. The stones at last breathed. Yet, through some as yet undisclosed agent an appreciation of the early solitude of the first inhabitants was passed from one Brightside to the next. Ernest's elder brother Jack felt it and it finally drove him from the house; from the pit even, to take up farming on the far side of Wakefield. Henrietta too, knew of it, indeed one might say enjoyed it. In the next generation the manifestation had already visited my uncle Lancaster by the time of his fourth birthday and certainly I can vouch for and attest the description given by my great-grandfather. I too have felt the depth of darkness in the stone. If not careful one could drown in it. That it is passed from one generation of Brightside to the next is confirmed by the simple fact that no lodger or visitor ever spoke of having experienced it, and indeed that the manifestation did not travel backwards through the generations is strongly suggested by the fact that great-great-grandmother had no experience of it either. Old Dr Cartwright who had known all the Brightsides well put it down to melancholia, which he had known to run in families, but putting a name to it really didn't seem to explain the phenomenon. After all, nobody seemed to experience melancholia outside of the house and indeed Jack, who was farming on the far side of Wakefield and his mother who still lived with him, had not suffered an attack since leaving our village. Henrietta, who was probably the cleverest Brightside who ever lived, put it down to history. History isn't that nonsense about long ago, she said. It's not about the kings of England, everyone of whom Mr Pettit knew by heart in chronological order, nor is it about battles and governments and dates and laws. No, history is about people. Not *the* people as some colliers now found it fashionable to talk of, not the amorphous mass of unwashed heroes. No, she said, history was about a life. Each life was a history. And not just people but things too. The stones which built the house had a history. They too had a life. Some of us can sense the history of the stones, the quiet, the darkness; others can't. That's what's passed on, she said. It's not melancholia, it's just an ability to appreciate the living history of others, of objects as well as people. All this came to her when she was eighteen years old. She had been sitting on the grass alone, by the river at Bottom Boat. It

20

had been summer, the flies and wasps whispering by the water. With her long legs drawn up and tucked beneath her chin she closed her eyes and thought of hearing the grass grow. She adjusted her straw hat, shielding her eyes from the strong sun, and watched the ichneumon wasps carrying spiders across the shimmering water and contemplated their grizzly end. She thought of how the wasp would deposit its eggs in the spider's body. How the larvae would grow, eating the spider from the inside but keeping it alive for as long as possible by eating the non-essential organs first. God is neither good nor evil, she said to herself, just clever. They are just two more different kinds of life, entwined but different. Not all spiders end up that way. Some, most even, have a different life, a different history. She then averted her gaze from the dazzle of the water to a group of stones half submerged by the bank. Moss green below, stone grey above, she thought how perhaps at one time they may have formed part of a way across the river, but then she dismissed the idea as being presumptuous. How should she know? What way? Where to? Whose boot on the stone? It was nonsense to guess. Like all of history, guesswork and lies, she thought. But the stones could be observed now. She watched them so hard they seemed to float out of the still water. She could observe them for as long as she lived, two different lives entwined again. She could describe them, record their subtle changes through the seasons. But how would the stone affect her? She supposed the very act of recording the stones would bring changes in her life. But was that enough? Was there more? she wondered. Again she closed her eyes hearing grass grow. Suddenly, a very familar feeling came over her. It wasn't pleasurable, but neither was it unpleasant. It was the feeling she sometimes got in the house – the feeling old Dr Cartwright said was melancholia. She could feel the cold and the dark and the terrible solitude. She knew now what it was, this feeling; she knew now what it was which afflicted the family so. The Brightsides knew what it was to feel like stone – wasp and spider entwined as one, the living spider being slowly absorbed into the wasp. She was sure now, eyes tightly shut listening to the grass, that she was experiencing a quality of being different to human or even animal. Henrietta was being slowly absorbed into the stone, and here was the empty feeling of stoniness, and although she knew not to, for she was an extremely clever girl,

21

she felt sorry for the lonely stones and started to cry. Stop it, she told herself, sniffling into the hem of her dress, such ideas will one day lead you to feelings for the spider and the ichneumon wasp and to question the intelligence of God. Stop it.

The morning after the episode with the cap which Elyahou had given to my great-great-grandmother, Henrietta sat at the table in the parlour writing up her journal and stamping the back of each written page with her name in indelible ink. The furious stamping heard during most of the period of the boot sale on the previous day had been Henrietta catching up and stamping the many hundreds of pages already written. The base of the stamp was about two inches square. It was supported by a polished thick wooden handle about four inches long. It bulged at the end forming a black rounded knob through which a long nail was sunk, holding the stem firmly to the base. Henrietta found that she could grip the handle, the phallic nature of which was not lost on the woman, very comfortably within her fist. She wandered off again into a distant dreamy land.

'C'mon girl. We'll be late,' said her grandmother.

Henrietta gripped the stem even more firmly and crushed the rubber to the paper on the table.

'I'm ready, grandmother,' she muttered. 'I've been waiting on you.'

'Hush, child,' the old woman tutted. 'C'mon. Mr Fox shan't wait for long.' Mr Fox ran a horse and carriage service from Kippax to Wakefield.

'Are you walking all the way into Kippax with me?' her grandmother asked.

'Yes. It's on my way. I can go that road to Bottom Boat.'

'To see the stones?'

'Yes.' Her grandmother nodded approvingly.

'Has thee a message for tha' mother?' she asked Henrietta.

'No.' Henrietta shrugged. Why should she have a message for her mother?

'What of your brother, Jack?'

'No.' Why should she have a message for him either?

'How long will you be gone, grandmother?' she asked.

'A few days, girl,' the old woman answered. Henrietta smiled contemplating the luxury of not only a bed to herself but actually

22

having a room to herself for several nights. It had never happened before. Until she was sixteen she had always slept with her sister Florence as well as the old woman. Before that she could vaguely remember sleeping in her mother's bedroom. But now her bedmate was going off to visit mother and Jack at the other side of Wakefield she could barely contain her joy. A bed alone. Then, as if she had read her mind, the old woman said, 'Don't go messin up my bed, mind. I want it neat and tidy when I get back.'

The two women walked the few miles to Kippax and Henrietta waved the old lady off in Mr Fox's carriage crammed full with trippers to Wakefield. She then made a detour to Bottom Boat, watched the stones a while, sketched them a little and made a few notes about a new species of lichen she had found growing on one of them, then returned home in good time to prepare the hot water for the menfolk, coming off shift.

That night Henrietta saw her brother Ernest and his family off to bed first. They climbed the stairs which led directly into the small bedroom shared by herself and her grandmother. She heard the interconnecting door close and watched the ceiling which told her when by the sounds of steadily filling chamberpots and the coiling of springs, the occupants were eventually settled for the night. Henrietta wanted no disturbance on this night, she wished to savour the peace of being alone in a room of her own. She lingered awhile talking with Bill Pettit and Mr Junkin, who recently had been joined by a third lodger, John Tregus, from Cornwall. As those above settled into moonful slumbers Mr Pettit who never would leave his knowledge alone, but who always had to unstack it and rearrange it in his head for fear that he might lose some of it, brought up again the subject of Ernest's new cap.

'I know it's that anarchist chap 'cos I read that 'e come over to Italy from Paterson specially to kill the king. Now what do you suppose that travelling man has to do with Bresci?'

Mr Junkin, because of miner's asthma was too breathless to reply. He just stared with vacant eyes into the glowing embers and spat a thick gobbet black as printer's ink over the coals. 'Gerout an' walk,' he said at last and turned to smile at Henrietta; then removing the rubber teeth he'd bought from Elyahou the previous summer he poured himself another mug of cold tea from the pot on the table. Tregus quietly accepted a refill too from the wheezing miner.

'I'll tell thee,' Pettit went on. ''Es a Jew. Must be with a name like Elyahou Tsiblitz. All them Jews are anarchists. Go about shooting people and blowing them up. Pound to a penny the man's an anarchist.'

Mr Tregus who was temporarily lodging in the area and was attempting to set up some education classes at the mission hall said, 'Now hold on, Mr Pettit, all anarchists don't go about shooting people and causing mayhem. Anarchy's not about violence, you know; on the contrary it's about peace and freedom.'

'Give over,' Pettit scoffed. 'They do nowt but kill kings and princes. Not to mention the odd working man who happens to be about when the bomb goes off.'

Tregus shook his large head. 'No, Mr Pettit, all they are after is the same thing that you want; freedom from tyranny. The only difference is that you would like to see a government of working-class men to replace the capitalists in parliament, whereas they don't want a government at all.'

'How can you not have a government, Mr Tregus?' Henrietta asked.

'The anarchists believe that if men were truly free then there would be no need for government. They believe that freedom would bring trust and self-help.'

'Like the cooperatives you mean,' she asked to the accompaniment of another crack of Junkin's black spittle upon the fire.

'Yes,' Tregus answered, 'like a huge cooperative movement all across the country. There'd be no bosses, no royalty, just people working in harmony. Doing what they want to do both to benefit themselves and others.'

'And how does tha' suppose they'll bring that about?' Pettit asked, derisively.

'By the overthrow of the state,' Tregus answered, undeterred by the man's scorn. 'By inviting the revolution of working people through their unions,' he went on. 'Maybe a solid general strike would bring down the capitalists. It would cease their trade, destroy their economic base. Then the working class could take over the factories and the mines.'

24

''E's an anarchist Jew, I tell thee,' Pettit responded. 'I met a Jew once,' Junkin said without averting his gaze from where his spittle sizzled on the coals, and surprising everybody with his intervention. ''E told me that one day the Jews would go back to Palestine and live in communes without government.' Tregus looked thoughtful a moment, then said, 'The Jews live here in communes, Mr Junkin; that's what our friend here mistakes for anarchy. If you had been chased from one country to another, never allowed to settle, wouldn't you look to your own kind for help? Wouldn't you seek cooperation to protect you from the threat of expulsion? Don't be too disparaging of the Jews, they have a thing or two to teach us about trust and cooperation.'

Mr Pettit for once could find nothing in his head to offer by way of response. He too stared at Junkin's rapidly shrinking phlegm, caught on the flickering coals.

''E's an anarchist Jew I tell thee,' he repeated, eventually.

When sure that all was quiet upstairs Henrietta lit her candle, (Ernest forbade the use of oil lamps considering them both dangerous and a waste of good money), wished the lodgers a good night and mounted the narrow steps to her room. She carefully closed the door, changed into her nightdress, snuffed the flame and spread carelessly across the entire width of the bed, long legs feeling for the endless limits of her comfort. With the pleasure principle so expanded too in her mind she soon drifted into a magnificent and open sleep. She was unsure how much later it was that she was awakened into a pitch blackness and an inability to cry out. The crude hand which tightly held her mouth and jaw made that impossible. The naked male presence, which now pressed upon her smelled pleasantly of grandmother's baskets. Perhaps because she had not moved her legs, spreadeagled still, as they had been when she fell asleep, it was quite easy for an unseen hand to ride up her nightdress and stroke the inside of her thigh. The visitor, sensing the passing of her initial fear relaxed his grip of her mouth and she immediately kissed him gently about the face. She could now feel that she was becoming very wet and with still spread legs writhed her buttocks slowly. The man was now kissing her ample breasts, occasionally gnawing on her nipples. Suddenly with a pain that made her all but scream out the man had entered her and was quietly thrusting deeper. She bit hard upon his shoulder, in pain as much as

25

with passion, but after the initial burning sensation she settled more comfortably to contemplate the thing which moved inside her. He now moaned softly, the first noise he had made since entering her room and it was sufficient to bring her to realize her situation. His moans seemed to bring from her the last entrails of sleep. Fully awake she knew she was being raped. Now, as I have said before, Great-Aunt Henrietta was a clever one. Crying out she knew would put both herself and others perhaps in mortal danger, so she lay there writhing, absorbing the thrusts of both man and thing into her long, strong thighs. But she was actually writhing towards the small table at the side of the bed and on which she had placed her indelible stamper. She supposed that if she could identify the man's nakedness it would at least give the police a good chance of catching her assailant. So, gripping the handle as she would have wished to have held the thrusting object within her, given the chance, she stamped the man's right buttock with the words 'Henrietta Brightside. Child of charm, poetry and love'. The touch of the rubber upon his bottom made the man only thrust the harder, which Henrietta hadn't expected and quite enjoyed. So she stamped his left buttock too with the same pleasant result. After the man had received perhaps twenty or so indelible stampings about his arse, my great-aunt must have been quite satisfied that the man could be identified, if he ever again dropped his trousers before anyone that is, but thought as the moanings continued that this whole episode really had to end. With great vision, she must have thought, she turned the stamper the other way up in her hands, holding it now by the square base, and in the pitch blackness carefully chose her aim and thrust as hard as she could. The wooden phallus then entered the man's anus with the most remarkable result. He ejaculated amidst terrible thrustings and choked screams muzzled by a pillow in which his head was now buried. These final thrustings however were something other than Henrietta had expected for they brought about her the most beautiful sensations of both mind and body which seemed to continue long after her assailant had ejaculated and ejaculated again. Finally coming to her senses amid the man's third ejaculation she realized that she was still wildly thrusting the handle of the stamper between the man's buttocks. She withdrew the object as gently as she could, continuing all the while to kiss the man deeply in the mouth, until passion and pain subsiding like an ebbing tide they both fell asleep, he first, she within moments.

When she awoke at dawn her assailant had left. She could hear her brother Ernest together with the three lodgers downstairs chatting over their breakfast. At first she thought of summoning her brother upstairs but eventually rejected the idea, for what if the companion who so recently had warmed her bed were he. She then thought of informing the police but quickly dismissed that notion too. Although the man might be identified quite easily (if he were ever to bare himself in public that is) how on earth should they ever set about facilitating that identification. Besides, the stamp bore her name which might, if the story got about, bring odium upon her. It then struck her that she had quite contentedly, if exhaustedly, fallen asleep in this man's arms, and indeed, he in hers. Perhaps, here, in its effects at least, was something other than a normal rape. Very suddenly, then, she was overcome by a terrible longing; the emptiness which she felt she must fulfil was not unlike that which Dr Cartwright had diagnosed as melancholia and which she defined as history. She felt that she was being absorbed once more, not into stone but this time into flesh. It was as if this person had taken something of hers and she were being invited to go out and find it. But where should she begin to seek? she wondered.

— 3 —

Three philosophies of the coalfield

When the John Brightside who nestled between my great-great-grandmother's legs said, 'Tha'll nivver go down t'pit again', he meant it and she knew he meant it too. Although older and a good deal bigger than the boy, she respected him for what he would become – a hewer of coal and master of a home. She wasn't too happy to spend all her time above ground where in the cold light of day people might dwell upon her ugliness but on the other hand she praised the Lord for her marriage and for sending her such a handsome and virile young man. And as her respect grew so too did her understanding of how to make something better of the hard life led by the pitman and his wife. Firstly, she said, they must limit their family to a single child. She knew this to be an awful risk for she was well aware of how the life of a babe might slip away through contracting measles or whooping cough or one of the many other diseases which ransacked the coalfield. But she also knew that with tender care and time to devote to just the one child the risk was worth taking. The problem was, however, that her young husband seemed to spend most of his time above ground nestled into her sumptuous thighs, and as her vow to do for him was to be the cornerstone of their better life you can see poor Jane's dilemma. What to do? she said. What to do? And then it came to her, the language of flowers, the secrets of plants and herbs. Some of it she knew from her childhood. More, she had to learn from old women, hags who lived alone, eking out a living from the sale of their potions and medicaments. So each morning Jane would swallow a draught of foul-smelling brew to keep away the babies, and each night they would nestle secure in the knowledge that the long slow hours of dark love-making would surely produce no progeny. Having a single child produced other economic advantages besides having only one extra mouth to feed. It provided room for more lodgers for example. At times they would have as many as a dozen men sleeping in the parlour below, each paying her twelve shillings a week for his board with food. All laundry was contracted out and they saw to their own hot water for bathing, not therefore disturbing the time she needed to devote to young James when he came along.

From the rents alone she was able to save three to four pounds a week. This meant that John only need work four shifts a week bringing in another pound and saving strength for older age and more nestling in her thighs. There were few pitmen who were able to live like that. Few families who were able to save money.

Then of course, she had the money from the sale of her potions, her female mixture as she called it. The fact that it didn't work for many, calling into question her own fertility, or that of her husband, didn't seem to reduce the sales any. Then there were other mixtures; for diarrhoea, for warts, an eye lotion for those miners with the terrible rotating eyeballs syndrome, and of course her bathing lotions for aches and pains. All this money too was profit, which the thrifty lady saved. Next, she laid down a few simple rules of the house, which applied as much to her lodgers as it did to her husband. No drinking. No smoking. No gambling. Jane had never been a great churchgoer but she could see how drink destroyed so many homes in the village. She wouldn't preach against the demon to others but if her home were to remain decent and economically productive, then the men would not fritter away their wages on beer and tobacco, although she did allow the occasional mug of yarrow beer purchased from herself at cost. 'Tha's just playin' into the coal owners' hands,' some prospective lodgers would say. 'They'd love a guaranteed, sober workforce. Good clean units of production, but tha'll work out the coal quicker that way missus. Then wot? When there's no coal?'

'If tha' think that, then there's no lodgin' here,' she would say and slam the door in their startled faces. But after all the planning and the loving and the saving, after all that brewing and book-work, infusing and cleaning, cooking and healing, the sky fell. Her John's skull – he was still only forty-five years old – was cracked open like a coconut. No more nestling in her beautiful thighs.

29

So it was in the summer of 1870, with Jack, Ernest and Flo already brightening the dark stone that Jane came from her village to the house of her only child, James Brightside, with a horse and cart and carrying in a small case the accumulation of her thriftiness. Aggie said, 'Let me take your case, mother,' but Jane hung on, went upstairs alone, and put the case upon her bed and no other comprehending soul has set eyes upon it, from that day to this.

It was soon after their marriage that John and Jane Brightside attended a meeting at The Greyhound (for so their local alehouse was named) to hear a Durham miner speak about self-help in the coalfields. The alehouse was an unsuitable venue for the meeting as the man was teetotal but the Greyhound was the only building in the village capable of housing the expected turnout. Besides, it was a Friday evening, and wages were to be paid as always at the pub. It was therefore with several colliers already roaring drunk that the Durham man took the floor. His eyes had an intensity which shone through the smoky fog. 'I'll make noo apologies for speakin' in an alehouse,' he said, 'but you should know that an ability to improve your circumstance and the drinkin' of this here ale are incompatible.'

'Stop the preaching and get on with what you have to say,' called Teddy Sloan, the landlord of the pub, amid supportive noises from the drunk.

Smoke billowed into the room from the stove-pipe near to the speaker, thickening the atmosphere and causing him to cough. He wiped the spittle from his mouth with his muffler and continued. 'How then are you to save your brass if you squander it on beer?' he challenged the rowdy element.

'Higher wages – that's what we want,' someone shouted.

'They'll come. They'll come,' he answered. 'But first we must put our oon house in order. What's the point in havin' higher wages if it only brings more drunkenness?'

'Piss off. You sound like the coal owners,' someone else shouted, applauded by Teddy Sloan.

The man put his hands in the air asking for quiet when another billow of acrid smoke enveloped both him and half his audience bringing forth enormous bouts of coughing. Taking advantage of the fact that many of his hecklers were now choking he weighed in, 'The first thing to do is build yourselves a chapel. Your chapel. With your money.'

'I'm no churchgoer,' young John shouted.

'You don't have to be,' the man's eyes gleamed through the haze, 'just think what this meetin' would be like in a clean room, with real chairs and without the drunkards. Not havin' to shout. No one chokin'.'

Jane nodded approvingly to her husband.

'Just think what you might learn in a room full of people who are there only to learn too,' the man shouted dodging a pot of ale flying towards him. 'Next, you set up a cooperative store.'

'What's one of them?' came the question from his audience.

'Instead of buying your groceries and provisions from the coal owner's shop, you set up your own shop in competition. You sell goods cheaper than he does, then if there's a profit at the end of the day you share it out; you pay a dividend.'

'Rubbish, we haven't the brass to build a store,' a thin young man said in a wheezy voice.

'Then do it from your home.'

'The coal owner's home you mean. If I sold goods in competition with the grocery me and my mother would be on the street,' the man replied.

'Then put the store outside the village, where he has no property,' answered the Durham man.

'It won't work.'

'It will work,' he shouted, eyes still glinting through the smoke. 'If you unite; if you stick together; if you cooperate, it will work.' He dodged another flying drink, the beer splattering his shirt and muffler. 'And there's another thing,' he went on, undeterred, 'home ownership. Own your own homes. Get out of the colliery-owned houses.'

'And good riddance,' someone shouted.

'Build your own,' the man went on. 'Those of you with the skills can build your own. Others form clubs, take out mortgages with the building societies through your clubs. But whatever you do save your brass. You'll need it.'

'Rubbish. Higher wages is what's needed.'

'Ay, higher wages,' echoed the landlord, and someone threw a mug of ale directly in the man's face. Amid great laughter another

31

billow of smoke wafted into the room enveloping all in a choking fog.

'C'mon lads,' shouted the landlord, 'there's a free pint. This one's on me.' There was a great unseen commotion as men disappeared with their pots and tankards into the acrid cloud. So it was that the meeting broke up, the Durham miner was howled down and my great-great-grandparents left the Greyhound with pandemonium filling their ears. 'It wasn't right, luv,' Jane Brightside said. 'They ridiculed that poor man yet he was speakin' good sense.' Her husband shrugged his boyish shoulders, unsure of what to think.

When John Brightside lay dead, the pit prop and his bust head like a bat and ball in the narrow roadway, his colleagues said the pit wasn't safe. The coal owners had insisted on the use of too few props for too long; something now had to be done. As their shadows stooped and flickered on the black coal walls, they huddled about their dead comrade and decided to invite a speaker from the Miners' National Union to talk about safety. So it was soon after the death of my great-great-grandfather and thirty years after the Durham miner had spoken at the Greyhound, Alexander Macdonald, the miners' leader, came to speak to an attentive audience at the mission hall which had been built in the next village. The wooden pews in the chapel accommodated a quiet group which included James Brightside and his mother. Macdonald first spoke at length of the needs for improvement in safety standards and inspection methods within the mining industry, but soon he was chiding his audience for their indifference and sloth, for very few of the men present and even fewer of those absent had ever belonged to a union. In the clean and cold chapel the men stamped their feet inside large boots trying to circulate a little embarrassed blood.

'We must organize to control the means of production,' he told them. 'To own the mines. They are your mines; we must eventually wrestle them from the coal owners.'

'How can we do that?' asked someone from the centre of the congregation. 'We can be imprisoned for striking, let alone stealing the pit.'

'Yes, friend,' Macdonald answered amid light laughter, 'But it isn't stealing, is it, if we can get a sufficient number of working-class people into parliament. If we can vote in a sufficient number of radicals and liberals who are sympathetic to our cause then we can change things through law.'

'Pie in the sky, man,' came the response.

Macdonald looked severely at the cynic. 'I tell you it can be done,' he said. 'It will be so, if you can organize your union properly. A well-organized union makes you less dependent on the bosses,' he shouted. 'Don't you see that?'

'Tell us,' shouted out someone else. 'Will it bring higher wages?'

'Yes. We can organize for higher pay,' Macdonald answered. 'And shorter hours,' he added. 'And more than that, you can pay yourselves sick money instead of having to rely on the smart money of the bosses. We can find assistance money in times of unemployment, and widows' benefit. With your support we can provide for your orphans and even for your own funerals.'

'What about strike money?' It was an immigrant voice asking in broken English. Macdonald's face suddenly became very serious. 'Beware the strike, friend,' he advised. 'Strikes can be good for us, they can teach the bosses a lesson, bloody their noses a little; but remember too, they can cause your union a lot of damage. If we have to give out strike pay over a long period we could run dry. Nothing for the orphans and widows; nothing for the sick. Strike yes – if it's justified we'll back you; but beware, that's all I'm saying.' The immigrant nodded his understanding of what had been said and murmured quietly to the well-dressed youth seated beside him. Even my great-great-grandmother would never, had she noticed it, have associated his face thirty years on, with the features of Elyahou Tsiblitz, whose father that day had walked him all the way from Leeds to hear Alexander Macdonald speak.

After the meeting most of the men present queued for hours in the cold chapel, creating a crocodile below the blue windows. Then, stamping into its communal boots, our village plodded into the union. James Brightside, standing with his friend Sidall Junkin, said, 'Good speaker, Sid.'

'Ay. Didn't 'ear much on what bugger 'ad to say, though. I were t'sittin' at back. Chap next me were nattering all while to his young lad in Polish or summat.' He coughed a lump of black phlegm into a clean white handkerchief, and looked hard at it.

33

'Got more bloody coal dust in me than there is in t'pit,' he commented wheezily.

Now at the head of the queue James turned to smile at the evening's speaker. Alexander Macdonald, sitting next to the lodge treasurer at a trestle table covered in green baize, nodded approvingly at the young Brightside. James never saw him again, but the Scotsman went away to secure the Mines Regulations Act a year or two afterwards, which brought greater safety to the pit, and then in 1875, he took his seat in parliament, sitting as a liberal; together with Tom Burt, the first trades unionists to do so.

4

James Brightside and how he learned
the notion of continuity

During thirty years of marriage John Brightside expressed little interest in anything other than his wife's body. When Jane was sure that she had enough money saved to enable them to build a house, he rejected her suggestion of it. When one night she suggested they build a shop instead, or even a small factory at which she could concoct her potions on a larger scale, he just turned over and went to sleep. She nattered for a time but her suggestions were always met with the same dull silence, so she soon stopped asking and just put her money into a small suitcase. Sometimes she would open the case and count the money in front of him but he never was interested enough even to enquire how much they had, and eventually she stopped doing that too. Their life was a round of hot nights and cold, lifeless days, which lacked inspiration; even with a parlourful of dossing colliers there was no more than a candle of pale light and a splutter of uneducated but temperate chatter. You could have chucked a bucketful of water over the lot, and they would have been extinguished along with the naked wavering flame.

It was a ghostly world into which young James had been born; solitary, almost unknown to his father he grew up amid quiet, broken bachelors who had nothing but their grey trousers and black boots to their names. So it was that the boy picked out very early in life two things. One was the lonely, ephemeral existence of the lodging collier and the other was the love of his devoted mother; the mother who had decided that it would be her son and not her husband who would own his own home and escape the coal owners' clutches. Yet, incompatible with hopes even for her son were the words of the dosser who had spoken to him as a boy, words which forever flickered in his ears like a trapped butterfly beating its slow and useless wings.

'No, mother,' he said, 'I wouldn't thank thee for a house of my own. Property is theft.'

'But that's not what the Durham miner said the night tha' father and I went to the Greyhound. He said build us own. Free thaselves from the tied homes.' She sounded disappointed. But James would hear nothing of his mother's pleadings and, aloof and proud, naive, misunderstanding and married, he entered in the rain the sombre stone house that would become my family home. Into the darkness he built simple cupboards from bits of wood. Aggie pegged a carpet for the stone floor and they bought a table and chairs to sit on, and finally they acquired a bed. It wasn't much, but as James argued if poverty were to be eliminated then luxury too would have to go; if there were to be no more hunger then there could be no more avarice. When the day of reckoning came and the oppressive coal owners finally were overthrown, he should be ready for it. Ready to receive a mean equality, a parity of possession and position within the society beyond the revolution. James Brightside was, in effect, preparing to receive his liberty.

We were a godless lot living there at that time, which might explain why a chapel was built not in our village but not very far away in the next one to it. It might also explain why it took so long for an intense idealist such as my great-grandfather to become a union man. Strangely, living slap bang in the middle of a terrace of colliery-owned houses gave him no sense of community, or equality. Well, at least it did in some ways and not in others. Of course, the occupants saw one another through various hardships; if it became necessary, food was shared. They did for each other, like laundry and baby minding, that sort of thing, but the pitmen had their own social structure, their own pecking order. At the top of the ladder were the men, like James Brightside, who hewed the coal; below them, and receiving less pay, were the putters who ran the tubs and the ponyboys who looked after the ponies. Then at the surface, and often receiving less pay still were an assortment of banksmen and weighmen, blacksmiths and joiners, general labourers and sorters who picked out the stones and sized the coal. These were often older men, clapped out hewers who could never go down to the coal face again and, because they were old and knackered, respect for them diminished. Unlike the respect shown to one's own father, which never wavered to the grave and beyond, the respect for one's elderly neighbours and workmates fell short like a diminishing light until there was no more than the black pain of age perceived as an abstraction. Looking at such people the future seemed black indeed. Now in that sense James felt no community; like his father he felt no continuity with these people. The generations proceeded and had preceded; but that's all they were, generations. Each huddled within the coal, black and bent, waxing and waning, then extinguished. To be a union man, you had to understand continuity, you had to have a clear sense of future communities, and how to fight for them and their liberation, even before their birth. The liberty which James would receive at the revolution would be a personal liberty; what all other liberated people would be doing was not his concern.

On the night that he went to the mission hall with his mother, the night he joined the union, the act was not performed with any particular political zeal. The talk of parliamentary revolution interested him but brought about no conversion from the narrow and selfish idealism which he felt. No, that was harnessed and given direction by something which happened at about the time Alexander Macdonald first took his parliamentary seat. That was the year the coal owners put the colliery on a three day week, because of the slump in trade. A shaft had been sunk, but the mine not much worked, at the foot of Hunger Hill; so for the sake of something to do my great-grandfather, together with Sidall Junkin, descended the shaft on one of the days when not working. They had no idea what they might expect to find but waded chest high in foul water through the narrow galleries, examining the walls of the dead mine in the pale glow of light from a couple of flickering candles.

Sid's wheezing, of which James was always aware, stopped suddenly and my great-grandfather turned to see the other, breath held and candle thrust out towards a crumbling wall.

'What've thee got there, Sid?'

'Dunno, come and see.' The reply resounded thinly in the empty arch above the water level.

'It's nowt but a sheep's bone,' James commented from his companion's side.

Sid wheezed a bit more then said, 'No. Sithee, James, it's too

37

big for a sheep,' and chipped away the rock from about the bone with a small pick.

My great-grandfather settled the candles on a ledge by the side of the discovery and helped his friend chip away the surrounding rock. After a couple of hours they had revealed a bone about three feet long running parallel to the gallery floor.

'It must belong to a bloody elephant,' Sid informed James from his rattling chest.

'I think its a pit prop that's become buried,' my great-grandfather confided.

'Nay, lad. Tha's not felt it,' Sid said with exasperation.

'Look, James, it's like stone – petrified.' He tapped the object with his hard pick to illustrate the point. The hollow noise echoed around the gallery. Sid started to cough. 'That's no pit prop' he added managing to squeeze the words between splutters.

'C'mon, Sid,' James said with concern. 'Let's get thee out of 'ere. This water'll be the death of thee if we stay here much longer.'

The two men waded out but waded back the next day, chipping away yet more of the rock and revealing an even greater length of bone and a second similar bone running parallel to it.

Throughout the two years of short working on each of two days a week they descended the shaft and chipped away at the bones slowly revealing a skeleton about fifteen yards long. The bones which they had managed to expose of course did not constitute the whole animal for there was little more than two feet in height between the surface of the flood water and the roof of the gallery. But nonetheless for the full run of fifteen yards they had exposed two feet of bones in the vertical dimension. They also had of course excavated back from the wall of the gallery some ten feet in all, and taken the height up some, in which area they had been able to work quite easily and even walk about, albeit with the stoop of apes.

The whole box-like cavern which they had created was a mass of bones, all of which supported magnificently the freshly created ceiling. The two huge feet were easily identifiable as was the area which Sid would insist on calling the rib cage; the head too, along with a mouthful of enormous teeth, could be recognized easily.

Sid, sitting between two rib bones, his head poking into the

38

cavern where the lungs might at one time have been situated, said 'I've never seen owt like it afore.'

'It's a bloody monster.' James replied.

'Do thee think we should tell?'

'Ay. We'll 'ave to tell someone.'

'Vicar?' Sid offered.

'No, he'll only preach on us.'

'Who then?'

James thought a while stooped in the same cavern in which the other man was sitting, their shadows licking the bones as the candles burned down.

'Dr Cartwright,' he said at last. 'He'll know what to do.'

Dr Cartwright was a small skinny man. The only hair to grow about his head was a sprouting of grey fluff which developed in his ears and curled about his hearing. He wore a squat silk hat and because of his extraordinary hair he appeared to have ear muffs beneath. When he had descended the shaft and waded through the foul smelling water he couldn't believe his eyes. He'd expected at best to see the remains of a bear of perhaps a rhinoceros but when confronted by the massive skeleton he said, 'My God, it's a dinosaur. Just look at those teeth'.

'A what?' asked James.

'A dinosaur.'

'What's one of them?'

'You know, a terrible lizard. They're extinct.'

'But where did it come from?'

'It didn't come from anywhere, James. It died there, where it is.'

'You mean it died down t'pit.'

The doctor smiled, wondering how he might explain the fossilized phenomenon.

'It's extinct,' he said.

'What's that?'

'It died millions of years ago, and so did all others like it.'

'No, that can't be, doctor,' said James, remembering what he'd learned from the little schooling he'd had. He'd been taught that the world had begun in the year 4004 BC. 'How can it have died millions of years ago?'

'The earth is many millions of years old, James.'

39

'Not 4004 BC?'

'No. Not 4004 BC.'

James looked stunned.

'A man called Mr Darwin wrote a book not many years ago showing how life evolves.'

'What's that?' James asked.

'One species develops from another. Higher forms evolve from lower forms.'

The other nodded, signifying some understanding. The doctor continued.

'The highest form so far developed is man and we came from apes.'

Watching the doctor stooped in the bony cavern, James found no difficulty in accepting that. He nodded.

'And this here's a lower form, that's now gone,' he said, looking about the cave.

'Yes. Good, you've got it.'

'So when God made the earth millions of years ago, there were no men around.'

'That's right. There were lower forms, still. Man eventually evolved.'

'And is this evolving still going on?'

'Yes.'

'Will there be millions more years of evolving, doctor?'

'Yes. Of course. But the most evolved form then will probably be as different from man as we are from this monster here.'

Suddenly in that dark cavern, he and Dr Cartwright bent like apes among the dinosaur bones, James had his first glimpse of continuity. He had an idea of what lay beyond the blackened old men of the village. He now understood what his father had not and was deeply moved by the revelation. He felt godless no more. In fact he had an overwhelming urge to kneel at the foot of the creator and thank Him for making him, James Brightside, a part of the grand design. So, the following Sunday, he took himself, and Aggie, and the children, Jack, Ernest and Flo, off to the chapel, and when the family returned to the house they found Dr Cartwright waiting. He first took Aggie upstairs to the bedroom and came down to confirm to James what the husband already suspected. His wife was pregnant. He then led James outside and told him that he had decided to inform a friend of his, a man at the Natural History Museum, about the dinosaur in the disused pit.

'What'll he do?' asked James.

'He may ask you to dig it out completely,' the doctor answered. 'I can't really say. Be grateful there's another on the way, James.' The doctor nodded towards the open door and to Aggie. He put his friendly hand upon my great-grandfather's shoulder, then he mounted his chestnut horse and rode off through the rain puddles.

Within seven days the man from the Natural History Museum had arrived together with Cartwright in a carriage. He wore a frock coat and carried a round knobbed cane. The monocle which occupied the space about his right eye flashed in the afternoon sun. 'Dr Cartwright suspects it may be the remains of an Iguanadon,' the man said in a tongue James had not heard before. 'It's all very exciting.'

'Maybe,' said James. 'I wouldn't know about that, sir. But I'd like to get it out complete like.'

'Yes,' said the man from London, 'but it's hardly your dinosaur, is it now?'

'I found it. Me and Sidall Junkin like,' James said possessively.

'No, it can't be yours. Firstly the pit belongs to the coal owner.'

'But it's not used no more,' James interrupted.

'But it's still his land, isn't it,' said the man, adjusting his monocle. 'And secondly, once found, a thing like this would immediately pass to the crown. I'm sure Her Majesty however, would want it housed at the Natural History Museum, for all her subjects to see.'

'You mean I can't dig it out?' asked James a little bewildered by all this talk of the queen.

'Well, you can't keep it, that's out of the question.'

'Can I dig it?'

The man looked uneasy then said, squinting at the sun, 'That's up to the coal owner; I'm on my way to see him now.'

'Yessir,' answered my great-grandfather, and the carriage rattled through our village out of the denaturing sun, taking with it the doll-like figures of old Dr Cartwright and the man from the museum.

41

The next day the coal owner sent for my great-grandfather who walked a couple of miles to the big house. When he got there the coal owner was waiting for him in the drive; the collier never would have been allowed to actually enter the house. My great-grandfather, big fellow that he was, removed his cap and towered over the boss.

'Brightside, who give thee permission to go down my pit?'

'Didn't know was needed, Mr Thwaite,' my great-grandfather said, wringing out his cap with large hands.

Mr Thwaite looked to the rustling leaves in the trees which lined the approach to his house.

'Well, tha' did and tha's done it.' He said aggressively.

'Yessir,' said my great-grandfather, still wringing his cap.

Summoning more aggression still he threatened, 'Brightside, I ought to take t'ouse away. Do owt like this again and I will, lad. Be sure on that.' He paused for my great-grandfather's quiet response.

'Yessir.'

The two men looked at one another amid the wind-stirred leaves. The trees seemed to echo the big man's lament. With courage he asked, 'Now I've started, Mr Thwaite, can I finish t'job? Get it all out?'

'No, tha' can't. Cheeky bugger,' came the quiet reply. 'First, thee 'ad no permission to go on my land there. No permission to hew out that skeleton. Second, if buggers from London want that thing they can get professionals in to do it, not soft buggers the likes of thee.'

'Yessir,' my great-grandfather said again.

'Now, clear off, Brightside,' said the coal owner, 'afore I set the dogs on thee.' He turned to go back to the big house.

'Mr Thwaite,' the collier called after him. 'Mr Thwaite, will I be able to help?' He touched the boss's arm.

The man turned and said venomously, 'Don't put tha' hands on me lad. Understood?'

'Yessir. Sorry, sir.'

'Let's get it clear, Brightside,' the boss said. 'Stay out of that shaft. That dinosaur thing's nowt to do with thee. It's my dinosaur on my land. An' them buggers in London will have it only if they pay my price. Otherwise it stays just as it is, in t' bloody ground. Is that understood?'

'Yessir.'

'Now stay clear of it, Brightside,' he said and turned a second time. 'I'm warning you, stay clear.'

My great-grandfather, crestfallen amid the warm sad trees, walked slowly back to our soot-grimed village, the butterfly in his ear flapping its useless wings once more.

James Brightside's philosophy had changed. The encounter with the dinosaur bones, and the subsequent meetings with Dr Cartwright and Mr Thwaite, and even the attendance at chapel, had all helped to change his views. The narrow idealist who couldn't see a world beyond his own death was able now to look to his children's future in a time without him; even the little devil stirring in Aggie's belly, the one he didn't yet know would, with luck, have a time beyond his own. He was also beginning to contemplate a better world for himself, beyond his own grave. The idea of heaven was beginning to appeal, realizing a different kind of liberty.

The butterfly too was starting to break free, at first painfully beating its useless wings, then cracking its wax encasement with such a rush, and flying blue and gold and all colours into the sun. Not one, but many, fluttering their paired wings into the sun, and liberating my great-grandfather from his naivité and misunder-standing. He knew now the message that the dossing collier was carrying. The property he had spoken of was not a house, or the useless baubles that went to fill it. No, the property he had meant was himself and his labour. It was the cruel use the bosses made of the colliers; stealing their labour and the fruits of that labour which constituted the theft.

'Two years of labour digging out that bloody skeleton, and not so much as a thank you,' he told Sidall Junkin.

'He's thieved it, Sid. Thieved it and going to sell it, and we won't see a penny of the price they pay in London. And why? Because it's his land and we're his slaves. That's why, Sid.'

'Maybe Union can do summat.'

'Union,' James puffed. 'Union's on its bloody knees. They won't do owt.'

'Alexander Macdonald, then.'

'Nay, lad. 'E's part of 'em, now. Lordin' it up in Parliament.

'E'll be 'avin' supper with that bugger with the eye glass. There must be some other way, Sid.'

He turned to his mother, Jane Brightside, and said, 'Mother, I was wrong. We'll get that house. We'll free ourselves from the bosses. I swear we'll do it. But first, I'll sort out that bastard Thwaite.' Now my great-great-grandmother had no idea what he meant by that last remark but taking Sidall with him, James left the house. The old woman was watching the remnants of Sidall's mucus tearing itself apart on the hot coals when she was roused by a deep explosion. She felt the vibrations from it push through her womb and knew then that her son was dead. My great-great-grandmother moved herself wearily into the street and headed for Hunger Hill. Halfway towards the old pit she met Sidall Junkin running and wheezing as hard as he could go, and coming to meet her.

'He's blown up the old pit, missus,' he shouted at her.

'Well, go and get him, lad,' she said quietly. 'Go on, go and see.'

'Yes, missus,' the man said, then ran back, arms and legs all over the shop.

She walked slowly to the pit head and waited. Eventually Sidall came out of the hole in the ground dragging a sack. Handing it to the woman, he said, 'It's all I could find, missus.' He was wheezing and spitting great black gobbets of muck. There were tears in his eyes and his clothes stank and hung heavy with the foul water.

After a time Sidall took the sack back from her and said, 'C'mon, there's nowt to do here. I'll take thee home.'

On the way back to the village they passed dozens of women, their heads covered in black shawls each bowed, passive and supportive. There were no tears, no words of regret, just a terrible silent agony conveyed through the spaces between them. Black, Sidall recalled it afterwards, just black and angular like the slagheaps reaching in the sky; stones at prayer to an awful God.

Once inside the house, Aggie took the children up to her bedroom and great-great-grandmother put some water on to boil. Then she mashed some tea. Sidall and she sat before the fire drinking from mugs and Sidall said, 'E's under a pile of stones, missus. All them bones have fell and crumbled into stone. It's not bones any more, missus, just rocks. You wouldn't believe that an animal could be so much rock. It's like it was sculpted out of stone then knocked down. All knocked down and broken, missus.'

My great-great-grandmother put her arms around her dead son's friend, kissed him on the cheek and went out of the house. By the time she had arrived back, Mr Thwaite was already in the parlour, lecturing to the assembled occupants.

'Condolences,' he said to Aggie and the children. 'It were a silly thing to do. Lost me a lot of money has this, a lot of money.' And he shook his head. 'Who's gonna pay the rent now,' he continued looking to each of the three children in turn. Then he said to Aggie,

'The orphans' fund and the widow's pension won't be enough to live on tha' naws.'

'No matter, Mr Thwaite,' said my great-great-grandmother, standing by the door. 'Tha's earlier than I expected.'

'Ah condolences, Mrs Brightside,' he said to the older woman warmly and moving to greet her. 'I didn't see thee come in.'

'Condolences, my backside,' she said in a matter of fact way. 'Here's twenty-five pounds for tha' trouble and a year's rent, Mr Thwaite.' The landlord looked surprised but took the money. 'Now I'd be obliged if tha'd leave us to grieve, Mr Thwaite,' she said, and showed him the door.

When the coal owner had gone, Sidall Junkin put his hand in his pocket and pulled out two stones which he held in his outstretched palm for everyone to see. 'Iguanadon teeth,' he said to a puzzled audience. 'They're all I could recognize.' The following day he parcelled them up and sent them to the Natural History Museum in London where they can be seen on exhibition to this day. 'I'll stay,' Sidall said, 'if tha' wants me to. Sithee all right through the night.' Great-great-grandmother agreed, and Sidall Junkin stayed in the parlour, sleeping each night in a wide winged chair until the time he passed away. The next day they buried my great-grandfather. Sidall never did reveal what or how much was in the sack and nobody cared to look, but the contents made a strange noise when the sack was put into the coffin, and rattled emptily when James Brightside's mates lowered it into the ground.

45

5

Mr and Mrs Gill's five little boys

Nobody in the family ever enquired how my great-great-grandmother came to be carrying such a huge sum of money in her pinafore pocket on the afternoon that her son died. Aggie supposed that it must have been part of the fortune which she was reputed to have brought to the house with her, but she had no idea where that money may have been stored for safe keeping. It could have been in some bank vaults in Leeds or Wakefield for all she knew. But Aggie was thankful, and Aggie cried with relief. At least for a time, she and the children were safe with a roof over their heads. The cruel irony in the timing of James's death had not escaped her mother-in-law's attention though. For how long was she now to carry the payment for her early sacrifices before it would be put to use and free her family? If she were a man it would be different, she'd perhaps buy materials and a little land and build a house; or maybe she'd join a club and pay a mortgage. Perhaps, even, she'd go right up to the door of one of the knobs, bold as brass, and offer them cash to clear out and leave the house to her, fine contents and all for there was enough. Enough to buy her family's liberty, big house and all. But she was a woman. Who'd accept the money from a woman like her without question? Where did it come from? How'd you earn it? It must be stolen, they'd say. Or ill-earned. Tha's taken a lot of strangers to tha' bed for this lot, luv, they'd say. She couldn't stand that. Not with her only genuine memory of it, being with her John, nestled in there, a little cock-sparrow between her legs. She realized she'd have to wait for her grandsons. Perhaps Jack or Ernest would be master of his own home. She'd wait.

Time passed in the village. Slump in the pits was replaced by good times. The boys growing into young men, began to earn wages. The union crumbled, then picked itself up as money poured in. Jack married a farmer's daughter on the other side of Wakefield, inherited a smallholding when his newly acquired father-in-law was gored by a bull on a carpet of bluebells, and left the pit and the village. Aggie, unable to bear the dark stone any longer, soon followed her eldest son and settled contentedly to the milking of cows and the feeding of chickens, leaving the young Henrietta in the care of her grandmother.

Ernest got religion. Following the example set by his father in the months before he died Ernest grew to be a godfearing man of the chapel, and he saw to it that his siblings too spent each Sunday in the bosom of the Lord. Pictures appeared for the first time in the house. Moses and Ezekiel adorned the parlour. Christ, Job and Ruth shared the bedrooms. The Bible with its heavy brass clasp, sat at the centre of a newly purchased sideboard, together with photographs of Henrietta and Flo in clean white pinafore frocks. The young family was comforted by the community, entwined eventually within it and all sucked to the teat of Methodism; the chapel took hold and they, like ivy, scaled the walls. Not just the Brightsides but most of the people of the terrace and the other pitmen's families too. Even the pit managers and eventually the coal owner worshipped at the same chapel. The amalgam was finally set when capital and labour were heard harmoniously singing together in the pews. Mr Thwaite smiled each time the minister urged his congregants to work hard, to be temperate, to be obedient, for that way lay their salvation; and Ernest too smiled at the thought of his being saved. Via the church's teaching, like so many pitmen before him, but unlike any previous member of his family, Ernest learned obedience, punctuality, industry, discipline, self-denial, abasement; in a word he was methodized. His labour was sanctified and he maintained grace. His poverty was blessed and in staying poor he knew himself to be saved in the next world. It was a mean business and my great-great-grandmother saw right through it, right to its rotten heart. She despised these ranters, preaching their sermons of everlasting hellfire and terrorizing the children, and so was relieved when Flo, at least, fell from grace.

Flo like her grandmother, but unlike her young sister, Henrietta, was an ugly woman. She not only shared the large, square frame which gave her body the solidity of a brute but she also had the face of one who might have been modelled in clay by a child. It

47

was the unfinished coarseness of her features which made her so ugly. It was she who, after her fall, would visit the public house each Saturday and following the prize given to the prettiest girl in the pub would be presented with the booby, invariably a short shrivelled black pudding. Thus was it unanimously confirmed by those unafraid to voice such opinions; Flo was the ugliest woman in the village. Now, I have already mentioned that along with Ernest most of the people who lived in our terrace had got religion, but there was one notable exception; the Gill family. Mrs Gill was a small dear woman who hardly deserved what the Lord had sent her; namely a crippled husband and their five little boys. Each of the five was built like a brick shithouse and inside they were twice as nasty. Mr Gill had been injured in an explosion years before when the oldest boy had been barely of an age to go down the pit. Since that time he had lain on a board upon the table in the parlour, his back broken in two places. There, he lived and slept, to be removed upon his board by two of his strapping lads only when it was necessary for the family to eat. The house reeked of the spoonfed old man's decaying excrement and once a week two of the boys could be seen at the village pump washing down the crumpled father and scrubbing his board with all the vitality of butchers at their block.

'Lord, deliver us from such evils,' Sidall Junkin at the window once said, seeing the boys delivering home their pitiful load after such an excursion.

'Amen to that,' my great-great-grandmother said. Although she had lost the two men most dear to her, at least death had come mercifully quick in both cases. There was not the slow dripping away of life as on the parlour table next door.

Yet out of their prostrate parent, and huddled about that table, the sons seemed to grow. Like giant fungi, shooting out of a confused mycelium, the boys blossomed. Blastospheres with much spores; spawning mischief as well as children.

On one particular Sunday, it was before Flo's fall from grace, indeed it was the morning of her twenty-fifth birthday, great-great-grandmother returned from a walk to Bottom Boat with a whole basket full of hemlock, to find the five Gill boys digging up the scullery floor with an assortment of pickaxes.

'We're looking for the money, missus,' said John, the eldest, by way of explanation.

48

'You wont find 'owt here,' she answered, and put some water to boil in a pan on the fire.

'Now tha' doesn't want trouble, does thee?' threatened Charley who was barely fifteen but just as large as his brothers. He brandished a spade in her face.

'No I don't want no trouble. That's why I'm going to have some tea. Now boys does tha' want tea,' she asked in a comforting voice.

'No, missus, we just want the money,' said John.

'What money? I have no money.'

'The money tha' brought here with thee, missus,' Barney chipped in. He wore braces to hold his massive trousers over a rotund and spreading gut.

'Oh, those stories!' exclaimed my great-great-grandmother, appearing to be hurt by such a reminder. 'It's not true. There is no money, Barney. Just tittle-tattle. Now have some beer. Come on, sit at the table and I'll get you some of my yarrow beer.' She was very calm and the boys sat one by one watching and mistrusting her all the time. She went into the scullery and came out clutching six bottles of her own brew. She gave one bottle to each in turn, then stripped a few leaves and roots from the plants in the basket. She tossed these carelessly into the pan of boiling water.

'They say tha's a witch, missus. Is that right what they say?' asked Charley, elbow on table and supporting his child's head in a big man's palm.

'No, child. I'm no witch,' she answered. 'Now drink tha' beer.'

The boys looked to John for a lead. At the nod of that older head it would not have been beyond them to have beaten her with their implements but John was thinking, and took a long swig from his bottle; thankfully the others quickly followed the example of their brother. Meanwhile, the old woman chucked a handful of tea leaves into the boiling water.

'If it's not 'ere, where is it then?' John asked, his voice already becoming thick from the effects of the beer.

'It's nowhere, John,' said my great-great-grandmother consolately. 'It isn't. Tha's mistaken lad. It's just a tale, I tell thee. There is no money.'

'Course there is,' Barney slurred angrily. 'Everybody knows it.'

'Now come on, boys, drink up,' she said calmly. 'Then we can have some tea and talk it over.'

'Over what?' asked the terribly stupid Benjamin.

'Over the tea, daft bugger,' Barney said, taking off his cap and hitting his brother with it.

'That's right, boys, let's get the beer down now,' she said, grateful for the diversion which Barney had set up. They all supped on the home brew until the bottles were empty. Their limbs had become decidedly more relaxed, their flabby jowls more shaky. My great-great-grandmother talked the whole while she was pouring the tea. She spoke of their father on his board, of how her only son had blown himself to bits in the disused pit, of their mother, and how good and kind a woman she was, and eventually she placed the tea in best china cups before the five drunken neighbours.

'Is thee not havin' any?' John asked suspiciously.

'Not yet,' she said. 'I'll have my yarrow beer first.' She smiled and put a bottle to her mouth.

Within moments of drinking down their tea my great-great-grandmother was able to perceive the flabbly jowls becoming more solid. No more shaking. The five fat faces were becoming rigid. Their stares became fixed. Inside, their brains were swimming. From without their heads were like the stone balls atop the pillars of the gates to the big house. The five fat faces were frozen. The old woman poked a long bony finger into the puffy cheeks of the eldest brother and when she removed it a white telltale depression remained in the flesh. A hand on the table twitched. She was unsure which of the ten it might have been.

'Now, tha great lumpkins,' she said quietly when certain that all were in a state of paralysis, 'tha've been given a little of the poison of Athens. Just enough for thee to be rendered harmless; not enough to cause any permanent damage, mind. But if I catch thee round here again I'll have thee put down like Socrates. Does tha' hear? Like Socrates.'

Suddenly, changing her tone she walked around the table to where Charley was sitting. Into the rigid face with its frightened eyes she said, 'So, Charley, tha've heard I'm a witch. Well, 'tis true dear. I am a witch. My spells have thee paralysed rigid. Come round here, frightening an old woman again and she'll have thee put down. Does th' understand? I'm going to release thee soon, boys, does tha' hear. Release thee from the spell, but

50

next time I'll let the poison do its work, all the way, does thee hear? There'll be no release next time, boys; remember, no release. I'll turn thee to stone, forever.' She looked into the frightened eyes and smiled. Another hand began to twitch and tremble. Both Barney and Benjamin were drooling, the saliva trailing over their fat chins as if a snail had passed unseen from their clamped mouths. She went on: 'Before tha' leaves, boys, there's another spell to cast. One of thee fine strapping lads will wed our Florence. I command it.' (Was this the one she had cast on young John Brightside fifty odd years before?) 'Now, which of thee shall it be, I wonder?' she went on.

The flabby jowls started to shake again indicating to her that the terrible effects of the hemlock were beginning to subside, though perhaps even in their drugged state the boys were showing some dissent, so horrible was the contemplation of marriage to our Flo.

'I'll count to ten,' she said quickly, and staring hard in turn at all five brothers, 'then tha'll be released from the spell and tha' can all go home. Does tha' hear?' She started to count slowly and on the count of ten sure enough the hands began to twitch, the feet began to stir. Soft moanings issued from their blubbery lips. 'Now, boys, let's be quick,' said my great-great-grandmother. 'Back to mother now,' and the eighty-year-old woman rushed each of the great big Gill boys unsteadily out of one door and in through the next. She then poured out the dregs of the poisoned tea, washed the pan out with clean water from the bucket and put fresh water on to boil, and all the while she could hear the awful wretching and vomiting of the Gill boys next door at their father's table.

Even my great-great-grandmother, I think, must have been surprised at the effects of the spell she had cast on the Gill boys. Florence, however, was undoubtedly the most surprised of all. The poor girl found that she suddenly had not one suitor, but five. They courted her on the common, in the fields, by the river, on the slope of Hunger Hill, even at the pit itself, and they fought over her too. They had their way with her two and three at a time (mercifully, never five) in the winding engine shed and even in the grounds of the big house at the very spot where her father had received humiliation at the hands of Mr Thwaite, and great-great-

51

grandmother double-dosed her morning and night with her female mixture. They paraded her at the public house where she regularly was awarded the black pudding but what should she care of that when she had five strapping lads snapping at her buttocks. Her grandmother, though, was worried. She feared that the spell had not taken hold and that all this multiple lovemaking was the boys' way of getting even with her. She feared that after a time, the boys would become tired of their game, and that Flo would be tossed aside, a shagged-out doll crumpled at the pit head. Thus it was with both surprise and relief that she learned of a proposal of marriage coming from the slow-witted Benjamin. Relief turned to consternation however when it became known that poor Benjamin had been beaten to within an inch of his life by John and the proposal withdrawn. John's counter-proposal, that he should be her husband, was met in the same easy manner by Flo.

'Tha'll do, John,' she said, and that was that.

Barney, however, protested loud and clear that because he was the biggest and the strongest he should have the woman for his wife and did he really have to beat the living daylights out of his four brothers just to prove his point. It was now that great-great-grandmother realized that the magic had taken hold after all, but not quite as she had intended. If she were not careful the potency of the spell was such that the magic would lay low all five potential suitors and the unfortunate Florence end up without a man at all. It was then that help arrived from an unexpected quarter. News of the predicament came at last to the ear of the prostrated father. From his position upon the parlour table the old man decreed that his sons must draw lots to settle the issue once and for all. So, grouped around their wizened and shrinking father, the boys drew straws from the old man's clasped hands, like hyphae from the fungal mass, the whole episode being witnessed by both Mrs Gill and Florence. The short straw was drawn by the quiet one, Arthur, who didn't say a word. He just walked out of the house with Flo on his arm, the brute of a girl giggling into the rain. The intent of marriage was announced immediately by Mrs Gill, and with the proclamation the spell was broken. The remaining four brothers sensing their release rushed into the street to congratulate the lucky Arthur. There are some days when it rains in our village, and the teeming water somehow

52

washes all the coal dust out of the air. Not only can one breathe more easily without having to taste the grit in each breath but one can see more easily too. The light for a whole while after the rain has ceased becomes bright and sparkling like clarified ale; it was such a time when the five brothers hugged and kissed each other, there in the street and each kissed the bride-to-be too. 'It was a day,' Charley told me many years later, 'when the Lord said, Let there be light.' Then he studied for a bit and added, thoughtfully, 'And tha' could see for fucking miles.'

My great-great-grandmother watched the commotion from the parlour window, pleased that it was the quiet Arthur who had won the girl. She never forgot that he had been the only one not to frighten her that Sunday when she had returned with the hemlock. The others, however, steered clear of the old woman whenever they could and never again was she pestered with the matter of the missing fortune.

After their somewhat hasty wedding (everybody went to great lengths to insist that the bride was not pregnant), the couple emigrated to Australia. The remaining brothers went on to take their positions in the greatest pack of forwards ever to grace the Northern rugby union and to make my father's early years a delight, basking next door in reflected glory.

Henrietta wrote constantly in a profuse exchange of letters with her sister. She passed on the news of how she had come to start writing the history of the Stones, and how it continued, of Ernest's love of God, of grandmother's experience with the people from the airship, of Sidall Junkin's asthma and of the arrival of Mr Pettit and his mind full of wondrous facts. From New South Wales, Henrietta learned of the love of Flo's new husband, of how much better was the organization of labour in the antipodes, of the New Unionism and the love of her husband. She heard of pregnancy and abortion and of strikes. Then one day Mrs Gill came round and informed Henrietta of the death of the man who lived on the parlour table and how she ought to pass the news on to her son in Australia. She then told her how she would have her husband cremated and have the ashes divided into five portions, one for each of her sons.

'Can I bring it round and tha'll send it for me?'

'Yes of course,' said Henrietta. 'I'm sending them some dried fruit, anyway. I'll put it in the same parcel.'

Though why she was sending dried fruit to the land of sunshine, she had not got the remotest idea.

Henrietta duly wrote her letter, accepting responsibility for the sad duty of having to inform Arthur of the death of his father and how she thought it to be for the better, releasing the man from all his suffering. She also told of how she would be enclosing the old man's ashes in a parcel to be sent.

The next letter which she received from New South Wales thanked her very much for the parcel of dried fruit which had unfortunately been damaged during the sea voyage. 'No matter though,' wrote Flo, 'we were able to scrape the lot together and make a lovely fruit cake – Arthur's favourite.' She also wrote that she was pregnant again. Henrietta hiccuped, put her hand to her mouth and waited for the next letter. It was much shorter than normal explaining that they had only just received Henrietta's last piece of correspondence.

'Arthur's quite upset at having eaten up his dad,' it said. Among other things it also mentioned that Flo had aborted again. Her grandmother found the latter comment of extreme interest, and wondered at the marketability of cremated remains.

6

Earth closets, ash pits and John Tregus's backside

After deciding not to inform the police that a rapist was at large, a rapist with her name stamped at least twenty times indelibly on his bottom, Henrietta wondered what her next move ought to be. A clever girl such as she knew how impossible life would be if she were merely to resort to pulling off the breeches of each and every man who crossed her path. She sat upon her bed and reasoned that firstly her assailant might try to wash off the offending ink marks, that is, if he was aware of their presence. After all, they were not exactly in a place where he normally might see them. What if he thought in the pitch dark last night, that the constant slapping of his bottom was Henrietta's way of encouraging him to greater passion in his sexual romp. Oh Lord, she thought, it gets worse. He probably had no idea that he was being branded, perhaps he thought that he was merely egged on by a love-sick girl. Then she reasoned that if he didn't know of the branding of his rear he would eventually learn of it from somebody else, and that meant gossip. Fortunately, or unfortunately for she could look at it either way, there were few solitary men in the village (she assumed him to be from the village if not from the very house in which she lived); most of them bathed in groups. Mates would enquire and chatter, laugh and eventually gossip. She'd know soon enough, she smiled, darkly.

That evening after each of the menfolk had bathed and not yet combed his hair, Henrietta returned to the house with her sister-in-law, Emily. There was no embarrassed chatter, no embarrassed silence, nothing to suggest that a person had been discovered with incriminating evidence tattooed upon his buttocks. All appeared, as always, to be perfectly ordinary. The smell of grandma's baskets hung in the steamy air, Sidall Junkin spat upon the fire; the damp men started to comb their hair. As the neat parting appeared at the centre of Mr Pettit's head he said,

'Tregus would make a grand wife. He washed our backs a treat.' And Ernest followed with: 'He's a mucky beggar though, seldom takes a bath he says.'

'Why, Mr Tregus,' Emily said, 'whyever not?'

'Oh, I do sometimes, ma'am,' Tregus answered uncomfortably. ''Course I do sometimes. It's just that not working in the pit I don't get quite as dirty as the others.'

'So how often do you bathe, Mr Tregus?' Henrietta asked with a boldness that shocked the others.

'Now steady on lass,' Ernest objected with a hint of warning to his young sister.

'No it's all right, Ernest,' said the big Cornishman. 'Fair question.' He thought a moment, smiling at Henrietta, then continued ''Bout once in six months, I suppose.'

'Six months,' the other men chorused.

'Bloody 'ell. We 'ave to 'ave one every day. Jane Brightside d'ave summat to say to thee.' Sidall complained and spat on the fire again.

'When do you leave?' Henrietta asked Tregus.

'Leave?'

'Yes. Go back to wherever it was you came from.'

'Oh, I see. Leave,' Tregus said. 'Long before I'm due my next bath, ma'am. Why I had one only last night, didn't I, lads?' He grinned, widely, Henrietta thought too widely, like a Cheshire cat.

A few days went by. Her grandmother returned from her visit to Wakefield. Henrietta still pondered how she might expose her attacker. She had for those few days even stopped visiting Bottom Boat so that she could spend more time in the village. She resorted to gossip. She would stop people in the street, call on others she'd not spoken to in ages, merely to engage them in conversation; but not once did she meet an irate wife or sweetheart, never did she come across a cheeky or knowing smile. As time went by it seemed more and more likely that Tregus was the only possible suspect. She had remembered the smell of grandmother's flowers when her attacker had entered the bedroom; the big hand over her mouth; the smell of bath potions on his massive nakedness. Had the Cornishman not

56

admitted to taking a bath that very night and had he not refused to have another one, ever again in our house, making some flimsy excuse that he bathed only once in six months. Not likely. Tregus was an educated man; it was his job to educate others. Was that the sort of person to take a bath only once in six months? And another thing. Was anybody likely to be able to sneak into the house past three lodgers in the parlour without waking at least one of them? At one time she thought it might be John or Charley Gill next door, but could either of those great big men possibly enter the house without commotion? No. It looked increasingly like one of the residents of the house. They had bathed together, all except Tregus, for four consecutive days now without a murmur reaching her ears. Besides, she knew, as if further proof were needed, that Junkin would have wheezed his way through the whole episode, Pettit would never have been able to keep his mouth shut, unstacking God knows what information upon her pillow, and her brother's wife would by now have spoken out having discovered something by the light of her small candle. But if it was Tregus how on earth was she to get him to expose himself? She decided that she would have to enlist the help of her nephew William, my father.

Now I'd better tell you about the earth closets. The earth closets were our toilets and they were at the back of the terrace of houses and their doors faced onto the back scullery of each house, about twenty yards distant. For some reason never explained they had been built in pairs. Ours adjoined that of the Gill family. Each pair was of a squarish brick structure, with two wooden doors. A thin brick wall separated each toilet, running from front to back, between the two doors. The toilet seat was made of wood and ran the length of the building running right through the dividing brick wall. It was about two and a half feet from the ground. The holes in the centre of the seat were perfectly circular which was all right if, like the Gills, you had perfectly circular bottoms. We Brightsides, however, were on the slender side, particularly the men. We found our earth closet seats less comfortable than the Gills did theirs. The earth closets were open to the elements, a blessing of doubtful value, for though the structure was ventilated in this way, defecation was a truly miserable affair when it rained or snowed.

In the interests of hygiene all the muck and excrement was raked out from the earth below the toilets on a daily basis. This was done from the back, the wall away from the scullery. In our house it was always Sidall Junkin who did this. He would go for a crap and rake out the accumulated excrement each morning at five, a chore he'd assumed since settling in to lodge following the death of his friend James Brightside. He would rake all the muck and excrement together than cover it with a bucketful of ashes from the fire. The area behind the earth closets was for this reason called the ash pits, and remained a smelly heap of mounds and craters until the midden man came in his midden wagon, at somewhat irregular intervals, to shovel and cart the lot off to God knows where. Nobody could ever understand why the midden man had entered his chosen profession and the children in particular stayed well away from him, watching from a safe distance as he shovelled the loathsome mess into his wagon. My father and the twins felt terribly sorry for the horse, a large blinkered beast whose white hair had been slowly turned grey-brown in the atmosphere of shit and dust. They used to dream of freeing the poor animal from its awful servility but nobody ever dared more than dream. The midden man was a powerful symbol of evil in our village and Albert, right up to his early twenties, was convinced that the stinking load was carted right off to be burned in a huge dump at the very centre of the earth. It was after one such emptying of the ash pits that Henrietta caught sight of my father playing around the earth closets and she there conceived her plan.

'William, dear. Come here a moment,' she called.

My father, ever ready to please, came running. 'Yes, Aunt Henrietta.'

'William, I wish you to help me in rather an unusual way,' she confided. My father, then nine years old, listened with obscene delight to the plan which his aunt had hatched. She wanted him to play a game. He was to hide in the space below the toilet at the Gill side (it was a good job he was small). Eventually someone would come and sit on our toilet seat and when William heard his aunt singing 'Ta-ra-ra-boom-de-ay' (a favourite among the children at the time), he should light his candle, directing the illumination upward and across and see if there was anything unusual about the sitter's bottom.

58

'Will it be you, Aunt Henrietta, sitting on the toilet?' William asked.

'It most certainly will not,' she said offensively and clipped her nephew about the ear.

'Who will it be then? Not great-grandmother.' He pulled a face.

'No, not at all. It will be a complete stranger, William.'

My father, who was quite unused to bottoms, then asked what might be so unusual about the sitter's bottom, and Henrietta, who now realized that she too had little experience of them, had to think hard for a time.

'William,' she said at last, 'it will be dirty.'

This, however, was like informing him that coal was black. To little boys all bottoms are dirty. The puzzlement on his face must have shown itself for she added, 'It will be quite black, I think, William.'

'Don't you know?' he asked.

'And it may have some words on it too.'

Now to my little father this was all too much and he burst out laughing.

'Be serious, William,' she chided, 'this is very important detective work.'

'But what will it say?' William asked, sniggering into his little grubby hand.

'I don't know,' his aunt responded, 'but you must promise me, William, that you will not try to read it. Promise me, William. Promise that you will not attempt to read the words.'

'I promise,' my father said, already enjoying the game immensely. 'But why are we doing this, Aunt Henrietta?' he asked.

'To help the police, William,' she answered putting her fingers to her lips and hushing him with her mellifluous eyes. After tea, his aunt directed William to take his place, match and candle in hand, below the toilet seats. And there he stayed while his ever so clever auntie busied herself in the garden which the Brightsides had cultivated on the land between the scullery and the earth closets. Soon Henrietta caught sight of John Tregus making his way to the toilet and William heard somebody enter the small building. He heard the door close and the lighting of a candle as the Cornishman settled down to read. From the garden came the coarse strains of his aunt's version of 'Ta-ra-ra-boom-de-ay'. William struck a match, lit his own candle and gingerly held out

59

his arm to cast light upon the sitter's bottom. From below the candle the boy peered into the ring of gloom. Lying, as he was, spreadeagled along the width of the two toilets, he was able to make room to gawp at the stranger's magnificent equipment. He was quite unaware of the songstress in the garden, reaching a peak of discord; to my father 'Ta-ra-ra-boom-de-ay' was not a song – only a game; it could not be played badly. You sang it, that's all. Then he was aware of the door to the Gill's toilet being opened, and suddenly a deeper darkness fell upon him as a second bottom cut off the circle of pale light above his legs.

'Hello, what's this?' It was Charley Gill's voice. 'Who've we got down 'ere then?' He felt a thick hand clutching at his trousers. Now, as my father later explained it to me, if you're being chased by the fastest second row forward in the Northern rugby union you move quickly, and he did. But there was only one way to go and that was to follow his hand and the lighted candle upwards. There was a terrible yelling as the Cornishman's magnificent equipment singed at the end of the flame. A welcome circle of pale light appeared as Tregus's bottom was removed like a lid from an Arabian jar and my father came screaming like a harridan, upward through the toilet, and away from Charley's awesome clutches. Tregus too startled, or maybe too injured to stop him, allowed the boy to escape through the door and into the arms of his gardening aunt who was still offering her grating refrain to the whole village.

'Did you see it, William?' she asked, excitedly.

William merely shook his head, his frightened eyes darting wildly around him. Eventually he left this island haven for the full comfort of his mother in the rooms above the parlour, sobbing uncontrollably for ages, before joining the others below.

Tregus then hobbled by, watched from the closet doorway by a bemused Charley Gill.

'Good evening, Miss Brightside,' he said, ever the gentleman. My father's aunt merely nodded and turned to follow the wounded man into the house. For the remainder of the evening my father refused communication with his aunt who, mainly through the agency of her beautiful brown eyes, kept on asking for information.

Unable to contain himself or the pain any longer, Tregus asked Ernest to step outside where he explained to a bowl of stars that he had been badly burned by an unknown person in a place which he didn't care to name. Ernest was sensible enough to tell his grandmother who offered the lodger her tender care. She was after all by now eighty-six years old and reputed to be a witch. So the big man put himself at her mercy and she got to massage his magnificent equipment at least once a day for nearly a month.

'Is there anything strange about his bottom, grandmother?' Henrietta asked.

'Why, child, what an odd question to ask me,' the old woman answered. 'Whatever would tha' be thinking? His bottom's burned, that's all.'

'But is there anything different about it, grandmother?'

'Yes, child,' she said. 'It's getting better, that's what's different.'

Mr Tregus gradually recovered, still unsure of how his rear end had come to receive its injuries. The imp which screamed upward and outward from the toilet had not been identified, and he cared not to discuss too deeply with those who might prompt him whether it was the work of child or spirit. For a time the earth closets, and in particular the structure shared by the Gills and the Brightsides, became forbidden territory to the children. The thing which lurked there, they reasoned, had probably been left by the midden man, who was assumed now to have an even greater propensity for evil than had ever before been imagined. Even Charley Gill grew to doubt whether the trouser leg he had grabbed that evening had any material content. Thus did the 'ghost of the earth closets' become absorbed into the folklore of our village. John Tregus remained with us for several months, setting up a programme for adult learning at the chapel in the next village. He managed to get started classes in History and Science which all the menfolk in our house attended on Tuesday and Wednesday nights respectively. Then, when he had handed over the running of the classes to local people, he left our house to do the same in some other area of the coalfield. Before he left he gave my father a shilling, the twins sixpence each, and shook hands in turn with each of the remaining members of the household. He urged Henrietta to continue to write her History of the Stones, for one day he was certain it would be an immensely important document. My great-great-grandmother thought him to be the finest gentleman she had ever met.

— 7 —

A mad way of looking at the mad, mad world

The one piece of furniture in our house which had not been either knocked together by the occupants or purchased for two and sixpense as a mass produced article, was great-great-grandmother's dressing table. It had been brought back from France at the time of the Napoleonic Wars by her father. A part of his plunder, although he preferred to call it compensation (for the loss of an eye and a foot). He gave it to Jane at the time of her marriage to John Brightside. It had been the only piece of furniture which she had loaded onto the cart and carried to her son's house at the time of her removal. James had had to winch it through the bedroom window at the time and he and Sidall Junkin had positioned it against the wall which adjoined the Gill house in the room in which his mother would eventually sleep. In those difficult moments during which the article was hauled into the house the oval mirror was unfortunately cracked diagonally, a fracture which remained always, splitting the image of the looker into a curious derangement from top right to lower left. One looked into that mirror and couldn't help but see the crazy side of one's nature; no matter how composed and sensible one felt a madman always stared back, mortal and deeply flawed.

The dressing table was not particularly large, nor was it very heavy, but it was different and so assumed a pride of place within the small cluttered bedroom. One had to walk around it to get from the top of the stairs to the adjoining door between the two bedrooms, always brushing the bed as one did so, much to the annoyance of both the walking and the sleeping. The article, however, was rarely moved, just on the odd occasion would it be trundled aside so that one might clean behind it. In the spring of 1902, Henrietta and her grandmother decided that it was about time that their room was redecorated and for the first time they should use anaglypta wallpaper for the hanging of which they would have to pull out the dressing table. Mirroring their every crazy thought and action they tugged the object alongside the bed, the two women eventually sprawling across the width of the mattress faces down and exhausted. When they had recovered they both went around the back of the piece of furniture to continue their decorating. They were surprised to find that a hole, large enough for a man to crawl through, had appeared in the wall adjoining the Gill house. It had been covered with a large slate at the neighbour's side.

'So that's how they came in,' my great-great-grandmother said.

'Who came in, grandmother?' Henrietta asked, feeling immediate discomfort at the revelation.

'Those five Gill boys, dear. The day they dug up the scullery floor. Do thee not remember?'

Henrietta vaguely remembered the occasion but it had been ten or eleven years ago and had made little sense to the young girl. 'Why did they do that?' she enquired.

'They were looking for treasure,' she told her. 'We must get it bricked again,' she then suggested.

Of course her grandmother's talk of the Gill boys gaining access to the house through their bedroom had given my great-aunt other ideas. It was not now so far fetched to think that Charley or John (the only two of the five still living at home) might have been her assailant. Good Lord, she thought, one must by now have seen the other, stamps and all. And she visualized the frantic rubbing and scrubbing away of the offending marks practised in clandestine brotherhood on each bath night. A practice accompanied no doubt by grandmother's potions, for she had also learned that Mrs Gill was an excellent customer of the old lady's medicaments. But to no avail she was sure; for indelible Elyahou Tsiblitz had said the ink was and indelible it proved to be. By way of testing the truthfulness of his view she had stamped a very small area of her upper arm with the word 'love'. Indeed she was certain nothing on earth could remove the cloying ink. She began now to contemplate the second plan which would involve her nephew William in dangerous detective work.

The four remaining brothers each formed part of a terrible eightsome playing professional rugby for the Castleford club. As I have already mentioned they were part of the greatest and biggest pack of forwards ever to step onto the turf. Now, in those days, there were no baths or changing rooms at the ground, so the men would change into their playing strip at home, walk or cycle to the ground (Wakefield had a hooker who ran the fifteen miles there and back with a bruising game between journeys), play up and return bloodied and muddied for a hot bath and a good meal. At the Gill house Saturday afternoons had become a ritual. All four boys, together with their mother, would after the game have a spanking meal, usually a sheep's head cooked in beer, which the woman would spend nearly all day preparing. Henrietta's plan was this. After the next home match when the boys had returned for their bath and the curtains had been drawn (always a sure sign that men were naked within) Henrietta would stuff a turpentine soaked rag under the scullery door and set it alight. William then, on her signal would approach from the front of the house shouting 'fire', and advising the occupants to leave immediately in fear of their lives. Meanwhile, Lancaster and Albert, both having been presented at the last Christmas with cameras from their great-grandmother, would be positioned at points suitable to photograph the ensuing flight and capture on film and forever any incriminating evidence about the back-sides of the Gill boys. In the furore, Henrietta would then slip into the house and douse the fire with the contents of the tin bath.

Well, the day arrived, Castleford were playing the massive team from Batley and my father, who had been to the game and seen his heroes mete out a terrible pasting to the men in blue, followed the Gill boys home. He was questioning whether it was righteous or not to carry through the plan and deceive the objects of his devotion in such a way. Detective work or not, he felt as if he were becoming a traitor, and he knew, from his father's preaching, what happened to them. He soon realized, however, that things were not going entirely to plan for walking up ahead with the four Castleford men were three others dressed in blue jerseys. His aunt had not allowed for the Gills' hospitality. These three men, almost half the opposition pack who only minutes before had been the object of his derision and hatred, were now, arms about their hosts' big shoulders, on their way to the Gill house for a bath and a share in the sheep's head. Treachery's a slippery thing, it can be passed like a rugby ball, my father

64

thought. Here now were the Gills behaving like traitors and he suddenly felt guilt no longer for what he was about to do. It was in such a frame of mind that he entered the village behind the giant neighbours and their guests. When the last rugby player had been clapped through the door (there was always a reception committee to greet them) and, the black curtains draped across the window, Henrietta went into action. She quickly set up the two tripods for the twin cameras. She gave each nephew their instructions and then covered them in a black cloth. With the late afternoon sun filtering the hazy air they looked like two beings from another planet set down on our common for a spot of gentle grazing.

Henrietta quickly went to the back of the house and gave my father the signal to go into action. 'Ta-ra-ra-boom-de-ay' wafted over the roof. My father, now feeling quite guiltless and sure of the direction in which treachery lay, started for the door and began to shout, 'Fire, fire!' He ran to the Gill house and beat upon the closed door with little fists. 'Get out, get out! Run for your lives!' The door burst open and seven naked men ran over my little father in a hasty retreat from the smoke which was billowing from the parlour. The four biggest forwards in the rugby union, plus three of the terrible Batley eight, poured like a blancmange in clogs over the pitiful William. Half a dozen dogs fielding at the boundary, including a long stop named Denton, then attacked the naked men in defence of the run-down child. The rugby players turned and fled with the dogs snapping at their heels. The cameras went off with loud bangs and a puff of smoke from each of the strange animals. Henrietta appeared in time to see seven backsides hurtling into the distance, smiled, went inside the Gill house and put out the fire. On coming out again, she gathered up the dazed William, pulled to her the strange animals now separating into twins and tripods, and cuddled them all the way into the Brightside home, watched by wide eyes set into the dirty faces of the human half of the village cricket team. That's how we come to have in our family photograph album two pictures, taken from slightly differing angles, of seven naked men haring across the common and each with a bottom as white as the day that he was born. What a disappointment for my father's aunt!

At her first glimpse of the developed photographs she went upstairs to her bedroom. She peered behind the dressing table, whose tulip wood and delicate marquetry had been covered in a wash of lime as part of the redecorating process, checking that the freshly bricked hole remained intact. Sitting on the bed before the cracked mirror, she started to cry. She watched tears rolling down her left cheek as far as the glittering scar, then disappearing only to reappear somewhere else, yet still down the same cheek. She adjusted her position on the bed, lifting her head and shoulders, in such a way that the crack ran through her chin. Now the tear drops seemed to flow right into it like a tributary to a river. She remained motionless, crying, watching the river which carried away her tears. The flaw on the right side cut right through her eye. She imagined it blurred her vision, as it was cutting her eye in two. How would the world look to such an eye, she wondered. The two eyes looked down to her left, down the glinting river watching the tears pool and flow. What a mad and frustrating world, she thought. Would she ever find her rapist? She watched herself watching the tears flowing down the river and out of the oval mirror, then looked back to the photograph upon her lap. Was it wrong to create such mayhem?

Or did the disorder exist anyway? Had she promoted the madness of the photograph, if indeed it were mad? Hadn't the selfsame seven naked men been naked moments before she lit the rags? Were they mad then? Was the situation then mad? No, she came to the conclusion that it was she who was mad. She lit the rags, that was an act of madness. Everything which followed, the men fleeing the fire, William being mown down, the dogs barking, the twins photographing the whole scene, even her entering the house to douse the flames (for which she was commended by an admiring Mrs Gill) were natural consequences of what she herself had set in train at the other side of the house – at the darker side she thought. And what of poor William? Her crazy schemes had put the boy in mortal danger now on two occasions. She would have to apologize to her nephew, she thought, and so went in search of my unfortunate father. Finding him on the common directly in front of our house, she drew him to one side, at the same time asking his flock of dirty friends to take themselves off to other fields.

'I am sorry, William' she said.

'What for?'

'For putting you in such danger at the earth closet and again the other day outside the Gills' house. I didn't realize that police work was so dangerous.'

'I don't want no more police work,' my father said in sudden panic.

'Don't worry, William,' his aunt consoled him. 'I shall not ask you again.'

With relief he said, 'I thought you were going to ask me. I don't like detective work, Aunt Henrietta.' He sobbed, and she tugged him to her bosom. 'Oh, William, please don't cry,' she said, biting her lip as the dirty flock of friends approached within a stone's throw of them.

'No,' he said, pulling himself from his aunt and composing himself with a large sniff, 'Don't tell anyone but I'm going to try thieving for a time.'

'Don't be silly, William. You'll soon be found out.'

'Not if I'm careful,' he answered.

'You'll be caught,' she stressed. 'The police can now detect the culprit from his fingerprints.'

'What's them?'

'It's true, William. The police now are able to identify the criminal by the fingerprints he leaves at the scene of his crime. I read it in the paper only last week.'

'Go on, you're kidding me,' my father answered.

'No, it's true. We each of us have a different print which can be shown up using a special powder. It's just like leaving a calling card. There'll be no more thieves running free, William.' Seeing the group of ragged friends advancing ever closer she added, 'You'd better tell them, too. Just in case they have any ideas.'

My father took to heart what his aunt had told him and steered clear of a life of crime, at least for the next five years. That was until the year in which Elyahou Tsiblitz paid his third visit to our village.

It was in those five years that the world beyond our village went absolutely crazy. President Roosevelt and our king exchanged messages by wireless, talking to one another over a distance of thousands of miles. An anarchist attempted to kill King Leopold of the Belgians. In London trains appeared which worked by electricity, then too the trams were electrified. Then in December 1903, as Duncan D'Arcy had predicted to my great-great-grandmother, a heavier-than-air machine flew for the very first time. Two American brothers in Kitty Hawk, North Carolina, had flown at thirty miles per hour on a flight lasting fifty-nine seconds. Then the buses were motorized; in London horse-drawn vehicles were becoming fewer. A man called George Rogers attached himself to the Russian army and sent back film he made during the Russo-Japanese war. Grand Duke Sergius of Russia was assassinated in Moscow, then somebody tried to kill the king of Spain in Paris, on two separate occasions within a few days of each other. A bomb was thrown at the Sultan of Turkey in Constantinople. Female agitators were ejected from the House of Commons, and then subsequently interrupted political meetings at Northampton and Manchester. Lieutenant Lahn won the Gordon Bennet Cup, flying all the way from Paris to Whitby in a balloon. Several suffragettes were arrested at the House of Commons and imprisoned. An anarchist made an attempt on the life of Alfonso XIII on his wedding day. The bioscope and kinema opened up in London and quickly spread to the provinces.

In our village, however, nothing happened. The men still hewed coal with picks and shovels and still bought candles from Thwaite. Accidents still happened. The dead were brought up if possible; the injured lay uncomfortably at home drawing a benefit barely enough to keep them alive. Ernest still forbade the use of oil lamps at our house, and the occupants still lived dimly within the halo of a candle's power. Henrietta, the incident of the rape fairly gone from her mind, continued to describe the stones. In her bedroom, the cracked mirror continued to monitor the sanity of those who cared to look into it.

The rise and fall of Sidall Junkin
and the fall and rise of the price of coal

It was back in the summer of 1873 that a great row broke out down at the pit head. Now ours was only a small pit employing fewer than two hundred men, so when trouble brewed it fermented quickly. And there was nothing like a bit of cheating on the part of the coal owner or his lackeys to get the brew started. A check-weighman by the name of Cotton who had been appointed by Thwaite had been caught on the fiddle. I'd better explain that the checkweighman, being the man responsible both for recording the tally of tubs filled against a hewer's name and for seeing that there is no underfilling of tubs (the fine imposed for such was to discount the whole of the tub) could afford no enemies. Nor, for that matter, could he afford to have friends, at least he ought not to have friends at the coal face. Impartiality was called for if the checkweighman was to survive.

Unfortunately Cotton had not the impartiality required for the job for he kept discounting tubs filled by our neighbours, the Hendersons. Worse still, it seems that on odd occasions he actually recorded tubs belonging to old man Henderson to the tally of Enoch Carpenter, himself a loathsome cheat and drinking partner of Cotton. Well, you can imagine the commotion that broke when suspicion finally turned to proof and Cotton was caught red-handed fiddling the tallies. He was spreadeagled and pinned to a door which had been brought from the joiner's shop, a pickaxe each through cuffs and trouser bottoms, while the men debated what should be done with him. Those who couldn't add up were quick to point to their certainty that they too had been cheated in the past, while those who were able to add but who were short on memory claimed likewise. It quickly got to the stage when all the hewers were claiming some shortfall in their cumulative tallies and clamoring for the blood of the unfortunate man spread upon the door. Sidall Junkin, who could both add up and had a good memory (a rarity on that day), calmed things a little when he pointed out that it was not possible for everyone to claim a shortfall in their tally. After all, if one loses then some other has to gain, just as Enoch Carpenter had gained one from Henderson. There was a general nodding of agreement with the logic of Sidall's argument followed by a quiet accusatory silence when the men realized that perhaps their neighbours, the very men who were now gesticulating vociferously by their sides, might be fiddling at their expense. This appeared a thought common to all at that moment and it was Enoch Carpenter, sensing the mood of the men and in need of friends if he were not to end up like Cotton, skewered to a board, who turned the situation to advantage.

'Seems like Cotton can't do the job. Seems to me he's been making mistakes ever since he started. Serves us right, I suppose, for accepting a checkweighman appointed by Thwaite.'

'Ay, he's right,' shouted old man Henderson. 'We should appoint us own. Someone we can all trust. A tallyman's position's too important for us to leave it to't coal owner.'

These two statements helped relieve the tension which the men were feeling. The cheat and the cheated were in common agreement with the unfortunate Cotton between, no more than an idiot doing his best. Nobody had been fiddled, not deliberately at least. The men breathed more easily. They ceased to eye their neighbours with suspicion. Cotton was released from his wooden bed of torment.

'Wait a minute. What if we've all been cheated?' It was Sidall Junkin's wheezy voice again. 'What if Cotton has systematically deducted tubs from all of us?'

'But tha' said there'd have to be gains,' James Brightside reminded him.

'Ay, perhaps the gains went to Thwaite. By not recording a tub and not awarding it to anyone's tally, who gains? It's still a tub full of coal, isn't it?'

'Thwaite,' came the chorused reply.

'Ay. Thwaite and that bugger Cotton,' Sidall shouted back. Now here was a man to be listened to. In a few moments he'd come forth with two first-class ideas. What did it matter that one contradicted the other? It was more important that one was viewed as an extension of the other. Sidall was seen to be thinking not just on his feet but on the move. These were the ideas of a man of action.

The unfortunate Cotton was again pinned to the board.

'Chuck bugger down t'shaft,' someone shouted from the crowd. 'No. There'll be no need for that,' Sidall wheezed holding his arms aloft and waiting for silence. 'We'll tek 'im to Thwaite, just as he is.'

'Ay,' they chorused amid laughter. 'Let's tek 'im to Thwaite.' With Cotton spread upon the door and his clothes in tatters, fifty men marched on the big house. They went through the gates where the giant boulders stood aloft the stone pillars and up the leafy lane which led to the coal owner's home. Thwaite was waiting, the door shut behind him.

'Thwaite,' shouted the young Henderson, 'we've come to sithee' 'bout this.' He motioned toward the board above the many outstretched arms, on which Thwaite could just see the lifted head of a man trying to make himself known out of the agony and the anonymity of crucifixion.

'It's Mr Thwaite to thee, lad,' the coal owner said with courage, before the mass of men and ignoring the prone man's plight. 'What is that, anyroad?' he eventually asked, pointing up to the board with his cane. The ragged man was set down with the care a family of Moroccans would exercise when showing a rare carpet. The men were aware now of his asset value, but the boss only too well aware of Cotton's changing fortunes prodded the prone tallyman with his stick.

'Been caught cheating 'ave thee, lad?' he asked. He tut-tutted, shaking his head and not taking his eyes from the unfortunate Cotton. 'A checkweighman really has to be beyond that sort of behaviour, lad. He really has.' Looking at the men he asked, 'What's tha' want me to do?'

'Tha' set him on, he's been cheatin' for thee,' Henderson said.

'Nobody cheats for me, lad. I can do my own cheating, thanks very much,' Thwaite replied with a light laugh.

'He's been under-tallying, regular,' Henderson said.

'Incompetent, is he?' the coal owner said, prodding Cotton again. A booted foot swung out of the crowd and struck the man on the leg. The crowd was beginning to realize what a useless asset they really had.

71

'I'm sorry, lads,' Thwaite continued. 'It was my choice, I admit that. I'll be more careful next time.'

'There won't be a next time, Mr Thwaite,' James Brightside said. 'We'll choose us own tallyman from now on.'

'Now steady, Brightside. Don't go threatening'.'

'No threats, Mr Thwaite. We choose us own. What have thee to say?'

'I'm sayin' now't, lad,' the coal owner said, holding his ground, and looking grimly about the mass of men. An immediate call for strike action went up from all the men on hearing the coal owner's response. Now Thwaite was nobody if he wasn't the supreme general; he knew exactly when to withdraw.

'All right, Brightside, who's tha' tallyman?' he asked, surprising the others with the allowed space into which they'd tumbled.

'Sidall Junkin,' my great-grandfather responded quickly. Perhaps too quickly for the colliers hadn't had chance to discuss it between themselves.

The coal owner studied Sidall for a long time, then he said, 'Tha's not a church goer, Junkin.'

Sidall shook his head.

'Tha's never been to a union meeting 'as tha', Sid?' he then asked. Sidall again shook his head.

'Tha's not a big man. Tha's not slow but I wouldn't say tha' was quick-witted either. Tha's a small wheezy man with black spit, Junkin. Take care tha' doesn't end up on a board like Cotton here. Start as checkweighman in't mornin',' the coal owner said decisively and went back into the house, closing the door behind him.

Cotton was released from the board halfway down the leafy lane, and he was kicked all the way back to the village. He had an extremely sore backside but no further injury befell him, that is not until he was maimed in a rock fall the following year.

Sidall, as instructed, assumed his new duty immediately and became a very popular and efficient checkweighman. Four years later at the time of James Brightside's death he was still the most trusted of the tallymen. When my great-grandfather was killed, crushed beneath the fallen fossilized bones of an Iguanadon, the pit was still working a three-day week, but soon after that the pit resumed full working. Due to the drastic fall in coal prices though, rather than work more short time the men had accepted a scale of pay which was related to the price of coal. Wages fell. When Jack went into the pit at the age of thirteen, he received no more than ten shillings a week, half of what he would have earned five years before.

The death of his friend wounded Sidall deeply. The day that he died, after leaving my great-great-grandmother and before descending the shaft to look for James, he had grabbed an old sack which lay on the ground at the holeside. Then, in the rising rotten flood water he had swum to where he knew the dinosaur bones to be. He could see a small light in the distance and knew it must be the flame of his friend's candle. 'I'm coming, James,' he shouted. 'Hang on!' The words echoed above the shortening chamber as the waters rose up the walls of rock. When he arrived at the flickering candle, however, he saw that it was still perched in his friend's helmet like a ghostly feather in an alpine cap. In the dim light he was able to see how the cavern had collapsed; the tons of fossilized bones lying in a great cairn, he assumed, above his buried friend. He reached his arm out of the water to grasp the helmet and as he did so the flame died. What he felt then was not a helmet but something altogether more soft, like flock he thought. He grabbed at it and stuffed it in the sack. In the dark, feeling about with one hand, he found other things and stuffed them too into the sack. Something touched his face lightly for a moment, then was gone. 'James,' he said quietly. 'Is tha' here, James?' There was no answer from the wet darkness, only the noise of the rising waters, lapping the rock.

Swimming for his life in the foul flood and lugging the sack of God knows what behind in the pitch black, he swore there and then to find a better way. There had to be a way beyond Thwaite to dig coal with dignity and in safety. A way to die in bed surrounded by children and not blasted to nothing in a foul pit, or spitting alone from a chair in the parlour. The day after they had buried the sack Sidall went to a lodge meeting at the mission hall in the next village. It was at a time when Union rolls were falling; there were five other union members present. Sidall spoke for the first time in public. He had no recollection afterwards of what he had said, only that he rambled on for at least an hour to an almost empty hall. He spoke of Thwaite and James Brightside. Of the iniquities of the wage scale and the need for strike action. Of the need for cooperation, not just amongst working colleagues but between lodges, between districts, even between areas. He was speaking of federation. And at the end of the evening he found that because he was a man to be trusted, a man with a job that demanded trust, he had been made lodge secretary. But he was secretary to a lodge whose numbers fell in a district whose numbers were falling even faster. At times there might be only himself and the treasurer at the meetings, but he stuck it out talking to himself, occasionally being rewarded with an audience of a half dozen or more who would listen docile and polite to his wheezy oratory. Soon he was delegated to the district committee of the Yorkshire Miner's Association and here his views received more than a polite hearing. He spoke to them of federation, of the strength in unity. Yes, they all agreed a national federation was needed, that would give them strength in their fight with the mine owners. In 1881 the Association refused any longer to accept the scale of pay related to the price of coal, and the following year the Yorkshire and Lancashire miners supported each other in their bargaining for the 10% wage increase. It meant strikes here and there, but Thwaite paid up without a struggle. Sidall Junkin was a hero, and the price of coal fell even further.

Then came Sidall's entry into the economics arena. Mr Thwaite met with him at the mission hall to hear his views. Outside a blizzard wrapped itself silently about the chapel. Quiet white footprints were filled in almost as quickly as they had been made. Inside, excited and frequently spitting into his clean handkerchief, the tallyman explained his ideas.

'Coal output's increased steadily, Mr Thwaite, so has the number of men employed. Nobody cuts any more coal now than he did fifteen years since. That means only one thing, over-production.'

'Ay, or over-manning.'

Sidall ignored the remark. 'There's too much coal chasing the same market, Mr Thwaite. Tha' can see that.'

'Ay,' Thwaite said stamping his feet beneath the table.

'Well, it must make sense to thee, a business man like thee, Mr Thwaite, to cut production.'

'Ay,' he said, and stamped his feet again.

Sidall watched the great sky without shedding huge blue flakes through the coloured window.

'What are thee suggesting, Junkin?' the coal owner prompted.

'The eight-hour day, Mr Thwaite. That's what I'm proposing'.

'Bugger off,' scolded Thwaite. 'Does tha' think I'm a muggins or summat? Nivver! If tha' wants to reduce production, and I don't think it would be too bad a thing mind, if we all agreed, tha' can have a three-day week like afore.'

'And three days' wages?' enquired Sidall.

'Ay, of course. Tha' didn't think I'd pay a full week's wage for three days' work did tha'?'

Sidall shook his head.

'Tha' wants it all, Junkin. Tha' wants federation, tha' wants more brass, shorter hours. There's nowt for thee, lad. With price of coal as it is, pot's empty.'

'But I'm givin' thee a way to raise the price of coal, Mr Thwaite. Tha' must see.'

'And what about the competition, lad? What about all t'other pits? Does tha' think all the coal owners will follow suit? Will they buggery! I'll tell thee what they'll do, Junkin. They'll bury me, and thee and tha' men. They'll bury us, lad, and good riddance they'll say.'

'So what'll it be, Mr Thwaite?' Sidall asked. 'Will it come to lay offs?'

There was no guile in the question, he merely tossed it like a bone to a dog – to see what Thwaite would do with it.

'Come on, Junkin, tha' knows I can't do that. We don't want anybody starving, do we?'

'No,' said Sidall. But for the life of him he couldn't think why Mr Thwaite cared that much for the men and their families. The dog hadn't even licked the bone.

'Tha'll have to accept a new scale in the end, Junkin. Either that or a three-day week. Now is there any more?' Sidall shook his head. 'Then I'll be off,' Thwaite said.

'Why don't tha' stay, Mr Thwaite?' Sidall asked. 'It's snowing hard out there. No point in going home in a blizzard.'

'Nay, lad, I'm not soft.'

'Well, I think I'll curl up here,' Sidall wheezed.

'Do as tha' please, lad,' Thwaite said. 'I said I'm not soft. I'll make my way back.' Then he stepped out into a cold, white and silent as the stars.

Thwaite was right though. The men had to accept a sliding scale, but before that Sidall Junkin was humiliated into accepting

75

a 15% reduction in wages. The men were locked out for six weeks until they capitulated, cold and hungry. The price of coal continued to fall. In her lifetime, Jane Brightside could not remember having seen so many starve, so many children going without shoes and breeches. The hero in the wide-winged chair was a hero no more. His eyes became sunken and black. His black spit became more tenacious, resisting for longer the flames of the fire. The men couldn't trust him any longer, not as their tallyman. Thwaite gave him a job picking out stones from the coal at the pit head. The job of secretary to the lodge went to young Oliver Henderson in whose term the price of coal began to rise; in whose term the Miners' Federation of Great Britain was founded, and in whose term 40% increase in wages was awarded to all the miners. Such was Sidall's luck riding on the price of coal.

But the price of coal is a switchback and within a year of the massive pay awards prices again took a tumble. The Yorkshire miners pugnaciously declared their wages were as low as ever they were going to be. There'd be no reductions and no scales negotiated. The capitalists would have to control their selling prices without affecting labour.

One Sunday Jack and Ernest, now both employed as hewers, took a walk. From chapel they decided to walk up towards Leeds. Leaving the taste of grit far behind they walked slowly through the meandering lanes about the Thwaite house. The sun filtered through the trees in the green leafy lanes, right down to the tracks, dry and rutted from the constant passage of cart wheels. What little grass there was appeared worn but it was a lush full colour like it always was away from the villages in the summer. The pink and white hawthorn hedgerows which hemmed them in for much of their walk broke suddenly to a field of yellow corn. At a bend in the lane they again tasted coal grit. It was Jack who noticed it first, his brother soon after. Then beyond the field of corn they could see rising and brooding over the flat fields stacks of coal. In the sun they shone black and brittle. They quickly crossed the track in the field and approached the steeply rising heaps.

'There's no pit here,' Ernest said.

'No,' said his brother, surveying the mountainous landscape they were coming upon. 'It must be a stockpile.'

They wandered about the awesome black pyramids wondering who on earth could own such mountains of their labour. The area seemed to extend for ever, black and brilliant and, from some angles, blotting out the sun.

'Thwaite,' Jack said. 'Thwaite's bloody stockpile.'

'Nay, this isn't Thwaite's land.'

'Who then? It's got to be Thwaite's.'

Ernest marvelled at the amount of coal set down in the middle of waving fields of corn.

'There's more 'ere than there is in't pit,' he said.

'Look on tha' labour, lad,' Jack advised. 'It's all here. As much as tha'll ever cut in tha' life. Thee and me both, maybe all lads in terrace. Thwaite's got us tallied up and saved, lad. There it is. Tha's been saved on earth lad, even as it is in heaven.'

When they arrived back at the house and informed Sidall Junkin of what they had found, his sunken eyes seemed for a time to lift themselves from their sockets. The dullness went and a gleam touched off from his dark pupils.

'I knew it,' he said with an enthusiastic wheeze. 'I told that bugger Thwaite years since he was over-producing and he knew it too.'

'No wonder price of coal is falling,' Sidall went on. 'Go get Henderson, Ernest.'

My grandfather ran from the house to bring home their illustrious neighbour, whose fortunes as lodge secretary were on the wave. The price of coal was falling again.

'Oliver,' Sidall said after Ernest had explained their find, 'tha' needs a miracle, lad. Make good use of it.'

''Ows tha' mean, Sidall?'

'We'll do Thwaite's job for 'im. We'll curb his stocks.'

'How?'

'We'll take it back, that's what.'

'What! Thieve the stockpile?' Oliver said incredulously.

'Ay.'

'Where'd we keep it?'

'Down't pit, silly bugger, where else?'

Oliver stared at the ex-secretary open-mouthed.

'Now, don't look like that, lad,' he continued. 'I don't mean down our pit, I mean in disused pit. Tip it down shaft on Hunger Hill where James is.'

'And how do we get it there?' Oliver asked still unbelieving.

'Call men to't pit, Oliver. I'll tell 'em 'ow.'

Sidall Junkin was now fifty-three years old, clapped out, wheezing and picking over coals at the pit head, but the glint in his eye convinced the young secretary, who was after all seeking a miracle, that perhaps he should do as requested. He called the men together at the pit head. It was the largest attendance ever to gather in the history of the village. The hero of 1882 was back, for a time, in the hearts of the people.

'Tha'll get carts and tubs, anything that'll hold coal. See the agriculturalists, get them to lend their beasts. Hosses, oxen, anything with four legs. You pit lads, bring up the ponies. We start tomorrow morning at four. Women and children too. Tha'll bring every bit of coal tha' can carry until that shafts full. Are we agreed?'

'Ay,' the men concurred, more enthusiastic than they'd been for years. 'We'll fill bugger's shaft brimfull,' Sidall shouted to the mob as it broke to seek out means of transportation.

The following morning the whole village turned out even to the youngest child and at a trot a strange train of wagons and carts set off up the rutted lanes leading to the cache of coal. Any wagon which broke down was simply lifted over the hawthorn hedge and dumped in the adjacent field. Horses had been borrowed from farmers and gypsies; there were even a couple of racehorses stolen from a stud at Wakefield. As they filed past the Thwaite house, the men and women jeered loudly. Eventually the coal owner came down his leafy lane to watch the procession filing by and to acknowledge the jeers with a smile. Even in such numbers and with such purpose the colliers were a little nervous of saying too much in the presence of the master.

To avoid congestion a route had been planned so that the procession filed in a great circle, creating a merry-go-round of enormous diameter. If only somebody had thought to have brought a steam-driven organ the circus would have been complete.

When loaded the carts continued beyond the stacks of coal to meet up with another road and proceed that way round to Hunger Hill.

'We'll not make much impression on this lot, Sid. Not like this,' Ernest said, shovelling the coal aboard his flat-backed cart with the red and silver tailboard as fast as he could. Sidall observed that all about him men, women and children were breaking backs in a strenuous effort to load their wagons as quickly as possible, yet the mountain of coal remained untouched towering above the labouring villagers.

'Keep shovelling, lad. Keep shovelling. Summat'll happen. I know it, tha'll see,' said the wheezing ex-tallyman. With the early morning sun, and maybe fifty loads already making the return journey, two strangers arrived at the stockpile. Sidall had seen them before but couldn't recollect where it might have been.

'Mr Junkin,' said the older of the two. 'I bring greetings from the Leeds Branch of the Social Democratic Federation.' The man's accent was foreign, his words lost in the scraping of shovels. 'We have brought machines to help.'

'Machines? What machines?' Sidall shouted.

'We have brought new rubber-belted machinery to convey the coal from the mountains to the carts. Your men will only have to shovel the coal onto the belts, the machines will do the rest.' He then turned to the tall young man next to him and spoke furiously in a foreign tongue. The young man ran up through the cornfield and disappeared out of sight.

'I told thee summat would turn up.' Sidall winked at Ernest. Then turning to the foreigner he asked, 'Has tha' got two?'

'Oh yes. We have one for here and one for the pit at Hunger Hill. When we have set up the conveying machine here, we shall join the train of carts and take the other across and set it working over there.'

Within minutes the tall young man had returned with several helpers in a cart. They unloaded about fifteen yards of shiny black belting which was wound on to an adjustable incline and positioned it at the lower end to the foot of the coal mountain where Ernest was shovelling. A steam engine was rigged up to drive the belt.

'There's a stream about twenty yards to our left,' the foreigner told Sidall. 'You must detail your people.' He threw several buckets down from the cart.

'You seem to have thought of everything,' Sid said, his eyes twinkling again.

'I didn't bring fuel,' the man said with a smile.

'No matter, we'll find us own,' Sidall smiled back broadly.

Ten minutes later coal was coming off the end of the belt and loading the carts at a speed greater than the dumbfounded colliers could ever have imagined.

'Here,' said the man from the Social Democratic Federation.

'I have room on my cart now. Please, you load me with coal and I join the train for Hunger Hill.'

In this way did the merry-go-round speed up. The carts and tubs were loaded after only a short pause then were on their way again, journeying at a trot to Hunger Hill and the disused pit. The first wagons were soon passing the gates to the Thwaite house for a second time and a bemused coal owner, whose sharp memory now recognized a second coming, began to wonder just what was going on beyond those gates. When he had acknowledged faces at a quickening turn for the third and fourth time he felt at last obliged to speak.

'What's going on Brightside?' he asked Jack as he passed again leading his gold-painted cart, pulled by a magnificent grey shire horse.

'It's a fair, Mr Thwaite. A fair, and a circus all in one,' said my jubilant relative.

'Any lions, or tigers?'

'No. No wild animals, Mr Thwaite. Just people. Enjoying thesselves.'

'Got a ring master, as tha'?'

'Oh ay. Foreign chap. Don't know 'is name,' Jack chuckled, and led his horse past the entrance to the big house. ''E's ring master and organ grinder all in one.' Then under his breath Jack said, 'And tha's bloody monkey this time, Mr Thwaite.'

The men, women and children of the village, together with their horses and oxen and their friends from Leeds moved mountains in twenty-four hours. The new rubber-belted machinery spewed coal back into the disused shaft at such a rate that within the rounding of the day it was filled to the top. Not another cart or tub of coal could be squeezed in. At the other end, the stockpile had been reduced considerably, mountains of their labour, as Jack had called them, had disappeared, pushed back to where they had come from. The moon shone pale on the black and straggled heaps which were left when Sidall, Jack and Ernest left the site at the back of the train for the last time. The huge merry-go-round had ceased and with the retirement of the village it too had to be put to bed. The animals were tethered to graze on the common, carts and tubs left about to be eventually returned to their owners.

Not a soul turned into work on the following day. At midday Thwaite arrived at our house.

'Junkin,' he shouted, 'this is tha' doin', I know.'

'Ay,' answered Sidall from the doorway and for all to hear he said, 'and I'm proud of it, Mr Thwaite.'

From among the nuzzling horses the coal owner yelled back, 'Well, Junkin, tha' knows me to be a man who speaks my mind, and I won't allow a turn good or bad to go by without a comment.'

'No, Mr Thwaite. I can vouch for that.'

Thwaite looked about the common where great pats of soft clap mingled with the harder bulk of horse shit.

'I hope tha's going to get this cleaned up, Junkin,' Thwaite said unexpectedly.

'Oh, it'll get cleaned, Mr Thwaite.' Sidall's voice was jubilant.

'Good man,' Thwaite shouted. 'Well, as I was saying I can't let a good turn go by without an appreciative gesture.'

'What good turn?' Sidall asked, with sudden suspicion.

'Tha' circus, yesterday, lad. That's what good turn. I like a circus, lad.'

Sidall suddenly found it difficult to converse with the coal owner. He couldn't understand Thwaite's game.

'Bags of excitement, Junkin. That's what I like. So I want to thank thee.'

'For what?'

'For fillin t'old pit with coal.'

Sidall laughed. 'Tha's welcome, Mr Thwaite. I knew one day tha'd see sense of reducing stockpiles.'

'Oh, that's not reduced stockpile, lad.'

'No?'

'No. Tha's increased it.'

Sidall watched the horses nuzzling each other. Saw the ecstasy of a scratched mane or neck. ''Ow come, Mr Thwaite?' he said.

'Weren't my bloody coal, lad,' the coal owner shouted. 'Still. It'll come in one day and it's a nice monument to tha' friend down yonder.'

9

Big twin, little twin, and my grandmother
Emily Brightside and her game with Russian dolls

Emily Brightside cuddled the new-born baby to her breast. 'He's a heavy one,' she told her husband's grandmother as she cleaned the blood from his face with a bit of rag soaked in warm water.

'Ay, heavier than William was,' the old woman answered. The two women had been closeted together in the bedroom for twelve hours, no other soul being allowed anywhere near.

'We were going to call the baby Victoria if it had been a girl, name her after the queen like. Ernest said we should call a boy Albert out of respect for the old queen's dead husband.'

'So it'll be Albert then, will it?' the old woman asked.

'I suppose,' she answered, still wiping the rag over the infant's nose and mouth.

The crying of the child had brought Ernest and Henrietta to the bedroom door. 'Out,' said their grandmother, pointing to the staircase up which they had trodden.

'Tha'll come and see when all's clean and well,' and she herded them back down the rickety wooden stairs. 'Yes, it's another lad,' she shouted down in answer to a muted question. She noted the small cheer which broke from the assembly in the room below, as the news whizzed in their circle like a ball in a roulette wheel finally coming to rest in a favoured slot.

'Keep tha' knees up, lass,' she recommended coming back into the bedroom, and taking the baby from the young woman. Suddenly she grabbed Emily's shoulder in an old and painful grip and said severely into her eyes, 'Now, Emily Brightside, tha' must do something for me. Tha' must give me one more push.'

'But I've just pushed all I can,' Emily answered, the clammy perspiration still clinging to her once white skin.

'Just one more, luv. For old Jane. Now come on,' the old woman coaxed, laying young Albert into his crib.

'Oh, I can't. No more,' Emily cried. Her matted hair stretched on the pillow like young eels.

'Yes, tha' can, lass. Tha' can.'

Suddenly Emily's back arched responding to a terrible pain within. Her face contorted squeezing and pushing; breath held tightly within her line of a mouth.

'Good lass. Good lass,' shouted the old woman.' Tha' can relax now.' And as she did so, Emily felt more of herself oozing away. A slithering from herself which she didn't expect, then a cry from somewhere down there in a space beyond.

'What is it?' she asked, raising her head a little from the pillow.

'It's another boy, luv,' the old woman answered.

'You mean I've got two, grandmother?'

'Ay, lass, it's twins.' She held up the blooded baby for the mother to see.

'E's much smaller than Albert,' were Emily's first words on seeing him.

'Ay, he's tiny,' she answered, 'but perfect, mind.' She turned him about in her hands as a potter would a lump of clay.

'He's been livin' in the shadow of that great puddin' there,' she continued. 'Born in his shadow too.'

The mother lay back, bemused, on the bed. 'Whoever would have thought, two,' she said.

The old woman cleaned him, then swathed the baby in blankets and handed him to Emily.

'He's wizened like an old man, grandmother,' she commented. 'Small and wizened.'

'He'll fill out, given time, luv. Don't tha' worry.'

'But he's so small.'

'No matter. What'll tha' call him?'

'I don't know. We didn't expect more than one. We only thought Albert.' She glanced across to where the large baby slept contentedly.

'Tha'll think of something.'

'I suppose. I just want to sleep now. I feel like I've been in the Wars of the Roses.'

'Why not call them York and Lancaster?' my great-great-grandmother smiled, putting the afterbirth and blood-soaked newspapers into a sack.

As the old woman was washing her, Emily said, 'That's a good idea, grandmother. The big one can be Albert York and this little chap here can be Lancaster. I like that.'

Afterwards, Ernest objected. 'But Emily, luv, it's coming the old duchess a bit, isn't it. York and Lancaster, I ask thee, it makes 'em sound like a couple of dukes.'

'And what about Albert?' she replied. 'Wasn't he a king?'

'A consort, lass.'

'Same difference,' she snorted and dismissed the subject forever. Thus did my two uncles became christened Albert York Brightside and Lancaster Brightside at the church in the next village.

The twins grew in their early years much as my great-great-grandmother had predicted, one in the shadow of the other. Identical in all but size they would sit side by side in their little and tiny sailor suits, Albert (York was soon dropped from the nomenclature) a bigger version of the same thing as Lancaster, and Lancaster a small edition of the same thing as Albert. Old Dr Cartwright put it in a less sinister way; he wouldn't hear of this talk of shadows. Two Russian dolls he called them, the very same yet one fitting snugly inside the other. Because nobody in the family had actually seen a set of Russian dolls and therefore had no idea what he was talking about, old Dr Cartwright made a present of some on the occasion of the twins' fourth birthday. The present consisted of a set of six wooden dolls brightly painted in yellow, red and black traditional costume. They screwed apart at their centres, one fitting snugly into the other, until the largest having eaten all the others stood stolidly alone but reflecting in all but size the exact appearance of the others.

Emily was both fascinated and horrified by the toy. The idea that Albert might one day gobble up his brother in such a manner caused the hairs to prickle at her neck. But just as horrifying was the realization that, although Albert might be represented by the largest doll, there was no way in which Lancaster could be considered number two. She estimated in fact that her smaller twin was only number four. Thus she named each doll in descending order of size, York, Devonshire, Westminster, Lancaster, Cornwall and Rutland; she had however to commit the sixsome to memory, for she didn't wish at any time to arouse Lancaster's curiosity and cause her youngest little son notions of

84

inferiority. Nor, of course did she wish her youngest big son to see himself as in any way superior. Nonetheless with the scale committed to memory she lived for the day when she might rename her son Devonshire. She then realized that Lancaster could not just jump a position. If there was any catching up to do he would first of all have to become Westminster. She was sure that Ernest would have something to say about that. Still it was a battle to be fought if and when the time came.

One area in which biological proportions were most certainly distorted however was the one which most Victorian mothers would have missed, that being the relative size of the boys' penises. My great-great-grandmother, however, who was definitely not Victorian but born in the reign of George III, schooled at the time of George IV, and had seen things which would have made sailors blush in the years of William, knew exactly what she was looking at. While Emily would smack small hands for messing with their parts, Jane looked on, allowing the stretching to continue and was delighted to note that Lancaster was capable of elasticating his white worm just as far as his brother's and if anything Lancaster's penis was thicker than that of Albert. Thus, with considerable satisfaction the old woman was able to assess that the boys were boys each like their forebears. For she had seen them all. They would both have their wives and their children like John and like James, like Jack and Ernest, all of whom were well endowed, for like I say, she had seen them all. (Though none would quite match John Tregus', she would soon find out.)

Anyway, the day that Dr Cartwright delivered the Russian dolls and on which Emily had mentally named them, a curious thing happened. The twins had been put to bed, together with their older brother, William. An hour later the remaining occupants of the house, who were chatting in the parlour below, were disturbed by a terrible shrieking from the room above. Ernest ran to the stairs and was halfway up when he was confronted by Lancaster, quite beside himself and hollering uncontrollably at the top. Each adult in turn tried to comfort the inconsolable child. His mother tried tender kisses while his aunt attempted to read him a tale from the *Arabian Nights*, but each failed in their attempts at consolation. His father promised a visit to the rugby football game and his great-grandmother promised money but again each was rejected with renewed bouts of shrieking. Finally,

Mr Pettit, who admitted to knowing the psychology of children, produced the six wooden dolls which Dr Cartwright had brought for his birthday (three of them belonged to Albert but nobody ever could decide which three belonged to whom). The adults held their breath as the bellowing, ceased on a sudden inspiration, from the child. It seemed so long before he expelled any air that his poor mother expressed concern that he would choke, but Pettit's idea had certainly worked. The boy coughed only once, grinned broadly at the lodger, and took up the dolls. Soon he had them lined up on the floor, re-enacting the battles at Magersfontein, Elandslaagte and Colenso, and sensibly utilizing the relative sizes to indicate the measure of battalion, catastrophe and victor, like any seasoned wargamer.

'Whatever caused you such distress, Lancaster?' his Aunt Henrietta asked.

'Dark' was all that he would say, occupied as he was with blasting his mother's Cornwall from the face of the parlour floor.

'What was dark, dear?' his mother asked. 'Was it a night dream?'

'No. It was dark in there.'

'Where, in the room.'

'No. Shut up, in there,' he answered.

His mother gave a short gasp and explained later to Henrietta her fears for Lancaster being swallowed by the magnum Albert.

'What nonsense,' Henrietta scolded. 'It's only the stones.'

'Melancholia, you mean, like your mother and your Jack.'

'Not melancholia, Emily, history. He has the Brightside ability to sense the history of the stones.'

'Sometimes, Henrietta, I think tha's quite mad. Thee and that book, God forgive thee.'

'Then you would rather it was your son who was mad.'

'I don't understand. What do tha' mean by that?'

'Quite simply, that you would prefer Dr Cartwright's definition.'

'Melancholia, tha' mean?'

'Yes.'

'Yes, I would that. At least I understand Dr Cartwright and I think he knows us Brightsides.'

'Emily, do you realize that melancholia is a kind of madness too?'

Her sister-in-law looked shocked. 'Never,' she said.

'Oh yes,' Henrietta responded. 'You either accept that madness runs in the family, afflicting us at random, here and there, including now apparently your Lancaster, or you can put it down to some special ability that we have, a sensitivity not given to many. As one afflicted, I know which explanation I prefer.'

Emily turned away but she never again suggested that her sister-in-law was mad, nor did she ever again imagine her son to be suffering from melancholia.

During the next couple of years the twins grew steadily. These were the two years in which Elyahou Tsiblitz first visited our house, revealing his magical inflatable costumes to the children of the village. And in these years, the relative sizes of the twins still, in Emily's mind, reflected a four-doll span. Nothing had yet happened to make her call upon a change of name. Both boys showed considerable talent in art producing many sketches and paintings in the period. They would draw the pit and the pit-men's houses, the terrace and the winding engine shed, dogs and the common, hills and slagheaps; all met their steady gaze. Sketches were often executed with the piece of coal found at their very feet. Then they would draw their relatives and friends, and finally each other, and it was in their portraits of one another that Emily found relief and the knowledge that she had after all been a good mother. None of her fears of inferiority and superiority for the boys had been picked up. They saw nothing but themselves in the portraits they produced. Albert's portrait of Lancaster and Lancaster's portrait of Albert were the same. Each would take up the same central area of a white sheet of paper, that is until the day they drew each other naked. It was a great surprise to his mother to see the feelings of inferiority expressed by Albert in his painting of Lancaster. And when she compared it to little Lancaster's painting of Albert she gasped: 'Goodness, whoever would have thought', and the only thing she could find to say to the hitherto unprotected larger twin was, 'Now, Albert dear, you mustn't be jealous', but to Mrs Henderson she confided one day, 'Best not interfere too much. Children have a way of sorting their own problems. In fact sometimes we put problems on them which they haven't got.'

'Amen to that,' said my great-great-grandmother who was

party to the conversation and promptly went out and bought two cameras with a small part of her hidden fortune. She gave one to each of the twins for Christmas, explaining that it was a way of encouraging their talent to grow in a new area. Of the two it was Lancaster who allowed his interest in film to expand and proliferate, indeed finding true expression eventually in that most novel and revealing of twentieth-century art forms, the cinema, about which more later. Albert, though, was grateful for his camera too, and as he grew continued to use it more in tandem with his blossoming talent as a painter.

It was soon after the incident of the fire at the Gill house that Albert became seriously ill. After a morning photographing his great-grandmother at the Roman wall on Hunger Hill, the rains came unexpectedly to marr their session. Albert caught a chill which developed into a nasty cough and all the old woman's potions were regrettably insufficient to prevent the development of pneumonia. At the height of the fever, spots appeared. Old Dr Cartwright diagnosed measles too and told Emily that the crisis was near. The house held its breath. Henrietta talked to the stones in the dark. The old lady with whom she slept thought she was praying and asked her what prayer it was.

'No prayer, grandmother,' she said in the pitch dark. 'Just a conversation with the house. Albert lives here too. The house will look after him.'

'That's a good lass,' answered her grandmother who knew nothing of it but believed it all.

Meanwhile Emily sat by the bed watching her son growing smaller. When the crisis came, young Lancaster was ushered to the bedroom to sit with his mother and watch the beads of perspiration scatter about the pallid skin of his dying brother. Emily looked to the smaller twin wondering how he had managed to avoid the illnesses which now so afflicted the one between the sheets; how had he managed to remain so healthy? Albert stirred and flickered his eyelids, attracting Emily back to the shrinking twin with the deathly pale mask.

'Will he be all right, mother?' Lancaster asked quietly.

'God will judge,' his mother answered.

Lancaster went downstairs again to sit with the others and await the outcome of the crisis. Old Dr Cartwright visited again and sat awhile with Emily at the bedside.

88

'He's shrinking, Doctor,' she said, 'just fading away.'

'No, Mrs Brightside,' he answered. 'Fading perhaps, time will tell, but shrinking's impossible.'

'I tell thee he's smaller than he was a week since,' said my grandmother.

Cartwright shook his head, 'But that's not possible.'

'We'll see,' she answered, closed her eyes and slept.

She was awakened by a quiet voice asking her for water. Struggling excitedly in the darkness to light a candle, she eventually cast the pale light on her son. His eyes were open, the perspiration had ceased. Feeling his forehead with her palm, she noted how his temperature had fallen. The crisis was over, the fever had passed.

'Can I have some water, mother,' Albert repeated and sat up in the bed. Jubilantly his mother poured water into his mouth from the spout of a stone invalid cup, calling all the while for the members of her family to come upstairs and witness the miracle of resurrection.

'Great God!' Ernest's voice broke and cried, as he knelt at the foot of the bed to pray.

My grandmother looked from the now smiling Albert to little Lancaster.

'Lord, look how he's shrunk,' she said, comparing the two.

'Nay, lass,' said my grandfather, hands still clasped in prayer. 'Albert's not lost 'owt. It's Lancaster whose gained it all during the last week or two.'

Could it be true? Emily stared again at the twins. Had Lancaster at last caught up? She compared the thickness of their arms, their thighs, noted the width of shoulders; even the size of their heads and feet seemed the same. Sure enough it was true. Albert hadn't shrunk after all, it had been Lancaster's growth spurt which had indeed confused her. Lancaster had swiftly moved to Westminster and on to Devonshire without her noticing. She pulled Lancaster to her, kissing him about the face and mentally renamed the dolls in order, Lancaster, York, Devonshire, Westminster, Cornwall and Rutland. In racing parlance, Lancaster had won by a nose except that, with their drawings in mind, Emily knew it to be not a nose but some other part of his anatomy which represented the winning margin. It seemed so much easier than renaming her children; and when I was born, my grandmother on first seeing me said, 'Goodness, he's a number four like Lancaster.' My father was quite uncertain of the meaning of this cryptic comment, and totally puzzled when Emily convinced my mother that I should be named Westminster, a name which in a mining community is not easily born with pride. Emily, the quiet one, who before the birth of her twins wouldn't have had the nerve to blow out a candle, was now as fully self-possessed as all the other Brightside women, and won her way. Thankfully, though, at school, I became known as Big Ben, much to the confusion of all, for I was never more than five feet three inches tall, and forever a genuine number four.

10

Elyahou as purveyor of ladies' fashion, and Bill Pettit shows his knowledge of the turf

The only difference between a man and a motor is one of the imagination. If you take a man, extend to him some wheels and a means of driving them, you have a motor, or a man motor, or even a man with a fashionable if rather expensive suit, which also happens to get him along much more rapidly. It is the imaginations of the men who developed the wheel and the engine which make the difference. Such were Henrietta's thoughts when she next saw Elyahou Tsiblitz. It was the first time a motor had been seen in the village and there was the Transylvanian astride an eight-horsepower Rover coupé looking terribly dashing in his mufti tweeds and breeches. The tall hat had been replaced by a fashionable light coloured cap not unlike the one he had presented to her grandmother six years before. And there's another thing, she thought, the way in which these motors were going to change our habits. Why, Mrs Agar at the end house was only now banging on the wall with her poker, far too late to avert a catastrophe Henrietta was afraid. A shawled representative from each house was already in the doorway having been alerted by the dreadful chugging noise of the engine as it sped by each door. Some other means would have to be found by which the villagers could warn of the approach of strangers, thought Henrietta. Speed would have to be deployed in dealing with the coming world, she thought, hurtling her gaze to the angular peaks of Hunger Hill and beyond. Yorkshire ranges and adjoining walls in Henrietta's mind were clearly things of the past already.

The women and children were already crowding around the vehicle touching and stroking the dark red-painted bodywork here and there and making it impossible for the motorist to dismount. From his seat in front of the cab and open to the elements Elyahou flashed his smile at Henrietta. She allowed her brown eyes to soften in response. The wild and bushy tash had gone. Elyahou had grown a pencil-thin moustache rather like that of her brother Ernest but, unlike the latter whose hair was always short and neatly parted at the centre, the Transylvanian's jet-black shock of hair remained long. It lopped across both ears without parting emphasizing that this man was still essentially a foreigner, no matter how English all else might seem.

He was still unable to dismount. The older children, re-membering that wonderful day when they had bounced about the common in ballooning animal suits, were clamouring for more, their thin arms like sticks penning him into the enclosure, in front of the red cab. The younger ones, who knew only of that day by the close following of folk tales put about by important siblings, waited hushed and expectant and fiddled with the shiny lamps, bonnet and radiator.

'Please, Mr Rubber Man,' a very young one was heard to begin to ask from a position in front of the radiator. Catching sight of the child directly before him Elyahou opened his mouth wide in an expression of mock wonderment. The child stared up into the rubber man's gaping chasm; he could see it to be filled with silver and gold teeth and beyond he could discern the flesh pink tonsils guarding the black hole out of which the true magic was bound to come. It was like the beginning of a new world. The orifice remained open wide for what seemed an eternity flashing its metallic bits in the sun, then suddenly it said: 'You want inflatable suits?'

As the cheers erupted Henrietta was as surprised and excited as any present; the words had been uttered in perfect English. Elyahou could speak; it was indeed a wondrous new world, she thought, and smiled at the tall busy man who had at last been allowed down from the motor and who was rummaging in the cab for the inflatable clothing.

'Youngest first,' he said, kneeling on the seat and poking his head on its long neck over his backside, so that he could see out of the cab. 'Line up, line up.'

The women lined up the children in order of age and, deft as ever before and in no time at all, Elyahou had half a dozen younger ones in rubber costume for the first time. Lion, tiger, sheep, horse and elephant were joyfully bouncing about the common while the fat child in the fat chicken could only succeed in rolling tamely on the grass. Some of the older ones took this as an opportunity to leave the line, deciding that a game of football with the unfortunate poultry was better even than the experience of dressing up. This was quite fortunate for my two uncles who otherwise would have been costumeless, being not among the twelve youngest any longer. My great-great-grandmother came down from a trip to the Roman wall just in time to see Lancaster yet again going up in the bees outfit. Emily who had not witnessed the flight of her son before asked, 'My goodness, wherever will he come down?' Then when it was apparent that nobody cared to answer, slung her eyes heavenward and shouted advisedly, 'Flap your arms, dear. Doggy-paddle' – as if she were advising him on how to swim. This Lancaster did but it only succeeded in taking him higher up and over the roof of the terrace and out of view of the congregation below, and from the worried eyes of his mother. Lancaster, however, was quite unafraid, this being the third occasion on which he'd donned the same costume. He was quite getting the hang of it.

'It's not fair, he always gets to fly and I never do,' said Albert, enviously watching his brother sail over the houses.

'Never mind, dear,' said his mother, 'you look wonderful in your Zebra suit. Now go and join the others on the common.' And off he bounced carefully bobbing his way among the footballers and avoiding getting mixed up in the match which was shaping up on the grass.

As the sun poured out of the sky that day the women watched and laughed at the childen and commended yet again the Transylvanian for bringing another enchanted afternoon to their dusty and dirty village. Laughter then turned to fits of uncontrollable giggling when Mrs Henderson insisted on trying to play 'God save the King' on the rubber bulb of the trumpet-shaped horn which clung to the side of the motor.

'Ladies,' shouted Elyahou, after this musical interlude, 'shall we have the sale?'

'As they all chorused in the affirmative, my great-great-grandmother said to Henrietta, 'I see his language has improved.' Then she shouted above the general clamour, 'Who's been giving thee lessons, then?' Catching sight of the old woman, the strange rubber man pushed his way through the crowd, shook her warmly by the hand and said, 'I learned in Turkey.'

'Oh, tha's been travelling again?' she asked.

'Yes. I went to Moscow, and then to Paris and to Turkey, and to America.' He counted the countries off on the fingers of his right hand then, as he touched his thumb with left forefinger, he added, 'Then I come back to my favourite place. But I learn my English from the Sultan himself in Constantinople.'

'Oh, tha's a waffbag,' said the old woman flirtatiously. The rubber man turned away, held up his hands to the crowd of women calling for silence then said, 'I am sorry that I haven't been here for six years but I have been travelling abroad. Russia, France, Turkey. Then America. I have seen something of the world to come. The motor, the aeroplane, cinema and telegraph. The world of new materials. Cheap goods at a price we can all afford. I shall bring you that world, I promise on each visit I make to you. I shall bring that new world. But always, like now, I shall bring you rubber.' He was silent for a moment and the crowd hushed expectantly. He could hear the creaking sound of the winding wheel caught in a gentle breeze. 'I have brought you waspee-waisties,' he shouted.

An anticlimactic murmur rippled through the crowd.

'What's waspee-waisties?' Mrs Henderson asked squeezing the horn and frightening the life out of Mrs Gill. Amid laughter he took a single piece of corsetry from a box and wriggled it over his slender hips.

'Waspee-waistie,' he shouted triumphantly to the sniggering crowd. Then he produced a large pad of sketches which he held high for all to see which illustrated how the garment would look on the figure of a woman. 'See how it nips in the waist, like real ladies,' he said indicating the waspish effect of the strong elastic. 'No strings. No difficult threading. No help needed. You just climb into it, ladies. I have all sizes.'

Interest was slow at first, reservations were apparent. Eyes wavered from the man in the corset to the children bouncing in the sunshine beyond. The women could hear the low excited noises of brand new experience. Lancaster reappeared and hovered above them, buzzing in his solitude. Pink clouds nuzzled into the azure sky behind him.

'Come, ladies, please do not be embarrassed,' Elyahou coaxed.

'They are only two shillings and threepence each. Now won't that be a small price to pay to be a lady? Here, you can try them on first. Take, take.' He started to throw boxes into the crowd.

'I'd like to try one,' my great-great-grandmother said.

'Me too,' said Mrs Henderson.

He threw to each one a box containing the largest-sized waspee-waistie. The two women retreated to their respective homes to draw curtains across their bedroom windows. Meanwhile the crowd below warmed and grew more enthusiastic, accepting at last the invitations to a free try on. Soon every upstairs window in the terrace displayed a curtain shielding a lady's modesty. From some houses came whoops of delight, from other cries of pain. In our house the cracked mirror thrust back fractured images of the consumers' madness. Nearly seven bob was going to be spent on undergarments which covered neither this nor that and which uncomfortably strangled the viscera into the bargain.

With all the curtains drawn against him, Elyahou from his perch at the steering wheel in front of the cab contemplated things away from the terrace. Firstly he studied the diversion on the common. The children were occupied, not with nature's bits of stick and stone but with manufactured goods. Playthings created specifically for the purpose. Why shouldn't adults too have such things, he wondered. What prevented it? His gaze was drawn to the winding engine, the black wheel in a red sun spinning nothing but dirt and danger. Why not put toys down the pit? Sophisticated toys like machines to dig the coal. What was the resistance to it? Why did those men risk their lives every day and break their backs in boredom, when they could have toys to both entertain them and to work for them? Who resisted, the capitalists or the workers? Surely it was in the coal owners' interests to have a happy workforce; poor, yes, but happy. Misery couldn't lead to efficiency, surely they knew that? What of the pitmen? Were they afraid that once introduced the machines would take over, oust them from their jobs? They had allowed conveyancing machinery to be installed without loss of labour. So why such resistance to machines for digging out the coal? What part of the system made them so frightened, he wondered. On each occasion that he had such thoughts Elyahou came back to the same place. The system. Both capital and labour were caught up in it. Equally the coal owner and the pitmen were enmeshed in a game which ensured the perpetuity of their relative positions both socially and economically. There was fear here too. The fear

95

of winning. The fear that somehow the winner might suddenly become the loser, never the reverse, mind. And in such circumstances best change nothing. It was a conservative view shared by most and bred by years of system. Best not meddle, radicalism might upset something, bust summat they couldn't put together again; then what of all this tender flesh and blood held in God's great hands. Winners? What did God care for winners, anyroad? Greed was a sin. Jesus Christ, those radicals and socialists poking their noses in where it didn't belong. Jesus Christ, they might bust summat. Jesus Christ, didn't they know that He might drop them, drop them from His big hands right through those hot cracks in the floor of the pit; right through to Australia.

The drawing back of curtains turned his gaze to smiling women at their windows. He'd devoted his life to change. He, a Transylvanian, now speaking an excellent English learned from the Turks, had no fear of those cracks; no fear of falling. The system could be prised apart. Men and women would be made to see a better world, made to be unafraid. Even as they smiled down at him from their small windows, even as the sun shone blood-red through the dusty haze on both himself and the bouncing children, on the joyful kicking, screaming children, on Lancaster alienated aloft and heralding the dawn of a new age, even as all this warmth and vitality filtered through his very skin, he could sense the fear which had seeped into the stone terrace of colliers' homes. But he and others, including that ugly old woman built like a horse, would change all that. There would be no fear in the coming world.

The women began to leak out from the doorways onto the grass, each with a waist a little slimmer than before. While each lady checked in her florin and pennies, Henrietta herded the ballooning animals back towards the motor. The now crimson sun was setting for the night and the children were stripped of their clothes. The unusual combination of the smells of rubber and sweat brought forth threats of soap and water from their mothers and when the last red rays had finally touched the Roman wall on Hunger Hill, turning the starry stonecrop blaze orange and the crevices secret violet, Lancaster fell like a stone out of the dark sky. He bounced for a moment then he too was stripped of his costume and taken indoors by a mother intent upon scrubbing memories from his sweating pores.

Jane and Henrietta Brightside remained outside to the last. Before leaving, the rubber man withdrew a long heavy package from the back of his motor.

'Be careful, it's very heavy,' he said, but still hanging on to the newspaper wrapped parcel he then asked, 'Do you still have the cap?'

'Ay,' the old woman answered.

'But, grandmother, Ernest lost the hat.'

'Nay, lass. You must be mistook.' The grandmother flashed her eyes angrily at Henrietta. The Transylvanian looked from one woman to the other letting his smile come to rest eventually upon the face of the old woman and indicating in this manner that it must be she who knew the truth of it. 'Good,' he said softly, 'I am pleased you still have it. Some things have too much value to be destroyed. They should be kept forever.'

'It's only a hat,' Henrietta said.

Elyahou now smiled at my great-aunt but the nature of the smile had changed. The smile said, 'Maybe one day you'll understand', then he said, 'Even some hats can be valuable.' My great-great-grandmother nodded, and Elyahou said again, 'Be careful, this is very heavy', as he handed the parcel across to her laying it lengthways in her cradling arms. 'Some things also are too beautiful, to be destroyed,' he added. Then he handed Henrietta a smaller packet similarly wrapped in newspaper. The three of them stood in silence for a while, as the darkness fell about them, then he cranked the motor; the engine fired and the man clambered into the driving seat of his car.

'I must go now,' he said, looking to the glow of candles lighting up the rooms in the houses behind the women.

'Why don't they put the motorist's seat inside the cab?' my great-great-grandmother shouted up at him.

Elyahou looked at the substantial piece of coach work behind him. It was true, the machine had been designed along the lines of a horse-drawn carriage. He shrugged, 'Perhaps it was thought that only servants would drive the motor.'

'Then why not have two cabs?' the old woman suggested 'with a dividing wall like the earth closets. Doesn't the motorist, even if he is a servant, deserve a little comfort away from the wet and snow?'

97

The Transylvanian shrugged his shoulders again. 'Progress even when it's fast is very slow,' he said smiling.

'Tha'll tell them,' she shouted up to him. 'Tell them about the comfort of poor folk. Tell 'em it's the same as their own. When they learn it's the same needs we've got then they'll start changing the world. Not till, mind. I'll sithee again, rubber man.' She turned into the house, sagging beneath the weight of her present. Henrietta, left alone with the foreigner, blushed into the colder night air.

'How was your present?' he asked out at her face haloed by light from the window behind.

'My present?'

'Yes. The stamper,' he explained.

'Oh, that. It was nice,' she answered, embarrassed, into the dark. 'It was nice of grandmother to have bought it for me, I mean.'

'Did you use it much?'

'I stamped what was mine,' she answered.

He shrugged again. 'Perhaps we'll meet some other time.'

'Yes, perhaps.'

'I must go now.' He squeezed the bulb of his horn. The motor honked as it drew away from the house and down past the lighted windows of the terrace. Henrietta waved goodbye and turned through the open doorway and into the parlour.

'Come in and close t'door, lass,' my great-great-grandmother said, 'It's turning chilly.'

'What've you got?' Emily asked of Henrietta excitedly.

'Grandmother first,' Henrietta challenged.

'Nay, lass. C'mon.'

'Yes, Aunt Henrietta, c'mon,' chorused William. 'Open it.'

My father's aunt slowly untied the brown string wrapped around the object in the newspaper while her three nephews hovered around her at the table. Several pages of the *Leeds Mercury* were removed to reveal a hexagonal polished wooden object.

'What's that?' asked William breathing at his aunt's neck.

'I don't know, William,' she answered irritably. She turned the object in her hands noting the circular base which was covered in green baize material. 'Now yours, grandmother,' she ordered,

98

looking to the old woman. My great-great-grandmother also took her time untying the string. She too eventually had discarded several sheets of the *Mercury*, before revealing a scrolled and decorative ornament of shiny golden appearance. The object was like a very elaborate candlestick, quite wide at the base, narrowing towards the centre and finally bulging out into the head of a mace in the upper section. The whole thing was surmounted by the small figure of a man with a cane.

'This must be the base for it,' William said, picking up the hexagonal object which had been given to Henrietta. 'Yes,' said Emily. 'Set the ornament down on it, grandmother.' Onto the plinth, which William held firm at the centre of the table, my great-great-grandmother plonked the ornament.

'It's lovely,' said Emily.

'It's a bit rich for our table, perhaps it would be best on the sideboard,' Henrietta suggested. Her grandmother agreed so the boys, moving the bible to one side, transferred the heavy object to stand on its base between the family photographs on the sideboard.

'Bloody 'ell!' exclaimed Bill Pettit who knew all there was to know about horse racing. 'It's the Ascot Gold Cup.' He had just come through the door with the other menfolk. Each blackened with grimy coal dust and clinging to an empty snap-box, they froze at the doorway immobilized by the radiant splendour of the object on the sideboard. It was as if they had been caught in the presence of angels.

'Where did you get that, lass?' Ernest asked of his wife in a soft voice which indicated that he was slowly breaking free of the captive rays. Emily looked to the old woman. Taking their cue from her, all other eyes turned upon my great-great-grandmother.

'It were given me,' she said defensively.

'But it's the bloody Ascot Gold Cup,' Mr Pettit repeated, the incredulity in his voice rising beyond the weight of knowledge in his head.

My grandfather turned to his lodger and asked, 'Are you sure, Bill?'

It was always a mistake to question Bill Pettit's knowledge in such a manner for, while erudition came forth full chapter and verse, it was always accompanied by the restacking of much

99

superfluous information like the taking apart of a Babbage machine.

'Ay. It were stolen at Ascot during the very race only two weeks since. The White Knight won from Beppo with Halsey up. Trained by Mr Sadler and owned by Colonel Kirkwood.' At this point, mercifully he stopped to consult a small book which he produced from his grimy waistcoat pocket. William wondered how Mr Pettit was able to read anything from it at all as the lodger smudged his licked thumbs through the blackened pages. 'I won myself three shillings and twopence on the race,' he continued, putting the book away and addressing himself again to his audience. Then before anyone could stop him he'd launched into reciting the previous winners of the race, starting at 1807, giving mounts and jockeys and breaking only to describe owners' colours where he knew them.

Shouting above the recitation to make herself heard my great-great-grandmother said, 'Mr Pettit, I didn't know you were a betting man.' This was uttered with such indignation that it completely upset the lodger who then had to start restacking his knowledge all over again. Taking advantage of the moment's silence, Ernest weighed in. 'For the Lord's sake shut up, Bill, and let's get back to the matter in hand.'

Sidall Junkin, also taking advantage of the broken recitation, spat upon the fire, and this indeed returned a kind of normality to the room. My great-great-grandmother, however, still with indignation, said, 'If tha'd been lodgin at my house when my husband lived, tha' wouldn't have been wastin' tha' money on horses. I've put up with tha' foul language and said nowt too long, Mr Pettit, but wastin' tha' wage on horses is really too much. I'll hold my tongue no more.'

'Now, grandmother,' said Ernest patiently, stepping in to rescue his lodger.

'I shouldn't take too high a moral position with me, Mrs Brightside,' the lodger said, ignoring Ernest's help. 'A bet now and then hurt no man, but tha's got stolen property there.'

'How can tha' be so sure of that?' Ernest asked. 'How can tha' be certain it's what tha' says it is?'

''Cos I seen it described in the papers, that's how,' said Bill, who was not going to lose the opportunity of displaying his talents. He shut his eyes and quoted the gold cup as having

100

scrollwork at the base and being surmounted by a small figurine depicting a man in a tailcoat and leaning upon a stick. All eyes turned to the shining object on the sideboard to confirm the true description being quoted at them by the man with the shuttered lids.

'Where did tha' get it, grandmother?' Ernest asked, the hint of a threat in his voice.

'It were a present' was all that the old woman would say.

'She got it from the rubber man,' William blurted to his father.

'Oh that explains it,' said Mr Pettit who had at last opened his eyes. 'Expect that Jew stole it.'

'Maybe,' Ernest said rubbing his chin. 'We'll 'ave to go to t'police.'

'Tha' won't,' said his grandmother. 'It's my present.'

'Now, grandmother,' Ernest cajoled, 'tha' can't go keepin' a thing like that. It weren't his to give you.'

'I'll bet it's worth a bob or two,' piped up the bright-eyed William, whose pupils reflected the gleam of the object over which he leaned. 'Why don't we take it to Leeds and have it melted down?'

'Ay, it's worth a fortune. A fortune,' wheezed Sidall. He spat on the coals again and shook his head sadly as the sputum sizzled.

'What a dishonest suggestion, William,' his Aunt Henrietta scolded. 'Put it out of your mind immediately.'

'Nay, tha's not melting it, lad,' my great-great-grandmother said. 'If tha' wants a fortune, I've an honest one for thee. No one's doin' owt with it. I were given it to keep and that I mean to do. Keep it safe.'

'Now, grandmother, tha' can't do that,' Ernest insisted.

'And as for thee, William, may the Lord forgive thee. In the morning we go straight for the law, tell them what we know, and leave it to them. No one in this house will have a bad conscience over the Ascot Gold Cup. Now let's get on with us baths and us dinners. Then it's an early night for all of us.'

Ernest had spoken with authority, even his grandmother was quietened. The women and boys left the house, the men set about their bathing and the Ascot Gold Cup shone like nothing had ever shone before into the gloomy parlour of our house.

Outside the old woman and Emily walked with the twins up

towards the big house while William and his Aunt Henrietta strolled in the other direction towards Hunger Hill.

'What did great-grandmother mean by that?' asked William.

'By what?' his aunt responded.

'She said that she had an honest fortune for me.'

'Oh that,' Henrietta said, putting her hand on William's shoulder as they walked along. 'Grandmother was supposed to have brought a fortune with her when she came to the house.'

'And did she?'

Henrietta shrugged. 'Maybe.'

'Did anyone see it?' William asked.

'I think my mother might have seen it. She told me that the money was kept in a suitcase.'

'Where does she keep it then?'

Henrietta shrugged again. 'Nobody knows. The Gills once dug up the scullery floor looking for it, but they didn't find anything. I expect they've looked other places too.' William laughed. 'Do you think it's true? Is there a fortune somewhere?'

'There's probably some money, somewhere.' She smiled at her nephew. 'Maybe not a fortune, just a bit put aside.'

'She must have something,' William said. 'She's always buying things for people. That costs, doesn't it?'

'I suppose,' Henrietta answered.

They walked on a little way in silence. The angry peak of Hunger Hill loomed above them from the dark mauve sky. She watched the twinkling of a star an instant, then said, 'It seems like today never happened. That motor, those silly suits, the rubber man, that golden thing on the sideboard. Nothing's changed here since I was a child, since my grandmother was a child.' She wriggled her bottom, suddenly aware of the discomfort about her body. 'Except waspee-waistie, I suppose.'

William giggled. He'd been embarrassed watching much of the sale, being now far too old to qualify for a rubber suit, yet just too young for a job at the pit.

'Does it make you feel any different?' he asked.

'No. I don't think so, except that it's uncomfortable now I think of it.' She smiled.

'Seems silly, paying good money to make yourself uncomfortable,' he said.

102

'There's a silly world coming, William. I think we must learn to laugh at it if we are to cope.'

'As silly as the dinosaur world down there with grandfather?' William nodded at the disused pit.

'Oh much more silly than that,' his aunt advised him. She looked again at the dark peak above them. 'I didn't know my father,' she told him, 'he died before I was born; but I'm sure that he would have been amazed at what we saw in the village today. But somehow we just take it all in our stride. Even grandmother saw it all as inevitable,' she added remembering the old woman's last comments to Elyahou. 'I think we should turn now and head back.'

Together they turned about and walked a while in the mauve silence.

'Why for me?' It was the boy who spoke.

'What for you, William?'

'Why should she have a fortune for me?'

Henrietta was silent a long time, trying to remember. Then she said, 'I think she was going to give the money to my father the day he died.'

'And then?'

'Well, he died in that accident. Then she must have waited for Jack and your father to grow to manhood.'

'And then what?'

'Well, perhaps she didn't like what she saw or maybe they rejected her offer; I don't know.'

'So, I'm next.'

'Yes. After your father you are next. Maybe soon she'll surprise you with a suitcase.'

He watched her white face moving along in the dark a while, and then said, 'I don't believe it. I don't believe any of it; there's no fortune. It's just stories like the ghost of the closets. People like us don't have fortunes.'

In silence and with tears in his eyes my father, who very soon would enter that gaping hole in the ground which beckons all the young men in a pit village, made his way home.

When they arrived back all the family were together and the table set for a meal. In the golden glow of the racing cup they ate heartily; the men washed and relaxed, the women fidgety in their new foundation garments. Ernest's promise of an early night for

103

all was kept and by ten o'clock the house slept. The following morning everyone awoke to hear Bill Pettit shouting, 'Bloody 'ell. Someone's stolen the Ascot Gold Cup.' He was probably right but thankfully his wondrous mind could add nothing of substance to the comment. Worse still, however, was the fact that someone had stolen our William also; at least, that's how his mother put it.

11

Sidall Junkin gets a new set of teeth

Whatever motivated my father to steal the Ascot Gold Cup for the second time was never revealed. He had crept downstairs in the middle of the night and obviously with an expert stealth, stuffed the object into a sack and left the house with the swag slung over his shoulder, and because of his small stature he looked every bit the chimney sweep boy. It wasn't true as most thought that he awakened nobody, for Sidall Junkin said that when the cup was put into the sack it was as if several candles had been snuffed at once. Sidall, however, thought that what he had witnessed had been no more than a dream, and he'd gone back to sleep in his wide-winged chair, eyes more firmly closed than usual.

Bill Pettit and my great-great-grandmother were certain that William meant to take the cup to Leeds to have it melted down exactly as he'd suggested the previous evening, but could offer no motive other than greed for such action. Henrietta plainly saw his motive as being material salvation. The boy was obviously terrified of having to go into the pit and the opportunity to gain easy money to forestall such a happening had tempted him to the crime. Ernest, on first realizing that William had not been stolen, as the boy's mother would insist, but had in fact done a bunk with the booty, dropped to his knees and prayed for all; unaccountably and particularly did he single out the twins for special mention. They, however, with memories of the previous day fresh in their minds refused to believe that the rubber man had become a robber man and would only accept that the object which had stood upon our sideboard as wondrous as anything from another planet, had been but a harmless present. They thought that the adult world about them had gone mad and sadly now it appeared that even the youthful world of their brother was beginning to crack a little. Perhaps it was an inevitable response to the approach of adulthood they reasoned most soundly.

'You can't go to the law now,' Emily pleaded with her husband.

'Emily's right,' Henrietta agreed. 'What could we say, Ernest?'

'The Ascot Gold Cup's been stolen?' Bill Pettit posed it to himself as a question then shook his head. 'They'd say we know that, it was in all the papers.'

'Good God!' Emily said, horror dawning on her face. 'If the police pick him up in Leeds with that thing, they'd think he'd stolen it originally.'

''Im and us,' Sidall piped up from his chair.

'Bloody 'ell!' Bill Pettit exclaimed. 'We'd better get 'im afore they do. Ernest, get off tha' bloody knees and let's get after 'im.'

My grandfather in a state of shock was helped up from the floor by Bill and Emily, dusted down, and sent into the street to air his addled brain. 'Prayin' all over the shop isn't going to help at this time,' his wife told him as she pushed him through the doorway.

In the house, all agreed that the boy had most likely set off to walk to Leeds and Bill Pettit was despatched immediately to the pit head to get a horse and cart. Henrietta explained, 'He won't be walking too quickly with that sack.' They all concurred that Henrietta was probably correct, the weight of the cup would hold him back. When Bill had returned with the cart they all piled excitedly on. It had a gaily painted tailboard and sides in rich silver and red and was pulled by a black horse with a sad white face and blinkers.

'Wouldn't it be best if I went alone with Sidall or Ernest? It'd be a bit quicker,' Bill suggested, but he was shouted down unanimously. Everyone wanted a ride.

Great-great-grandmother who was sitting up front with Bill said, 'It'd be a lot quicker if we had one of them motors.'

'And where would we get one of them?' Bill asked.

'From the rubber man,' she answered folding her arms into her ample lap. Bill pulled a wry face but thought it best to say nothing. Ernest was tugged aboard still in a daze and lay with his head cradled in his wife's lap, murmuring softly to himself. Then with a self-assured 'Giddyup!' Bill cracked his whip and the cart, dragged by the sad horse set off across the common to link up with the road to Leeds.

'We're 'avin a day off,' Bill shouted when the neighbours came out to investigate the commotion caused by my family. 'There'll be no sick pay,' shouted the young Henderson. 'Bugger sick pay,' shouted back Bill as the cart wheels gathered a little speed and the sun peeped from the early morning mist.

Once out of the narrow, rutted lanes the horse was able to travel at a fair old lick and within two hours of setting off was trotting over the River Aire at Leeds Bridge. They then carried on into the main, wide, cobbled thoroughfare of the city. Briggate was a thriving street bustling with coaches and horse-drawn trams, there were also a fair number of motorized vehicles jostling for position. Men in suits as dark as their pavement shadows were everywhere, thronging the street with their billy-cocks and canes. A few ladies flitted about in satins and dark lace like silhouetted butterflies in the sun.

Just beyond the bridge, my family fell upon the public conveniences. Here, at the lower end of Briggate, Bill called the horse to a halt and with much relief, and amid great jubilation, the excited contingent descended from street level to use the underground toilets. It was the first time that both the twins and Sidall Junkin had seen a water closet and each occupied a cubicle for longer than he should to flush and reflush the white porcelain bowls, and great-great-grandmother finally had to draw them to order when Albert had climbed to perch at the top of an interconnecting wall there to view the newspaper-reading public at its duty. Eventually the cubicles emptied, chains swinging madly after one last communal and noisy flush. 'Why can't we have water closets instead of those smelly earth closets?' Albert asked, ascending the steps to the street and feeling the weight of the old woman's hand about his ear.

'They'll come,' she told him. 'Wait and see, lad.'

'Put thee out of a job, when they do,' Bill told Sidall Junkin at the top of the steps. Sidall eyed his fellow lodger humourlessly, moved the rubber teeth around in his mouth, and spat his black spit onto the cobbled street. 'Tha' wants to think on, Bill. I'm a good bit older than thee. When I'm gone it'll be tha' turn to clean closets.'

As the group was remounting the cart and arguing busily which direction they should take to start looking for William (even Ernest had recovered sufficiently to present an opinion) fate took a hand and solved the problem for them; William came to them. He suddenly stepped out from behind a horse-drawn tram looking dirty enough to have already swept three chimneys.

107

'There's William,' said Lancaster, pointing across the street as he was being hauled onto the cart. He had said it so conversationally that at first nobody paid attention to the remark.

'Where's William?' his mother suddenly asked realizing at last that the object of the twins twisting gesticulations was the very thing they were seeking.

'There, there,' answered Lancaster, picking up some of his mother's excitement.

'Where?' the others chorused.

Dangling in mid-air, neither on the cart nor on the street, the twin shouted, pointing awkwardly.

'Behind me. Across the street, it's William.'

All eyes turned and at the same time the hands which had been bringing the twin aboard, relaxed their grip and Lancaster fell to the ground. I only mention this because it seems to me that my uncle Lancaster's life was full of nasty tumbles from the air, culminating of course in that final terrible fall during the Battle of Britain. Then, within seconds, feet were landing heavily on the cobbles all about him as the occupants of the cart jumped down to give chase to the errant William. He was caught up with outside Stead and Simpsons' shoe shop, above which was the largest piece of advertising that anyone had ever seen. It read in letters each two feet high, and taking up all of the space between the top of the doorway and the roof of the building:

MACDONALDS TEETH MACDONALDS
HIGH CLASS TEETH ENGLISH AND AMERICAN
ARTIFICIAL TEETH TEETH ARTIFICIAL TEETH
WITHOUT PLATES PAINLESS SYSTEM
MACDONALDS (ENTRANCE KIRKGARE) MACDONALDS

Leaving the squirming child in the hands of his parents and the sack securely in Bill Pettit's grasp, Sidall Junkin made his way round the corner to Kirkgate and to Macdonald's emporium, to reappear minutes later at the cart displaying a dazzling new smile. Mr Junkin's mouth appeared to be overfilled, Albert thought, as if he'd stuffed too much food into it. Nor could the boy help wondering how many different pairs of teeth he'd had to try on before settling for the ones now offering the big new smile. Worse still, Albert concerned himself with the notion that they might be second-hand. Meanwhile Bill Pettit, mounted aloft, had his head thrust deep within the coal sack trying to establish that the trophy was still there without of course drawing the attention of an as yet unconcerned public. William, sitting dejectedly at the back of the cart, was receiving alternate kisses and chastisements from his mother. Ernest, however, told him only once that he would be dealt with when they got home, then proceeded to sulk.

'It's here,' Bill Pettit said finally, lifting his head from the sack like a satisfied horse. 'Shall we take it to the police?'

'No,' said my great-great-grandmother, gathering the sack up from the lodger's lap and dumping it in her own.

'But be reasonable, Mrs Brightside,' Bill said. 'Look, did tha' ever ask thissen' why the rubber man should have stolen the Ascot Gold Cup only to give it to the likes of us?' she asked him.

Even with his marvellous knowledge, Bill Pettit couldn't answer that. 'I don't know' he sighed.

'No. And neither would the police,' she answered. 'In short, they'd never believe the tale. Why should anybody go to the lengths of stealing a valuable trophy only to give it away to strangers?'

'Grandmother's right,' Ernest said. 'We'll 'ave to think on it.'

'Well at least while we're in Leeds we can call on't bugger and 'ave it out with 'im,' Bill said.

'That's a good idea,' Ernest conceded. 'What's address?'

'I know,' Henrietta offered. 'It was on his stamper that first time he came to our house. You remember, grandmother?'

'I'm sayin' nowt,' the old woman said, clutching the sack even closer to her.

Henrietta thought a moment with eyes tight shut, as the others nudged her memory with unhelpful suggestions.

'Ship's Yard,' she suddenly shrieked, opening her beautiful brown eyes wide as they would stretch. 'That was it, Ship's Yard.'

'Right,' said Bill dismounting. 'I'll go and get a bobby.'

Sidall Junkin snorted and tried uncomprehendingly to say something. His gutta-percha smile flashed in the sun as he too dismounted. After a couple of minutes they both returned.

'There is no bloody Ship's Yard,' Bill told them angrily.

'Well I'm certain that was the address,' Henrietta said. She felt disappointment.

'Ay. Well, it's false,' Bill went on. 'Bugger's given us a wrong 'un.'

'He's given us the Gold Cup, hasn't he?' my great-great-grandmother reminded him.

''E's still leadin' us a right dance,' the lodger said, climbing back aboard and helping up Sidall Junkin.

'I'll bet 'es not given us his right bloody name either.'

'Ay, whoever heard such a name. Elyahou Tsiblitz,' said Ernest.

'I'll bet he's not even a Jew,' the old woman mused.

'Ay, that's right,' said Bill. 'That'd be bloody typical of 'em', and with that he gave a loud 'Giddyup!' and headed off up Briggate and away from the public convenience.

The journey back to the village was memorable for only two things. One was that it rained heavily for most of the way, the weather turning about half an hour out from Leeds. Secondly, and probably because of the wretched rain, Sidall Junkin suffered a very severe attack of asthma. It was so severe that, as my father told me years later for he was sitting next to him in the back of the cart, he feared that the poor man would die there and then. Unable to find his breath for what seemed like minutes but could have only been seconds at a time, the man with the new smile turned purple in the face, threshing about his arms and legs, searching for an airway. The huddled soaking mass of people in the back of the cart did what little they could for the ailing man but their discomfort was compounded by the knowledge that whatever they did it was not going to be enough. As Ernest said he just wanted to rip a hole in the man's neck to let him breath. In short, they were all frightened for him, as they clapped him heartily on the back and at one time poked their fingers in his throat. Sidall's condition seemed to have improved a little by the time the cart had arrived back at the house, at least sufficiently for him to slip back into his jaws the new set of teeth which had been removed during the worst of the asthma attack. He was helped into the house and then upstairs to the bed shared between Henrietta and my great-great-grandmother, they both having insisted that he sleep there for the night. Then the old lady sent Lancaster to get old Dr Cartwright. After examining his patient the doctor proclaimed that the lodger was about to die at any moment, shook his head sadly and said that there was no more that he could do. My great-great-grandmother sent for a cooked ham which Albert brought from Mr Doyle who kept pigs. The experienced old woman well-trained in the rituals devised to attend the dying organized the making of sandwiches while she set out the Ascot Gold Cup once more upon the sideboard. She then sent the boys and the men for a walk. After an hour or two, Sidall appeared at the foot of the rickety stairs. He looked very much better.

'By, that ham smells good, Mrs Brightside,' he said.

'Now, Sid,' said my great-great-grandmother,' the ham's for the wake. Go back to bed, lad, and get on with tha' dyin'.'

But Sid's face registered a terrible hunger. So my great-great-grandmother sliced him a plateful of best boiled ham while he rummaged in his waistcoat pockets, finally producing his new teeth which he inserted once more into his jaws. With his plate of ham he turned smiling to the stairs, trying to wish a goodnight to the ladies through teeth which fitted his mouth to overflowing. That was the last anyone saw of him alive. In the morning Ernest shouted, 'Quick, quick! Sidall Junkin's dead.' Then the house fell into silence and even when Bill Pettit shouted, 'Bloody 'ell, the Ascot Gold Cup's been stolen!' – for the second time in twenty-four hours – it didn't seem to matter. Both statements were true of course. Dr Cartwright came and examined the body and said that it was probably Sidall's new teeth that had finally killed him. They were far too big for his mouth, he said. The man must have choked on his evening meal for the doctor drew attention to the half-eaten sandwich still on the plate in the bed, and to the tell-tale crumbs which spotted about the corpse's mouth. Then with a final wretched search for the over-burden of proof, he prised his bony finger into the gap between the teeth and ripped out the dentures with a powerful tug. Half-masticated bread formed a glutinous mass which kept them together still biting hard on the doctor's outspread hand. As the teeth came out there was a great expulsion of trapped air and the face caved in to the customary lugubrious countenance of Sidall Junkin. Albert thought how Mr Junkin had not stopped smiling since he'd bought the teeth despite the asthma attack. 'He must have died happy,' he told the doctor.

It was also true that the cup had been stolen for the third time, but nobody had stolen William. Nobody had gone but for Sidall

Junkin, and nobody seemed to care that the trophy might have gone with him.

At the funeral service in the church in the next village Jane Brightside, who was now ninety-two years of age, listened to the ranters awhile then stood up and shouted back, 'Thee and tha' kind sicken me. Tha' fright the children, tha' fright the grown men but tha'll not fright me. If tha' must preach, preach on a new world, not that old sad place in your minds. God fell out the sky and showed me a new world at Kettle Flat. God's come to our house three times now, the last time in a motor, who knows what wonders will be next.'

'That's not God, it's Mammon. The devil of covetousness,' the ranter raved back.

'Nonsense. It's the god of convenience,' she shouted at him. 'What is this better world tha' talks of if it's not going to be convenient?' She looked about her at the congregants. 'Isn't it convenient to make tha' lives here on earth easier to bear? Machines and motors may cost now, but if tha'll show tha' wants them and tha' know how to use them, the Lord'll make them cheaper for us. Design is not an art, it's an inevitability once tha' tell Him what tha' want. Design is a sign of the coming world. Design is a symbol of what tha' can have. Don't kick God backwards. God's an engineer and a sign of what's to come. He's been to our house.' She walked out unsteadily on the arm of her granddaughter. The neighbours thought the old woman had gone mad, but at her age you might expect it they said. It's been a long innings. The two women walked home, away from the funeral service, watching the dark peak of Hunger Hill, and each resolved not to think of Elyahou Tsiblitz again.

12

Of Lancaster's two passions, flight and the cinema

Soon after Sidall Junkin's death, a shelf was erected in the parlour. It was put up specifically to house the family library. All but Ernest's bible that is, which remained dark, brooding and closed with a brass clasp, occupying the spot which once had been reserved for the Ascot Gold Cup upon our sideboard. The books on the shelf were not many but included the family photograph albums and of course Henrietta's *History of the Stones* which was now running into many volumes. She still, almost every day, visited Bottom Boat looking for changes, and incredibly was still able to find the imperceptible moves which caused her book to evolve. But these changes only reflected her solitude and the isolation of not only herself but of the village, this place nestled at the foot of Hunger Hill and bounded to the West by the big house. But now even Henrietta was becoming anxious for more rapid changes; she had a plan for the stones but the time was not yet right to put it into operation.

Then there was H. G. Wells' *First Men in the Moon* and the same author's *The War of the Worlds*, and a book about fly fishing between the pages of which were tiny scales which glinted gold and silver blue when turned in the light. There was the *Colliery Manager's Handbook* dated 1906 and a slim volume by Henry M. Stanley, the famous explorer, entitled *Through Ukwere to Useguhha*. Nobody knew where this book had come from and it remained unread until I was well into my teens. There was also a volume of beautifully printed reproductions of *100 Favourite Paintings*. This marvellous book in full colour had been given recently to the twins by their great-grandmother as a birthday present and to encourage their steadily developing artistic talents. In fact at the time of the erection of the new shelf Albert was busily copying Gainsborough's *Blue Boy* onto a canvas the exact dimensions of the original. This information was of course given beneath each reproduction in the book together with the gallery at which the painting might be seen. It would be several months before the copy could be completed but the boy's dedication and remarkable talent were given wholehearted encouragement by all members of the household, especially his twin, who was beginning to be left a little way behind in his ability to paint. Not that Lancaster lacked talent, it was rather that he was turning that well of ability more in the direction of photography. Also, more dreamy than his brother, Lancaster nurtured at odd moments, his notions of flight. At the age of twelve he managed to convince my great-great-grandmother that her first and, as it would turn out, her only visit to the nation's capital city should be to view the International Balloon Race. Through the sole agency of the rubber suit Lancaster had become obsessed with the notion of flight, and yet to date he had never seen an air device in the flesh so to speak. The old woman had the advantage of him, for at least she was able to see, just for a few seconds before it almost tumbled on top of her, the airship of Duncan D'Arcy and Lady Anabelle Kerr that morning at Kettle Flat. Without hesitation, the old woman agreed to take my uncle to London. Why shouldn't he too experience the wonderment which she had then felt?

So it was that the strange pair set out in their best clothes taking Mr Fox's now grimy carriage to the station at Wakefield, and there to meet a train which would carry them on to London. Unfortunately, the train was delayed at Grantham because of repairs being carried out on the line, thus when they did finally arrive at the capital the race was already under way. Unaware of where they were or of how they should get to Fulham where the race was to have started, they wandered uncertainly into the Euston Road, whereupon their eyes were immediately directed upwards primarily because every other living soul they could see were cricking their necks in an effort to view the sky beyond the high buildings. The sight which met their gaze was totally beyond even the imaginings of the old woman and her charge. As Duncan D'Arcy had predicted my great-great-grandmother was at last seeing her sky full of flying men. Dozens of balloons were tossing silently above the metropolis. The steep-sided buildings only accentuated the height at which the lofty airships anchored into their spaces, for without wind they hung about like fish in deep waters giving no hint of their journey. Like the blue sea, the sky too teemed with life, and up there beyond the spires and towers built by the earthly Londoners, small men in baskets were waving; raising glasses to their glinting eyes and waving. After several minutes of sheer wonderment and with a pain in the back of her aged neck by great-great-grandmother hailed a horse-drawn cab. Then, with heads resting upon real leather cushions and with eyes slung heavenward, my two relatives scanned the skies all the way to Fulham, and all the time they were followed by the colourful balloons which now drifted on a sudden breeze, like so many ideas, across their lines of vision.

At the park it was apparent that several competitors had not yet managed to inflate their craft and therefore that Lancaster would have ample opportunity to inspect some airships at close range. Paying off the cabman they set off to view a small red, white and blue striped balloon which had caught their attention and which was slowly inflating in a flat area guarded at the back by a clump of dense trees. They were suddenly stopped in their tracks by somebody shouting. It was not the voice which was familiar, but the words immediately attracted the old woman's attention. 'Hey, Yarrow beer!' the message repeated again. My great-great-grandmother turned to see the instantly recognizable Duncan D'Arcy. 'Hey there, Ardsley,' he shouted, changing his coding in the hope that both the drink and the place combined would touch off the old woman's memory. He needn't have bothered, of course, for Jane Brightside had never forgotten him. He ran through the crowd from behind her waving his arms about in an alarming manner.

'I thought you'd be here,' she said to him, though it had been more in hope than certain knowledge.

'No flowers, madam? No basket of Yarrow beer?' he remarked.

'No champagne?' she challenged back, and he laughed.

Lancaster gawped at the man's velvet jacket and the lace cuffs of his shirt, which ruffled through the sleeves.

'No,' he answered her, 'not any more. It's not a game any more. We sail these things for real now.' He glanced towards heaven.

'Yes, I see,' she said. 'Tha' was right. The skies are fillin'. It'll soon be like fish in t'sea.'

He smiled, then looking at Lancaster, he said, 'And who have we here, madam?'

115

'My name's not Yarrow beer, nor is it Ardsley, by the way. It's Jane Brightside, and this 'ere's my great-grandson Lancaster Brightside. Say 'ello to the gentleman, Lancaster.' She nudged my uncle.

'Pleesetomeetcha,' said Lancaster, awkwardly offering his hand. As the balloonist took my uncle's hand in his firm and large grip, the old woman said, ''E's mad about flyin'.'

'Oh, did you ever fly in a balloon, young man?' Lancaster shook his head, shyly looking at the ground. Then stirred by a sudden attack of vocabulary he blurted out, 'No. But I will. One day I'll win the Gordon Bennet trophy.'

'Yes, and so will I,' said Duncan D'Arcy. 'Perhaps we'll do it together.' Then he laughed that same hearty laugh Jane had heard when he'd downed the yarrow beer.

Lancaster's eyes brightened as he warmed to the big stranger. 'Did you enter in the race before?' he found the courage to ask.

'Oh yes, I was in the first race, a couple of years back. Set off from Paris and came down in the English channel. Had to swim the last five miles.' He laughed again, slapping the boy on the shoulder.

'Lahm won that one,' mumbled Lancaster.

'What, boy?' said Duncan D'Arcy, bending down closer to my uncle's face and turning his ear to the boy's mouth. His moustache was stiff and waxed.

'Frank P. Lahm won, sir,' Lancaster shouted.

'Know your stuff, eh,' said the balloonist stretching back up to his full height and poking a long finger into the ear which he'd so recently offered to my uncle.

'Flew 402 miles and came down on Fylingdales Moor.' Lancaster confidently continued to air his knowledge.

'Quite right, young man. Had to leg it in to Whitby and didn't know for days that he was the winner. What a place to come down, though. Whoever would wish to set anything down on that blasted heath, beats me.' He laughed again, even more heartily than before. 'Tell you what,' he went on, 'how would you like a ride in my airship?'

'What? You mean go up in it?' Lancaster asked excitedly.

'Not only that – not just go up and down – have a bit of a ride, what.' Lancaster was so excited he could scarcely contain his joy.

'Yes, yes,' he shouted, dancing round the gentleman. 'Would you, please, please?'

As Lancaster, now ignored, continued to jig on the grass, the man asked my great-great-grandmother, 'And you, madam? Would you do me the honour?'

'But I'm ninety-three years old' was all that she could say as he took her by the hand.

'Then you shall be the oldest person ever to have flown in a machine. It'll be a record worth having.' He laughed again. 'Tell you what. I'll take you home, back to Ardsley or wherever it is that you come from.'

'Oh please, great-grandmother. Can we? Will thee?' pleaded Lancaster.

'Of course we shall,' Duncan D'Arcy answered for the old woman, and led her by the arm to the red, white and blue striped balloon which was now full of gas and which swayed like a large drunken sailor in the rising wind. The old woman was helped unsteadily up some steps and into the basket, then the boy and gentleman quickly followed. The balloonist shouted instructions to his team of helpers outside the basket. The wind was rising quickly and as Duncan D'Arcy discarded sandbags from the sides of the basket the men ran round untethering ropes. With one last heave, the man in the velvet jacket discarded another bit of ballast and within seconds, and without noticing how they had got there, Lancaster saw that they were above the trees.

The balloon quickly picked up speed and sailed over central and north London soon to be crossing open country.

'It's strange,' said the old woman. 'I thought it would be noisy up here, but it's silent as the grave.'

'There's no noise because we sail on the wind, madam. You see, in effect, there is no wind up here at all.'

Looking down from the silent basket to the even more silent farms and lanes Lancaster thought that the whole of England must be asleep. Then as if stealing his very thoughts Duncan D'Arcy said, 'It's been like that for thousands of years. But change is coming, look there's a motor car track,' he pointed excitedly. Sure enough, the boy could discern a trail of disturbed dust winding through an old lane as if a snake had gone by. Then a motor was actually seen puffing up a little dust as it throbbed its

117

way home. They all waved and shouted as the motorist waved back.

'What time will we be home?' Lancaster asked.

'Oh,' said the balloonist, taking out his fob watch, and looking to the hazy sun, 'You'll be home before dark.'

'What! It were near four when we left,' said my great-great-grandmother.

'Yes,' he said with a shrug. 'With this wind we'll be there in less than four hours. If we climb higher it'll be quicker still.'

'No. This is high enough, thank you,' said the old woman, and they all laughed.

While Duncan D'Arcy took out his maps and compass and read them on the floor of the basket my relatives continued to watch the sleepy land below where only the balloon's shadow seemed to move. Lazy farms with lazy hens and lazy cows came into view and disappeared just as quickly under the balloon's black shadow. Duncan D'Arcy, having taken his readings, stood up and leaned over the basket and with hands cupped shouted, 'Wake up, England!'

The wind picked up again hurtling the balloon with its strange band of occupants into the unknown. 'For God's sake wake up!' he then muttered to himself as he wrapped a blanket around my uncle. He then put another about the old woman and sat her on the basket's floor.

'We're asleep. We're all asleep,' he said to her on his haunches, and twirled one side of his moustache.

'What does tha' mean?' the old woman quizzed him.

'I mean what I just said. What I just shouted. We have to wake up. This is not the magic land of Merlin any longer.'

'Less of the we. We're awake in our village,' she admonished.

He thought for a moment, twirling his moustaches now with both hands. 'I'm not so sure,' he said eventually. 'The government sleeps. Those with the money sleep. The working class sleep. We all slumber on. Why?'

The old woman shrugged, then yawned. 'All this talk of sleep is making me tired,' she said, and her shoulders sagged back to the walls of the basket.

'It's all too cosy,' he said. 'Amidst the greatest changes ever seen, nobody wants to change anything. That's a recipe for disaster if ever there was one.'

118

'Oh, just take us home, luv,' she said. 'I'm all done.' Then she fell asleep.

Lancaster, chin resting on the backs of his hands which in turn were supported by the side of the basket, was astonished by the silence. He had never before in his life heard nothing so clearly.

The balloonist stood up and, next to my uncle, hollered down through cupped hands again, 'You can't stop progress, you know. Governments can't reshackle us once we've tasted freedom,' and the land shouted back a mauve and green stillness deafening the two watchers above. By the time the balloon had been whisked into Yorkshire my great-great-grandmother was awake. Duncan D'Arcy offered round cucumber sandwiches and lemonade then, the short meal done with, by carefully manipulating the valve to let gas from the envelope which stretched like the great dome of a cathedral above, he controlled the descent of the contraption. About a mile from the house he allowed the basket to trail through a thick hedge almost tipping the three occupants to the ground. But the desired effect was achieved in that the balloon slowed to almost nothing and, hovering two feet from the ground, he pushed out his two passengers.

'Thanks for the ride,' shouted up my great-great-grandmother.

'See you again sometime,' said the balloonist and blew her a kiss from the back of his hand.

'Will tha' not come in for some cocoa?' she asked him.

'Madam, I'm in a race remember,' he said allowing the basket to hover just above the ground, then he clumsily tipped a sandbag from the craft and the balloon soared away in silence towards Hunger Hill. He waved once, then was gone.

'By gum, grandmother,' Ernest said as they entered the parlour, 'them locomotives get faster all the time. I didn't expect thee home till after midnight.'

'Nay, Ernest. We didn't come ont' train. God brung us home in 'is chariot.'

Ernest laughed, and Lancaster didn't enlighten him to the true means of their transportation. Not then at least, and my great-great-grandmother is still unofficially the oldest person ever to fly in a balloon. Duncan D'Arcy didn't win the race but landed on that blasted heath called Fylingdales Moor, and from all accounts was glad to do so, in winds approaching sixty miles an hour.

119

Some months later old Dr Cartwright came to our house. He'd been sent for to tend Ernest's leg which had been fractured in a roof fall at the pit. The doctor arrived in a blue forty horsepower Crossley motor with a shiny gold radiator, and my great-great-grandmother was pleased to see that it had a soft hood which protected the motorist from the worst of the weather. The old medic spent several minutes watching Albert painting and studied the half-finished portrait of the *Blue Boy* carefully; then he told Emily that her son had a rare talent which needed careful nurturing. He made it sound like a disease which had to be treated. He then flicked through one or two books on the new shelf and, thumbing through the slim volume by Mr Stanley, he informed Lancaster, 'It was Gordon Bennet who put up the money for Stanley's expedition in search of Livingstone, you know.' Lancaster stared at the old doctor blankly.

'Come now, Lancaster,' he said, 'I know how interested you are in aviatrix.'

It sounded like another disease. 'Flying, boy,' he bawled at my uncle. 'It's the same Gordon Bennet, lad.' He threw his two hands into a great circle describing a balloon.

'Yessir,' said Lancaster as the doctor replaced the book upon our library shelf. 'Livingstone reckons sunspurge to be poison to zebras, you know,' the old doctor then told him. 'You are still interested, lad, aren't you? Still keen to have a go in a flying machine?' he went on in an alarmed voice.

'Yessir,' Lancaster said, nodding at the old man.

'Good boy. That's the spirit.' He smiled and put his hand on Lancaster's shoulder and eyed him paternally. 'Now, did you hear that Mr Cody had flown a heavier-than-air machine down at Swann Inn Plateau in Hampshire?'

Lancaster nodded although unsure of who Mr Cody might be and definitely uncertain of the Swann Inn whatever it was. Had this Mr Cody flown inside a pub he wondered.

'Yes. Flew at a height of thirty foot for twenty-seven seconds before crash landing,' the doctor droned on. 'Covered about one third of a mile distance. Mind you, it doesn't compare anything with what the Americans are doing. I see that Wilbur Wright was up in the air for over an hour only the other day. An hour, boy, in which he flew forty-six miles.'

Lancaster nodded again, watching the careful brushwork of his twin seated at the canvas. Deep blue pigment seemed to be everywhere; on his smock, on the pallet, some on the floor, and on the canvas of course; but nowhere did it appear more than at the tip of his black horsehair brush. There it resided like fire would at the end of a burning poker, ready to spread his blue inspiration.

'Took a passenger up with him too. Even that damned Frenchman Delagrange has been up for half an hour,' the old man went on. As the doctor searched our ceiling in a kind of mock exasperation, Lancaster continued to eye his brother's brushwork, noting how he was folding the blue paint into the subject's satin suit. Then Lancaster, turning his back on the old doctor, picked up a brush and without comment smoothed some paint into the same fold on which his brother had worked. If there was any resentment on Albert's part it wasn't shown and Emily noted how her sons were working as one, like Russian dolls for a while, painting Gainsborough's *Blue Boy*.

During the next several months many things happened to bring changes to the lives in our house. My great-great-grandmother brought home a phonograph which she had purchased in Wakefield for five shillings. It was the first in our terrace and music was heard wafting across the common for the very first time. It seemed to cause the dogs more concern than the humans, for long after the colliers and their families had grown used to the strange noises the dogs would cease their playing and chewing each time the records played. Then they would slowly come forward to the front of our house, ears pricked and heads quizzically tilted, perhaps to hear the better. Pedlars then came selling everything from picture frames to three-piece suits with rich satin linings. You didn't have to pay for them either, not immediately that is, for the pedlar was quite prepared to allow payment to be made over a period of two or three years. All the men, including William and the twins, had them for Sunday best, and even at the outbreak of war they had still not been paid for. *The Blue Boy* was finished and framed in gold. Ernest hung it above the mantelshelf sideways, for the painting was too tall to hang in the vertical dimension. Surprisingly it looked just as well and Bill Pettit retitled it *The Sleeping Blue Boy*, and Emily called it *Little Blue Boy* for she thought it just like the boy in the nursery rhyme. Occasionally a car would visit our village driven by a salesman, or a flashy relative, but Elyahou Tsiblitz was never among them.

Then at the start of the new year, 1909, my great-great-grandmother drew her pension for the very first time from the post office in Kippax. She put the five bob into her pinafore pocket and along with many others shouted 'God bless Lloyd George', then treated the family to a trip to the cinema in Leeds. Ernest, whose leg was mending nicely, stayed home with Bill Pettit, but everyone else piled into Mr Achibold's motor bus and for the sake of a penny each way saved their shoe leather. At the Assembly Rooms, right at the top of Briggate, they saw a half-dozen short films. There was a film of a boxing match, and of a horse race, and of some ladies shooting bows and arrows at Beddington in Kent. Then came a film of a train entering a station and everyone gasped as it almost ran them down; the film froze for five minutes then continued with pictures of the passengers alighting from the coaches and walking along the platform. This was followed by a short comedy about a man trying to open a door. Then came footage of Winston Churchill's wedding and more of the king opening the Franco-British exhibition. Then came the evening's main attraction, a very short film about fruit-picking in East Africa. It was while watching this last film that Henrietta learned that the stone balls atop the pillars at the gates to the big house were actually pineapples. So pleased was she to learn of it that she wrote it into her *History of the Stones*. It had been a typical programme for the cinema of the time, an Aladdin's cave full of magic. Nobody thought then of it being a little short in material content. What the heck, they were pictures and they moved. So what if the movement was too quick and jerky to be real – did that matter? One had seen East Africa and the king and they existed for sure and so too did pineapples.

From that night my family became regular cinema goers, travelling at least once a week to shows in Leeds and Wakefield. Always, initially, seeing the same sort of programme as they had seen the day my great-great-grandmother drew her first pension. Then one day they saw a film which was different and which changed their lives completely. The film was called *Rescued by Rover* and it had been made by Mr Cecil Hepworth at a cost of £7.13s.9d. The film is acknowledged to have been the first to tell a real story and, although made in 1904, it was just coincidence that my family saw it five years later and it happened to be their first experience of a story on celluloid too. Suddenly the anarchy of the real world, of their lives, was gone. Here was something else, each Brightside was embroiled in the lives, yes the mortal lives, of others and yet these lives were no more than an illusion which disappeared as soon as the noisy projector was switched off or the film ran itself out.

Ernest never would go to the shows. He thought them to be the work of the devil, illustrating in one thousand and one ways how we might abuse ourselves and others. He stayed home with Bill Pettit who thought the cinema, like roller-skating, to be no more than a passing craze.

But Bill didn't count on the greedy need the human race seemed to have discovered for seeing and being cast with those big seeing eyes right into the epicentre of these celluloid implosions. For that's what they were, little eruptions deep within oneself calling us to account for the misery and joy of others. We were all film stars now. To illustrate the true involvement she felt, when Ernest asked his sister which were the most memorable moments during a particular film, Henrietta answered, 'I'll never forget that poor woman's screams, Ernest. They pierced me to the very heart.'

'But I thought those films were silent,' said her brother in exasperation.

'Oh, they are, Ernest. They are silent, but for the piano, that is.'

'What piano?' he asked, opening wide his deep brown eyes.

'Oh, they've taken to having a piano player to drown the noise of the projector,' she said.

'Isn't that off-putting? I mean, doesn't it spoil the film for thee?'

'No,' she answered. 'Somehow the piano helps you to hear the players.'

'I give up, lass,' Ernest said, shrugging his shoulders. 'It beats me how tha can waste tha money on such things.'

'It's just a craze, I tell thee Miss Brightside,' Bill Pettit said.

'Oh, can you be sure of that?' she asked, rounding on the lodger. 'Can you be certain of that, as you are of all else, Mr Pettit?'

'Ay. I'll give it another year or two, like roller-skating,' he said with confidence.

123

Even as he spoke, two more cinemas were being opened in the city not ten miles away, and Lancaster listening, as only a youth could, to the conversation which had just passed in our parlour thought how the cinema was neither music, not photography, neither real nor yet unreal, and resolved to find in those silent pictures the source of his aunt's wonderment at a lady's scream.

A few days later a letter was delivered to the house. It wasn't from Australia, nor was it from Wakefield, but it had been franked in London. It was addressed to Master Lancaster Brightside. The twin opened it excitedly, wondering who on earth would write to him from London, and withdrew from the envelope a stiff white card, scrolled around with gold leaf. The golden copperplate printing invited Mrs Jane Brightside and Master Lancaster Brightside to be the guests of the Honourable Duncan D'Arcy and the Doncaster Aviation Committee at the First Aviation Meeting to be held in Great Britain at the Doncaster Racecourse. They were asked to join their hosts on any day they cared between 15 and 23 October 1909. In a short note which accompanied the card Duncan D'Arcy explained that Mr Samuel Cody, who had recently flown a distance of one mile, would be there along with several other well-known aviators. He also thought that England was at last perhaps waking up.

'Waking up, my arse', said Bill. 'With two-thirds of the population now slumbering at the picture shows, who's he trying to kid?'

As part of the minority not attending the cinema Bill knew what he was talking about. Bill Pettit knew that when they entered those dark and smoky places the patrons were encouraged to leave their real selves at the door. How else could one explain the good-natured way they would put up with sitting for hours on end on uncomfortable box-wood seats in a filthy, choking atmosphere? How else could one explain Henrietta's hearing voices which weren't there? And, what's more, they never on any occasion, when leaving the cinema, recollected their whole selves. No, a little bit went missing after each subsequent visit. It was like collecting their coats from a cloakroom each time to find that a little more had been cut from the hem. Bill could see it but they, unfortunately, could not. It wasn't only the folk in whose house he lodged either but it was his workmates too. He'd seen

124

the eyes of colliers, glazed like ham, as they moved into a new persona. Dreamlike, they made love with imaginary women, slaughtered their enemies in a thousand different ways, rode horses, drove locomotives and cars, flew aeroplanes. And their wives were no better, idling through their days with a handsome cowboy or a rich Arabian prince. It seemed to Bill that, apart from Ernest and himself, the whole working class was drugged on the craze, for it hadn't escaped his attention that the one-third of the population not attending the cinema shows were the rising middle and upper classes. No, they have it all sorted out, he thought. They needed their hold on reality in order to govern. They'd got the worker both out of the pubs and into a comatose state in one move. Clever. It might even be a Jewish plot, for weren't the film makers Jews, and weren't the cinema owners all Jews? Weren't they feeding unreality to the host population in darkened places? Who knows what might happen in the dark where you can't see the face even of the one sitting beside you? But for poor Bill, progress was thundering along too quickly. The old stacks, housing his information, were too cumbersome. More input was needed even before the rearrangements were complete. Picture palaces appeared. Big posh cinemas opened with seats more comfortable than a pasha's throne. Places where you got a cup of best tea at the interval all thrown in for the sixpenny price of your seat, and that brought in the toffs. Poor Bill, those with the money had only been waiting for the opening of palaces where the entrance fee was one which they could afford. Now the whole country slumbered in celluloid dreams. What's more, my great-great-grandmother, seemingly with money to burn from her five bob pension, was able to move her family upmarket and treat them all to the luxury of the sixpenny picture palace every Thursday.

13

Pause for a photograph of my father

'It is in the nature of those with enquiring minds to discover more facts,' said old Dr Cartwright from the deep sanctuary of one of our wide-winged chairs. The small man appeared lost in the comfort, hands clasped before him by a roaring fire. 'How in heaven's name should I be able to diagnose the Brightside melancholia were it not that I recognize the facts? Fortunately, child, I am able to recognize a scientific fact when I see one, but that is my calling. So too, I think, it is with you.' He was talking to Henrietta and tapped the open volume of bound papers which perched precariously on his knees. 'In your study, you also are seeking scientific facts. And finding them, I might add. Yes, finding many.' He nodded his small head and tapped the book again with bony fingers before linking them once more in desperate prayer and staring again into the flames.

Was that true? Henrietta wondered. 'Am I?' she found herself asking. 'Almost certainly you are, my dear. Each day you observe, hoping that the stones and their environment will yield more of their mystery to you, don't you? Well, what is it that they yield and which you faithfully record?' Here again he tapped the open volume in his lap. 'I'll tell you. It is facts, child. Scientific facts.' The old doctor had just carefully read several pages of Henrietta's beautifully written-up observations with their accurate illustrations, each one meticulously labelled. Henrietta was shaking her head as he adjusted the reading glasses on the end of his long thin nose.

If it was scientific fact that she required, Henrietta was quite aware that all she must do was lift her head from the study of the stones. If it was facts that she was after then they were all about her at Bottom Boat. Her journal would then have been quite different. She would have recorded pilewort in flower, frogs spawning, the yellowhammer and the pied-wagtail in song, blackcurrant in leaf, different species of ladybird depositing their eggs on the gooseberry leaves, the brimstone moth on the wing and the foxglove flowering. She would have recorded hearing the cuckoo and the redpole, she would have heard the grasshoppers singing in the night and drawn long ears of barley and oats, described grubs suspended by threads and counted the spots and hairs on each of their abdominal segments. Spindle tree, guelder rose, wild hop, eyebright, bellflower, sainfoin, milkwort, field madder, red clover and cocksfoot grass would all have been lovingly described. She would have rejoiced in the variation among the birds; stonechat, chiff-chaff, swallow, sand-martin, redstart, blackcap, landrail, tree pipit. For she had already dis-covered variation to be the engine which pulled evolution along, hence her fascination for the imperceptible change. But facts, for sure, did not lead to truth and truth was what she was after, although she was very unsure of how one did arrive at such a thing.

'But it is not science that I study, it is history,' she told Dr Cartwright as he slammed shut the book with his skinny knees.

'Historic facts then. You look for historic facts.' He beamed from his spectacles.

What on earth was one of those, she wondered. Was 1066 an historic fact? And if 1066 why not 1142 or 708 B C? Was everything historic fact? Yes, she could accept that every moment of her life was indeed an historic fact, but who chose which to highlight and why? If some anonymous biographer were to choose the historic facts in her life would they choose the day she first sat down to write her journal? Cartwright probably would. Or would they give equal weight to the thousands of other days she had sat by Bottom Boat? Would they choose the night of the rape, or one of all the other nights she had spent in her bed? Was it an historic fact that she was unmarried and did it matter? Who was it who made history – Cartwright's sort of historic fact history? Was it the people about whom the history was written, or was it the historian? 'No. No. It's not that kind of history,' she said. 'I don't observe facts'.

'A history without facts. That's a funny kind of history.'

'I've told you, my journal is not about facts.'

'Then what is it about?' he asked, adjusting his eyeglasses

127

again and heaving the book onto the table without rising from his comfortable perch.

'I think it must be about causes.'

'What sort of causes?'

'The why things happen kind of causes.'

'Is that not the domain of God?' the old man asked, shuffling in his chair.

'Not exclusively. If he knows then why should we not know too?' The doctor tut-tutted into the red glow of the fire as Henrietta continued. 'Take your diagnosis of melancholia for example. Simply calling it a name doesn't satisfy me. Not without an explanation of how it comes about.'

The old doctor suddenly looked alarmed. 'You're on dangerous ground here, my girl,' he said sternly.

'Yes. I know,' she answered. 'You too share that ground. I'm sure you see it too as a dangerous path.'

'Bless my soul, child, whatever are you talking about? I am a doctor, this is my ground. No, I'm as sure-footed here as a mountain goat in the Alps. But you, child, you are like a horse on the same terrain.'

'Don't be such a stuffed shirt,' she said to the old man who was becoming quite agitated and finding it difficult to settle on a permanent spot in the wide-winged chair. 'You give me a name which describes the condition, and hope that the name in itself will be explanation enough. Well it isn't. I want to know the cause of this condition.'

'I've told you, girl. It's in your family,' he said irritably.

'But neither is that an explanation.'

The doctor paused a while, searching the fire before him. 'Juices, physiological juices,' he exploded, looking into her soft brown eyes. 'Perhaps your family has some strange ferment which is passed in the generations. I can't say more. Would that satisfy you as a cause?' He cocked his head to one side like a bald cockatoo. Henrietta nodded. 'Perhaps.' Then as the doctor settled smugly back into his wide-winged chair, hands clasped before him, he closed his eyes. 'But how can you be sure?' she asked, jolting his eyes open again. He again thought a few moments, then said, 'Why, bless my soul child, I have no idea.'

'Then can't you accept that this thing which afflicts the family and which you call melancholia may have an external cause? Will

128

you not accept that the cause may reside here in the house, in the stone?'

'Nonsense, girl,' he interrupted her. 'What on earth could there be in the stone which would cause such a thing.'

'But you ask me to accept the cause as some juice which is passed to me at birth.'

'Yes, I do.'

'Then what about Lancaster?'

'What about Lancaster?'

'Who passed it to him at his birth?'

The old doctor looked shocked and, had I been there, I should have asked, Yes, and what about me? Who passed it to me? That would have added a bit of weight to my great aunt's argument; but by the time that I was born, Dr Cartwright was preparing a different set of answers to those he was about to give. Henrietta filled in the silence of the coming years.

'It wasn't his mother or his father, for neither Emily nor Ernest suffer from the melancholia. So who, doctor, who passed it?'

'I don't know child,' said the old man shaking his head. 'All I know is that it can't be the stone. For me to say so would be – unscientific. Science is only just beginning to understand the techniques for extracting chemical substances from living tissue. Perhaps when we have identified the offending material we may then see how it's passed, but it will call for much experiment over the years.'

'Experiment!' Henrietta pounced on the word excitedly. 'That's exactly what my journal is, Dr Cartwright, It's an experiment.'

He looked perplexed. 'And I suppose Bottom Boat is your laboratory,' he said kindly.

'Oh no. Not if a laboratory is a place where controlled experiments take place. I have no control over the river. The elements come and go as they please.'

'Then I fail to see the experiment,' he said dismissively.

'I am the experiment,' she assured him, tapping at her bosom. 'I and the stones both; we constitute an experiment. Our interaction is the experiment.'

'But, my dear girl, there is nothing of you in these journals.' He waved his hand towards our library. 'You describe the stones and their changing environment, beautifully I might add, but that's

129

all you do. Like it or not, Henrietta, your journal is nothing other than a collection of facts.'

'Well, it seems that you see only facts, Doctor. I write the book, yet you don't see me. Between the pages, between the days of observation, I am there and I'm constantly changing, yet remain hidden. For you, it would appear, the facts obscure the book. The stones and I are entwined throughout, changing together. Don't you see?'

'Bless me, child,' he said, 'well no, I don't see.' He shook his old head slowly. Henrietta gazed for a long time, penetrating the thick lenses of the doctor's reading glasses.

'It seems that the facts get in the way,' she said at last, and with some frustration. 'I shall have to move the stones to another place where the experiment might yield up results which you can clearly see.'

'But what is it that you wish me to see, child?' he asked now with mild exasperation.

'The truth, doctor. The truth about me.'

The old man shifted uncomfortably, staring into the fire, the heat from which now flushed his face. Bless my soul, he thought, the woman is mad. She's quite mad, I'm sure.

In the days immediately prior to the Doncaster aviation meeting the rains came. They tumbled incessantly from a leaden sky and tasted of metal. From the parlour window Lancaster watched his father and Mr Pettit now joined by William stomping across the soggy common in the direction of the pit. He thought how small and vulnerable his brother appeared to be, tucked as he was between the two strapping colliers and gripping his wretched snap box in slender coiled fingers. The boy had to scuttle, half-running, in order to keep pace with the two long striding men. It appeared though that William had settled quite happily to life in the pit. He had a pony of which he was very fond and was always pleased to exhibit his blackened face on the common just to let the younger ones know that he was now a man and drawing real wages.

Albert, having completed the *Blue Boy*, had turned his attention to the *Mona Lisa* and, sitting at his candle-lit easel like a flower-bearing visitor to a shrine, he would lay his colour onto the canvas, pushing it this way and that with a certain brush. In dark

130

Leonardo strokes it moved about the fabric, stopping only to draw a brief moment's admiration from his mother or his aunt Henrietta. From the window Lancaster watched with a sharp eye pushing the brush, with unseen movements of his head, in the direction it should move, and dreamed of meeting Samuel Cody.

The American's plane had by now stayed in the air for over an hour. It seemed almost every day that news reached Lancaster of some wondrous feat performed by the aviators, each one of course bettering the others. And only yesterday he'd learned that Lord Northcliffe, the newspaper proprietor, was to offer £1000 to the first Britisher to fly a British-made machine a distance of one mile. It was not only Duncan D'Arcy who was urging us to stir from our slumbers; here indeed was inducement of a more positive kind.

From behind Albert's shoulder at the easel, Henrietta quietly watched more candles flickering in the scullery beyond. There her grandmother was busily preparing tinctures and extracts in shiny buckets and bottling others already expressed into glass storage jars which dimly reflected the wavering smoky flames. Here, in our house, was another shrine, a vestry in which Jane Brightside played. The liquids straw yellow, red, brown, bright yellow, rose and black shone dully in their glass containers. Henrietta thought of old Dr Cartwright's words about juices and ferments and realized that her grandmother had been extracting juices from living material for years. Plant material maybe but to extend her dispensary to cover expressions of animal tissue would not be beyond the old woman's wit or calling and, looking across the room from one shrine into the other, Henrietta thought how science, if it was about anything at all, was concerned with unknown principles. Like the unseen energy released at the burning of coal, so unseen agents accumulated and grew in the leaves and roots of grandmother's specimens. So too, according to Dr Cartwright, did juices (or perhaps even spirits, she thought) pass in the generations of men.

And did it matter that you called it melancholia or history as long as you were aware that something was passing unseen? Perhaps here was the great task for science and scientists, identification of unseen agents. Isn't that what the doctor had said? She supposed, pompous as he was, the old man really was a scientist; he knew the way ahead. But not her, she was convinced now more than ever that her mode was history. But for some reason this historian needed a laboratory in which to work. She needed to prove something by experiment.

Emily watched her son. As the rain poured into the lush grass of the common, she watched his boots putting in two steps to his father's one. The three figures receded towards the ridge of green, then to the dip which would take them down to the winding-engine shed. Above the rough wooden structure the wheel cycled wet and noisily. As Lancaster moved from her side Emily wondered how, now the bill was law, an eight-hour working day would affect their lives. Precious little, she concluded, and sniffed. It had been such a long fight, something Sidall Junkin had urged almost all his working days without success. And now they had it, too late for Sidall, it didn't seem much. Eight hours plus winding time. But the colliers claimed it as their greatest victory. It was, they said, a testament to the durability of the mineworker. For more than a generation they had been banging away at the doors at Westminster finally to have them flung open. A victory for the working man, Ernest had called it. More like a testament to the slothful in parliament, she thought, an illustration of the snail's pace progress of parliamentary processes. Meanwhile the Miners' Federation had become affiliated to the Labour Party and wages were not rising fast enough to account for the increased cost of living, not that they'd starve. The old woman in the scullery behind would see to it that they didn't starve.

Emily watched Lancaster setting his camera upon its tripod. She saw the young boy, now beyond the window, rain dripping from his cap, direct the lens towards the three disappearing figures. From the candle-lit room she peered hard into the metal-tasting rain, and watched the magnesium flare momentarily brighten the gloomy sky, and realized the truth of her man and boy captured forever, disappearing from view to the hidden pit beyond. Walking from view. Running from view by the window. My father running from the window to catch his father. My father two-stepping to meet me.

Lancaster knew the truth of that image. It was a black and white photograph for a National Photographic Museum one hundred years hence. It was an expression of now and then. Then past and then future. It was the advertiser's dream, timeless. Emily already knew it as shoe-blacking, in time it would become custard, oven cleaner, deodorant soap, cornflakes, brown sauce, and she would know it as all those things. Then after her death the image would continue to represent washing powders, frozen foods, gadgets. The advertisers would of course use more modern images, the new, the chic, the trendy, but always they would return to the image that Lancaster captured that day on film. For they knew the truth of it.

But Lancaster put the photograph in the family album and promptly forgot about it. His mind was on free running passages. Kinema was in his blood and as his young heart pumped, the idea of film wound itself in his brain. Static images, backtracking staccato fashion, were not for him. There could be no settling of Lancaster's mind until cameras were turning in his hands. It was an urge to overcome the truth and head straight for the lie beyond.

Like any good storyteller (my father reckoned I inherited the ability from my uncle), he needed to relate the whole story. Nothing could be left to the imagination, the terrible focus of truth.

The next day Lancaster and my great-great-grandmother went to the Doncaster aviation meeting. It was the sixth day of the show and poured down. Along with 50,000 other drenched spectators they watched Samuel Cody swear the oath of allegiance before Doncaster's town clerk. The American was now British, a curious conversion but for the lure of Lord Northcliffe's £1000. The band then played 'God Save the King' and Duncan D'Arcy from beside my uncle raised three hearty cheers for Cody. The ex-American's biplane was housed in a great shed which Duncan D'Arcy called the Cathedral but the press, through some misunderstanding thought D'Arcy, was referring to the name of the plane.

'No,' shouted the balloonist to *The Times* aviation correspondent, 'The airplane is to be called Lancaster Brightside,' but it was too late. Cathedral had already been telegraphed around the world, and all settled for that version of the truth. Not only were the newspapers reporting events, they were promoting and now making the news. D'Arcy thought it a dangerous turn of events.

The biplane remained in the shed all day as two days previous its nose had been damaged when Cody crash-landed, so Lancaster unfortunately didn't see Cody fly. But Duncan D'Arcy went up in a small monoplane based on the Bleriot model, circled for ten minutes or so, and was warmly applauded by the wet and appreciative crowd. Back at home, Lancaster cried because of the lack of understanding among the stupid pressmen. His Aunt Henrietta told him that it really didn't matter for it wouldn't have been he who was famous, but the aviation machine, and that names were unimportant anyway.

14

Water comes to the house
and the reordering of the Stones

When the snows came the Airedale Water Company sent a man. He called himself a dowser and carried a V-shaped willow twig. The sun came out but the thermometer registered temperatures below freezing all day. Henrietta, welcoming the sunshine, wrapped herself warmly and sat out in a deckchair. Her bottom pushed the canvas red, yellow and black broad stripes almost to the level of whiteness beneath her.

She watched the man cross and recross the common many times, divining the water and leaving thousands of black tracks in the crisp snow. The man whose hair was almost as white as the snow itself kept shaking his head when the willow twig refused to divulge the presence of what he had been sent to find.

'I don't think it works,' she said to him on one occasion when the line he walked took him close by her striped deckchair.

'Oh, it works all right,' he said. 'There isn't any water here, that's all.' His two eyes were close together and appeared high up on his forehead, although in reality the man had hardly any forehead at all. If she squinted slightly the two eyes came together giving him the appearance of a cyclops.

'But how?' – she pointed to the twig which he held lightly in both hands – 'how can a silly thing like that tell where the water is?'

He shook his head again, 'Dunno, miss. But it works. My father was a dowser and his father afore him. It runs in families tha' naws. If there's water we allus finds it.'

She focused her attention behind the one-eyed man to the whereabouts of the Roman Wall which lay buried under a cap of snow on Hunger Hill.

'Doesn't the snow interfere?' she asked.

'No. It's only water under t'ground that matters.'

'And isn't there any here?' She looked back at him without

135

refocusing her gaze, all the while amusing herself with the man's single eye.

'Don't look like,' he answered and took himself off from the strange squinting woman to see what he might discover below the ash-pits and spawning many more small dark prints on the way, all in a perfectly straight line.

A month later, with a deep layer of snow still covering the common, the Airedale Water Company sent six Irish labourers. They dug many holes out of the frozen ground in the common and a long channel which ran all the way down the terrace from Mrs Agar's house at one end to the Waltons' home at the other. Some days it snowed persistently, covering up whatever tracks there were on the common, but this didn't deter the navvies. They just continued to dig into the hard earth like burrowing animals tunnelling from one hole to another, linking everything together and bringing their tunnels to the walls of the houses themselves. Then they went away and left us with an inverted black and white maze about five feet deep. The children played soldiers in these trenches, heaving great rocks from one area to the next, and when the snows thawed, coating the playful military in slithery liquid earth, horse-drawn wagons arrived with miles and miles of cast-iron piping. The pipes were laid out on the grassy bits which remained between the trenches and when spring arrived the Airedale Water Company sent a dozen men to lay them in the prepared holes. Now, one of the men included in this batch of newcomers was black as the ace of spades and was called Mr Ndolo. He said that he was a prince from West Africa. It was the first time that anybody from our village had seen a black man and they were all a little afraid. However, on learning that Emily was the mother of twins he developed an irrational fear of his own. He claimed the village water pump to be contaminated as he had seen Emily, this mother of twins, drawing from it and refused absolutely to take its water. Furthermore, he told everyone what a good thing it was for them to be having water brought to their homes, not least because Emily could no longer pollute the general supply. My grandmother was very distressed when she heard this story and Bill Pettit told her that the black bugger didn't know what he was talking about and complained to the Airedale Water Company who had Mr Ndolo replaced by an Irish labourer. Eventually, the pipes were laid all the way to the river, via the little pumping station which had been quickly built, and right up to the houses in the other direction. Then after all the holes had been filled in, they sent the plumbers to us. They put tanks into the houses and fitted shiny gold taps into the walls above the sinks in the sculleries. Then they fitted waste-pipes and drainage, and one day in late summer Ernest turned the tap to great cheering in our house and out flowed turbid water which was of a pea-green colour and smelled of cucumbers.

The handle of the village pump was then removed. The authorities, after all these years, had decided that the water which came from it was unfit for human consumption. Mrs Henderson was greatly relieved for she believed Mr Ndolo's fear to be not without foundation. The water had not been quite the same since those twins had been born, she said. She was never heard to pass an opinion on the condition of her household water though. However, my own family had much to say about it.

In the first place it frequently changed colour. Its natural state seemed to be somewhere between the pea-green liquid, which had oozed out on that first tap's turning, and murky brown. On occasions, however, it appeared pale blue and, even more alarmingly, red. Then, they complained, it smelled strongly of cucumber but sometimes of violet and even geranium. The greatest complaint was reserved though for when the water was heated. At about the mid-point between room temperature and boiling terrible sulphurous fumes would fill the parlour, choking the occupants and encouraging giggles from the twins who put the smell down to their great-grandmother's frequent bouts of flatulence. The water also had a permanently bitter taste and it sometimes brought on debilitating attacks of diarrhoea.

'Drink more water. You must replace the fluid loss,' said old Dr Cartwright when brought out to attend Emily who had been smitten.

'Can't something be done to reactivate the old pump?' Ernest asked.

'Don't worry, you'll all get used to it eventually.'

'But what's in the water to cause such terrible diarrhoeas?'

'Algae,' the doctor answered without hesitation. 'And they will also be causing the smells, and the changes of colour too.'

Seeing the lack of comprehension in Ernest's face, the old man

137

offered to bring over his microscope so that the family might understand something of the life with which their drinking water teemed. The following day he came back with the apparatus, placed a drop of water upon a glass slide, covered it and lay it upon the microscope's platform. He then lit a candle close by the mirror so that the light reflected upwards illuminating the water on the slide. He then focused the lens and invited Ernest to peer into the eyepiece.

'What's that?' said my grandfather, tearing his eye from the glass and registering a look of amazed horror.

'Euglena, I think,' said the doctor with his face all screwed up and looking back down the tube.

'But it's moving.'

'Yes, it would. It's alive.'

'You mean we swallow them things live?'

By now everybody was wanting to view the marvels which the microscope was bringing to life and eventually, after much twiddling, they were all given a glimpse of one or other of the darting animalcules which lived in our water supply. There were also long green sticks and worm-like things which, despite their shocking appearance, at least managed to stay in one place. By the time Dr Cartwright's biology lesson had finished my assembled family were mostly close to hysteria. Bill Pettit had also managed to commit to memory the new words: spirogyra, stigeoclonium, arthrospira, synura and gomphospheria. There were many others which had tripped lightly from the doctor's tongue which even Mr Pettit couldn't recall.

'Facts. They are all there,' the doctor said for Henrietta's benefit, pointing down the microscope tube. Then he went on speaking to Ernest. 'They should have been filtered out. Perhaps they're having trouble at the plant. I'll have a word with them.'

'I should hope tha' will,' said Mr Pettit, none too keen on the words which had found their way into his head.

'No matter. As I've said before, you'll all get used to it. Give it a few more weeks.' Cartwright went on, 'At least there'll be no more hauling buckets of water all the way from the pump. You'll be glad of that, I expect.'

Henrietta nodded. Since the installation of the supply she had taken to filling the sink almost full with cold water, adding a few soap flakes and washing dishes for hours on end. And during these long hours of dish-washing she would ponder the stones, their history, science and meaning, while her arms to a level above the elbows slopped about in sudsy water.

Some of the time she contemplated her new laboratory. Where it should be and how she would move the stones from one place to the other. She was unsure of exactly when such a change would come about when an incident at Bottom Boat forced a decision from her.

She had, as usually was the case, been sitting on the bank watching the stones and drafting a few notes, when she caught sight of two dead fish floating on the current and being taken downstream. At first she imagined nothing unusual for she often saw and recorded dead fish, especially if their bodies were caught up among the stones, but gradually more appeared. Soon her eye was taken with dozens of dead fish floating along, their bloated sides turned pink and upward to the sky. The river water was slowly turning pink too. Minutes later there were thousands of dead fish choking the surface of the river from bank to bank, all carried on a foamy red tide.

Her first thought was that it was the untreated waste from the village, which she knew to be poured into the river about a mile upstream, that was polluting the water. But what could there be in their household waste to cause such devastation? As water toilets had not yet been fitted, the waste returned to the river consisted of dirty water, being mainly the washings from the villagers' baths and their dinner plates. Henrietta quickly walked upstream to the place where the village effluent was emptied into the river. The water here was almost blood red and beyond, further upstream and floating down to meet her, were more dead fish looking very pale in the crimson rush. The foam too was becoming heavy. Following the river around passed the pumping station my great-aunt came eventually upon the source of the pollution. Simmonds' dyeworks. It was a small factory with a tall brick chimney which continually puffed out clouds of black smoke which smelled of marzipan. Henrietta went inside through a wooden door which bore the company's name in white lettering and demanded to see the owner. She was kept waiting for an hour then eventually a man in a straw hat arrived who explained that Mr Simmonds was in London but that he was the company chemist and would help if he could. Henrietta explained her concern at the red stuff which was being released into the river and killing all the fish. She also explained that since the introduction of the water supply she and her family had to drink water from the river.

The straw hat which was slightly too large for the man's head moved a little as he spoke, and he kept having to readjust it with the red thumb and index fingers of his big hand. There was a pink area on the brim which suggested that this was a regular man-oeuvre, and the smallness of the rosy patch was testimony to the man's accuracy in hitting the same mark on each occasion.

'It's a chemical which takes the oxygen out of the water,' he explained, 'so the fish are unable to breathe. We humans take our oxygen from the air fortunately, so it won't affect us. Don't worry, your water will be perfectly safe for drinking.'

She thanked him for his assurances and he smiled swivelling his hat ever so slightly. We had red water for a while and two people living in our terrace died that week. Others vomited into their sinks and flushed away the sickness with gushings of cold water from their golden taps. Old Dr Cartwright thought the deaths due to food poisoning and blamed Mr Doyles' pigs for both the deceased had consumed pork in the day before they died. The diarrhoea in our house ceased for a while and Ernest believed, as he had been told by the doctor, that everyone was getting used to the water. Of course, nobody was, and had they at that time put a drop of water on one of Dr Cartwright's slides and presented it to the microscope, they would have seen that all the little animals had been stained red and that none of them were moving.

The episode with the dead fish and the pollution of the river water made Henrietta see that she must act quickly. The stones had to be moved. So her journal dated 30 August 1911 was headed 'THE REORDERING OF THE STONES' in large capital letters and described how William and Mr Pettit brought the stones to our house in a wheelbarrow in six journeys and dumped them on the common just outside our door. There were 147 of them altogether, far more than she had ever counted before, but as William explained they kept finding stones underneath those which had been visibly available. The next day, the day of the start of a month-long strike, and also the day on which Albert finished his painting of the Mona Lisa, my great-aunt went outside with two pots of paint, one red, the other yellow. She then proceeded to paint all 147 stones choosing at random those to be painted red and those to receive the yellow paint. Watched by scores of out-of-work colliers who had little else to do, she covered the stones on all sides in the coloured paints. She then dispatched a dozen men with an assortment of implements and the wheelbarrow to dig up from wherever they could find them as many stones as possible of a similar size to the ones which had been brought from Bottom Boat. When the first barrow load of stones arrived back at the common my great-aunt immediately painted them with pitch on all sides and left them to dry on the common. This she did with each succeeding load until she had about six hundred stones, all black as pitch; then she went indoors and wrote up her journal.

She tested her indelible stamper, the stamp from which was becoming slightly faded, on the back of Albert's recently finished canvas, which lay on the parlour table. This she did only once, breathed on the inked rubber, and stamped the pages of her journal.

The following morning a congregation of about thirty men appeared in groups about the two piles of coloured stones and wandered aimlessly among the strewn-out black ones. Henrietta, after breakfast, went outside and told the dumbfounded miners, who looked as if they had stumbled upon the Easter Island monuments, that they were going to build a wall. Thus were the stones reordered with my great-aunt supervising the placement of the red and yellow stones amongst the black ones as carefully as an Egyptian architect would have seen to the placing of blocks in the building of a pyramid. The wall abutted to the front of our house at both sides and formed an enclosure taking in a part of the common about ten yards long by five, the latter measurement being the width of our house. With her laboratory complete and the stones identified and trapped amongst their dark and anony-mous neighbours Henrietta brought out her deckchair with the matching striped canvas. She placed this just in front of the gateway which had been left in the front wall and in line with the doorway to our house. She then invited Albert to come and paint her sitting outside her laboratory. She ordered Lancaster to come and photograph, and asked Dr Cartwright to come and see. From the far side of the common, the coloured stones shone out like jewels. Dr Cartwright, always concerned when in the presence of madness and genius and never easily able to distinguish between them, blessed his soul again and diagnosed mania. But the woman seems harmless, he thought, and did no more about it.

Elyahou Tsiblitz was soon to arrive outside our house. He was driving a 28 horsepower Lanchester car. It had a hard covered roof but no glass windows and within the coachwork was so splendid it looked as if it might have been built for royalty, for the padded cushions were puffed up in kingly red.

'It was,' explained the rubber man when asked, 'built for the Jam Sahib of Nawangar. He had six motors built for royal occasions by the Lanchester company. As I was supplying the tyres I asked if they could manufacture an extra one for me.'

He was standing in Henrietta's laboratory. Behind him the body of the vehicle was quite visible through the gap in the wall and my great-great-grandmother could pick out the Jam Sahib's coat of arms painted in black and gold on the two doors.

'Will tha' come in for some tea?' she invited as a crowd began to collect about the motor. He nodded and followed her into the parlour where Ernest and Mr Pettit sat reading the newspaper in the wide-winged chairs. Beyond, in the scullery, Henrietta was deep in thought with her arms to the elbows thrust in the sink and covered in foamy bubbles. Mrs Gill, banging at the back boiler with her poker, caused the two men to look up from their reading.

'What's he doin' 'ere?' Ernest asked.

'I invited him,' said the old woman possessively.

'Gerrout.' Ernest nodded towards the doorway through which the two had just walked. 'We don't entertain thieves.'

'Ay. Go on, 'opit,' said Mr Pettit, imitating Ernest's movement of the head.

The Transylvanian looked towards the open door but remained where he was as the old woman held him stubbornly by the sleeve of his tweeds. He could see the top halves of many people as they stood about his motor.

'I'd better leave,' he said to my great-great-grandmother.

'Nivver,' she said. 'Ignore them. They've no understanding.'

'Yes. It's for that reason I'd better go,' he smiled.

'No.' She tugged at his sleeve. 'Tha'll stay.'

Bill Pettit stood up and approached Elyahou, 'Go on, clear out,' he said up at him, for he was a good six inches shorter than the tall rubber man. 'Tha's not wanted here.'

The old woman rounded on Bill. 'Mr Pettit sit thee down. If there's any leavin' to be done, it'll be thee that goes. Remember, tha's only a lodger here thissen'.

'Grandmother. Watch 'ow tha' speaks to our lodgers,' Ernest warned.

'Ay, and tha' watch how tha' treats a guest, Ernest,' she countered. The two men feeling the embarrassment of a family affair nothing to do with them now looked at each other with neutral eyes.

'Sit down, Bill,' my grandfather said softly, still looking angrily at the visitor.

'Tha' must tell us sometime 'ow tha' came to pinch the Ascot Gold Cup though.'

The tall man shrugged and gave the old woman a look which suggested he had no idea what her grandson was talking about. He was spared further pressure to stay, however, when a chant went up from the children outside the door.

'We want the suits, we want the suits,' they chorused.

Then as Lancaster appeared with his twin in the freshly walled compound before the door, it changed to 'we want to fly, we want to fly'.

Elyahou went through the doorway and stood beyond talking to the now hushed and expectant children. 'There is no more flying suit. No more bee,' he explained. 'It was damaged by a stupid parent down near Barnsley only last week. The child went up over the roof and the man went pop.' He squinted into the imaginary sights of an imaginary rifle held in his hands. 'The child came down unhurt, thank God, but the suit is beyond repair. So, no more flying, I'm afraid.'

As the moans went up around him Elyahou shouted, 'but everything else is here' and he ran to the motor. Out came the same old battered suitcases and as always the children were quickly dressed and soon bouncing around the common.

From his side my great-great-grandmother asked, 'What have tha' to sell us today, then?'

143

'I've nothing today,' he said, spreading his hands and smiling into her disappointed face.

'I have made my fortune in car tyres, Michelin, Dunlop and now Tsiblitz. I need nothing more.'

'Then why didst tha' come?'

'Courtesy.' He shrugged.

'Tha's a liar,' she smiled. 'Tha's got summat for me.' The smile developed into a small giggle.

He laughed as she touched the red bodywork on the motor and ran her tongue over her lined lips.

'Come on. Get tha' tea,' she said, gently tugging him by the sleeve. Reluctantly he followed the old woman.

On reentering the house they quickly passed through the frosty atmosphere in the parlour to the scullery where Henrietta was still dibbling in the sudsy water.

As the old woman filled the new black kettle with water from the tap and took it into the parlour to boil on the fire, Elyahou asked Henrietta what she was doing.

'Thinking,' she said, blushing deeply.

'With your hands?' he enquired with concern.

'I just find it helps me to think,' she said. 'Having my hands in water helps me to think,' she elaborated.

'I never heard anything like that before,' he said.

'No. Perhaps.' She smiled nervously. 'But it works.'

A few years later he happened to explain Henrietta's habit to a Cambridge philosopher called Ludwig Wittgenstein who tried it out as a means of thinking. Wittgenstein took up the habit and washed many a dirty pot, hours on end, thinking about thinking. Because he developed a contact dermatitis the philosopher then asked Elyahou if it would not be possible to make a glove out of his damned rubber so as to protect the hands of the washer-up. They sat down together and designed it there and then.

Left and right. Elyahou made yet another fortune as the inventor of the washing-up glove, but one rarely hears of the part Wittgenstein played in its development.

'Tha'll get nowt but chaps, lass,' her grandmother said, coming back to the small room and searching among the bottles shining out of the shelving.

'Here,' she said at last, plonking a fat bottle down on the tiny wooden drainer by the sink. 'Rub tha' hands with glycerin and rose water, it'll sooth tha' chaps.' Ignored by the granddaughter the old woman turned to Elyahou.

'I've been thinking 'bout tha' motor,' she said.

'What about it?'

'It's a grand motor is that. Will tha' sell it to me?'

The rubber man looked away to study the labels on the neat rows of glass bottles behind the old woman.

'Tha's not answered me,' she told him.

'You couldn't afford it,' he said still with disinterest.

''Ow should thee know?'

He looked back at her searching her gnarled face 'Did you sell the cup?' he asked. A moment's panic crossed his face. 'I didn't believe you'd sell the cup.'

'The cup's safe enough, don't tha' worry,' she assured him. 'How much for the car, rubber man?'

'Three thousand three hundred pounds,' he said still searching her face.

'Don't go away,' she said and went as quickly as she could from the house. Not that Elyahou had any thoughts of leaving, imprisoned in the scullery as he was by the hostile stares from the men in the parlour. For the while he felt safe where he was. It was a place for women. The men, he knew, would not transgress. He watched them reading their newspapers an instant then turned his gaze back into the scullery.

'What do you do in the house all day?' he asked Henrietta, his hands thrust deeply into his trouser pockets. She half turned towards him at the sink.

'Oh, I write my journal, boil the water; sometimes I cook. We take it in turns, Emily, Grandmother and I. Emily always bakes the bread though. I wash the dishes, but I enjoy it, now we have water to the house.'

Then, as if to prove the point, she sloshed her arms even deeper into the cold suds.

'Did you never think of work, going into service or something like that?' he asked. His hands were still thrust into his trouser pockets and she could see by the way he made unseen bulges with them that he was holding up his trousers with tight fists. Turning her head back to the sink she thought for the first time in a long time of the rape. She thought too of grandmother's baskets, sniffing the perfumed air in the small room.

145

'Ernest wanted me to go into service but when I started to write my journal grandmother forbade it. She said I should be free to concentrate on my writing.'

'She is an enlightened woman, your grandmother,' he said. She turned her head again towards Elyahou and noted how his trousers were too long for his legs. Although the Transylvanian had very long legs, his trousers seemed to have been built for a giant of even greater proportions. She allowed her eyes to lift slowly from his shoes to the area about his crotch where they lingered awhile. Elyahou, suddenly uncomfortable, hitched the trousers up about his waist by means of the hidden bulges at which the woman was staring. She smiled.

'Is it true that you have made your fortune selling motor car tyres?' she asked now with her back to him.

'Yes, I have a factory making tyres in Berlin.'

'Are you rich, then?'

He shuffled a little then said, 'Reluctantly, yes I am rich.'

'Whyever reluctantly, Mr Tsiblitz?' she asked, busily scrubbing a plate for the umpteenth time.

'Because, as a socialist I always believed the working class to need the fruits of technology, and I always thought that I might provide some of that harvest.'

'And so you did,' she turned and told him.

'But I did not intend to make myself wealthy. I did not intend to become a capitalist; employing labour, accumulating profit and all it entails.'

'And have you become a capitalist?'

'Yes. Well, no.' He struggled with his thoughts. 'I suppose I still think like a socialist.' He hitched his trousers again.

'Mr Pettit thinks you are an anarchist,' she smiled.

'That too. I used to believe in anarchy. No more government, the human race attaining its natural moral state without political masters. I still do really. I still think that way, but I've been overrun by success. I wanted to give rubber to the people and they gave me money in return. Perhaps I should give it all away.'

My great-aunt turned from the sink drying her long slender fingers on a towel.

'Grandmother has been trying to give away a fortune for years. It breaks the old woman's heart that no member of the family will

146

take it from her.' She unstoppered the fat bottle which her grandmother had left on the drainer and poured the viscous liquid into her palm causing an effusion of roses into the atmosphere.

'How come a woman like your grandmother has a fortune to give away?' Henrietta rubbed the emollient between her palms, wringing her hands in the process. It made the soft intimate noise of flesh being squeezed into something other and looking again to the visitor's crotch she noted how a third bulge had suddenly appeared between the other two.

'As you said, she's an enlightened woman,' Henrietta answered, while undoing Elyahou's fly buttons. Hardly daring to breath the man pressed his back up against the shelves of bottles out of view of the men in the parlour. He could hear the turning of the pages of newspaper as my great-aunt proceeded to reveal his stiffly erect penis from among the folds of his large trousers. Stroking him lengthily with her glycerin and rose-water hands, she was on this occasion at least going to send him away with a cock smelling of roses. His own small responses following the movements of her hands caused a trembling to be set up in the wooden shelving which was immediately transmitted to the rows of bottles which rattled brittly against one another. This caused the whole of my great-great-grandmother's stock to sing at such a high frequency that the dogs on the common started to bark and howl in tune to the quiet masturbation which was happening in our scullery.

'Must be another stranger coming,' said Mr Pettit looking up from his newspaper and lending an ear to the cacophony on the common.

How true, Elyahou thought, while ejaculating into Henrietta's saponified palms, and unaware of the strange vibrations which were eddying through the coloured liquids above his head. In embarrassed silence the rubber man quickly made himself decent and, unperturbed by the dangers beyond, scurried from the room at the earlierst opportunity leaving Henrietta with her arms thrust once more into sudsy water, although on this occasion she was washing herself rather than the dishes. My great-aunt hadn't felt so good in years. 'Next time I'll bite it off,' she said softly to the accompaniment of a bottle of red liquid falling from the top shelf and being dashed to smithereens on the stone floor.

''Ey up!' said Mr Pettit from behind his newspaper and, as Elyahou ran from the house, 'There goes another one.'

Ernest smiled, but didn't move from his seat. His sister would clear the mess.

15

Jane Brightside buys a motor
and how the stones came alive

In the popular imagination the typical collier is a rugby-playing,
beer-swilling mountain of a man who can withstand, because of
his job, all that brute nature has to throw at him. We tend to think
that all of them will have been spawned by the Adam and Eve
who shared our earth closet; Mr and Mrs Gill. Nothing could be
further from the truth. In our village at any one time the majority
of the men were knackered. Like Sidall Junkin, they were asth-
matic and breathless or, like old man Gill, they lived with their
broken backs, thighs, necks, arms and all. There were few who
didn't suffer rheumatism or rupture and, because of the cramped
conditions in which they worked, the constant scraping of knees,
hips and elbows caused the joints to fester. The most pitiful of all
though were those with the terrible rotating eyeballs. Unable to
fix their gaze on anything for very long their eyeballs would
swing wildly in their sockets sometimes causing their eyes to
disappear completely, and giving them a ghoulish appearance,
setting up panic and fear in friend and stranger alike. When
my great-great-grandmother returned to greet Elyahou, her
deep pinafore pocket stuffed full and clanking with coin of
the realm, she knew exactly the use to which she would put the
Jam Sahib's motor car. She would take the crippled and the
unfit and unwell for trips into better areas. She would take
them for a day away from the grit and smoke; she would see
to it that they breathed more easily, that their pains were
eased.

'I'll take them to Burnsall Fell where I once went as a lass and
show them a river that's clear, and air that doesn't need rain to
wash it clean,' she told the Transylvanian as he watched the
inflated animals playing cricket on the common. He had taken
himself off to watch the children in an attempt to recover from
Henrietta's attentions.

'You can have the motor. Have it for nothing,' he said without humour.

'Nay, lad, tha' must tek payment for it.'

'But I don't want to. I have enough,' he protested.

She would not hear of it and, remembering the words of the granddaughter, he felt an obligation to put an end to the breaking of an old woman's heart, and with some reluctance but an overwhelming sense of duty, he went to the motor and took one of the battered suitcases from the back seat. He knelt on one long knee at the woman's feet exactly as he had done on his very first visit to our house, and opened the case. Standing above him, she let cascade from her pinafore a noisy assortment of guineas, florins, half-guineas and pennies. As the coins tumbled past his face, and pulling apart the sides of the case in such a manner as to create more space while it filled ever higher with my great-great-grandmother's fortune, he felt himself becoming locked into a charade from which he could see no escape.

'Tha's earned it,' she smiled at him. Although that was about the last thing he wished to hear, he smiled back.

'You must let me give you something now,' he said when the metallic cascade had finally ceased and he'd closed the lid on the pile of cash.

'I knew tha' would,' she grinned expectantly.

Elyahou stood up, put the case back into the motor and opened the second case from which he took a wooden tube. He removed a rag plug from one end and started to extract a scrolled canvas.

'Is it a map?' she asked, not able to hide her excitement. 'Buried Treasure!'

Elyahou shook his head and continued to extract the object. When the scroll was finally free of the container in which it had been rolled, he handed it to my great-great-grandmother. Unravelling it between her wrinkled hands, she had no difficulty in recognizing it for what it was.

After all she had been looking at a steadily developing copy of it for several months. It was the *Mona Lisa*. Taking the wooden tube from the man, she asked him to wait a moment and went into the house. As Ernest and Mr Pettit were still occupied with their newspapers the old woman had no difficulty in exchanging unseen Albert's copy of the gift which Elyahou had just made to her. Returning to the Transylvanian she then told the only

150

downright lie of her long life. She said, 'No thanks, Ernest thinks I shouldn't keep it' and, putting the copy into the container, handed it back. Elyahou shrugged, told her that he understood and arranged immediately in his mind for it to be returned to the Louvre. They must have been pleased to receive their precious Leonardo back in one piece but they must have wondered why it had been returned with my great-aunt's name on the back. Perhaps they knew it to be a fake (although I should stress that it was a very good one) but thought it hardly worth making too much fuss as the good citizens of Paris would be none the wiser if they covered it with glass, housed the painting in poor light and gave prayers at the cathedral of Notre Dame. The citizens proved to be very thankful indeed.

The original hung in a rough pine frame above our sideboard until the next time the pedlar came to our village when Ernest bought a fine golden frame for it. It fitted a treat and he hung it back on the wall centred against the bible with the brass clasp which remained darkly shut immediately beneath.

When the men in our house learned of the family's new acquisition they were very angry. My great-great-grandmother didn't let on that she had paid for the motor but allowed them to think that it had been given her as a present, like she had been given Brescis's hat and the Ascot Gold Cup. Naturally, though, they thought that it had been stolen. Mr Pettit made enquiries first in his head then with the police. No, the Jam Sahib of Newanger had not reported the theft of a motor. A detective was sent from Leeds to look at the vehicle and take fingerprints, and my great-great-grandmother took him for a spin around the neighbouring villages. She sounded the throaty horn as they passed by the Thwaite house just as the coal owner was taking a walk along his leafy lane. The old capitalist didn't see who was driving it but thought what a magnificent machine had just passed by his gate with the pineapple balls. The detective went back to his inspector to report that the old woman believed that she had received a gift from God and he couldn't see, at this moment in time, any reason to doubt her.

William, though he approved absolutely of the use to which the old woman was to put the motor, was nagged by thoughts of her having squandered the family fortune. Perhaps it was because of something which his aunt Henrietta had said that he disbelieved the old woman, but he felt certain that the motor had not been given to her. He therefore decided to confront Jane Brightside alone.

'Don't worry, there's more,' she told him, when he'd informed her that he understood the fortune one day to be his. 'And anyroad tha's had tha' chance with the Gold Cup. Great softee, tha could've hung onto that. Had it melted any time tha' liked.'

'I would had tha' not come lookin' for me,' my father accused.

'Nay,' she said, 'tha wouldn't William; tha's too honest, lad.' Then she started to laugh, great loud raucous laughter. She laughed and she laughed, tears streaming down her face and her mouth open wide like a barking dog. In mid-laugh she suddenly stopped. Her old gnarled face seemed to collapse in on itself; her mouth closed then the rough dry lips parted as if she were about to say something. She might have been about to say that the real *Mona Lisa*, not Albert's *Mona Lisa* but Leonardo's *Mona Lisa*, was hanging above the sideboard. Or she might have revealed the whereabouts of the Ascot Gold Cup or of the suitcase with the money, but she didn't say any of those things; she just said that she was glad and asked to be put to bed for she didn't feel right. She couldn't remember who she was or anything but kept repeating that she was glad.

Ernest and Henrietta put their grandmother to bed wrapped in a white cotton nightdress and bonnet and resting on a blanket of cotton wool. Her face was sunken and olive green, the black lines showed the coal grit of nearly a hundred years. She kept mumbling that she was glad and couldn't remember anything.

William took a load of cripples to Burnsall together with his brothers, and they swam in the Wharfe with the disabled on their backs. They climbed the fells with them on their shoulders and described what they could see to the blinded. Where the river widens and snakes through the village by the pub they paddled and drank ale, and the man with the terrible rotating eyeballs syndrome who couldn't focus on anything for more than a few seconds at a time disappeared his eyes into the top of his head and didn't frighten anyone anymore.

The following week he took the asthmatics to Ilkley Moor in the motor, the finest in Yorkshire, and in the heather heard them breathe more easily. Like Sidall Junkin, they wheezed and spat great gobbets of mucus black as printer's ink, all over the pink and violet heather; but there was a spring in their strides which they never displayed in the village. He took some heather home to his great-grandmother and noted that her skin colour was as green as the plant and he told her of the trip to the moor. She said that she was glad, and with the cotton wool haloed about her head she looked like a dead angel. My father continued for as long as I can recall to take a car load of the less fortunate each week into Wharfedale.

The motor remained parked on the common at the side of Henrietta's laboratory and was washed twice a week. On only one occasion was it vandalized, and that was when a boy from another village stole a headlamp. It found its way to a pub at Middleton where the landlord, realizing what it was, returned it to William and apologized for the thief's bad behaviour. Such was the fame of the Jam Sahib's motor.

The imprisoned stones yielded little information to my demented great-aunt. At night they shone white and mauve from between their black neighbours, appearing a ghostly mosaic under the moon to those who viewed from across the common. During the day, however, the coating of soot which they quickly collected gave them a dull and grimy look, that is until it next rained, when they were again washed clean. Then they glistened as cold stone does and the moss beneath the coat of paint stretched itself. Seated in her striped deckchair Henrietta waited and prised time apart. She created a continuous present pulled high as the laboratory walls and from that safe limbo she was able to see that everything which had passed carried the historian's stamp of inevitability; yet there was nothing at all inevitable about that which was to come. Here in her waiting room, walled off from the world in both space and time, she would wait. Was she waiting to bring history to an end she wondered? Here in this super present would it all finish? Or was she waiting for some accidental happening to nudge events along? And what of God? Was she waiting for the Almighty to cause the unfolding of some great plan, or even perhaps for Him to tumble her Jericho there and then in her extended and stretched present, just as He must have tumbled the dinosaur bones onto her father?

Hadn't Mr Darwin put an end to that nonsense though? Wasn't

it now quite acceptable to see both history and nature travelling an unbroken line from their beginnings and on into a never-ending and disappearing future? Ah, beginnings she thought. Where is the beginning of history then? Man's consciousness, she supposed. When nature was conscious enough to influence events, that's when history started. Isn't that what she had meant by her journal being a history, a book of causes? It was her own awakening consciousness that had first made her aware of the stones. But what had become of her since that first day, after the beginning of history? What line did she travel that old Dr Cartwright could not see the woman she so earnestly hoped would be found lodged between the stones in her journal? Her book of facts as the old doctor called it, her description of nature. Had she influenced the stones at all? She was beginning to doubt that she had; yet they had undoubtedly influenced the events in her life. Day by day by day, hadn't they? But what if the stones constituted an ever present even before the building of the laboratory, before the now. Perhaps they formed a present in which she had grown very old. Was her life to be but one day in the existence of the stones? Was the waiting room no more than a selfish indulgence which, like with her father, in the end would destroy her? Would she herself, too late, bring down the walls of Jericho? Too late because she had not even begun to do what she knew she must, and she returned again to thoughts of bringing the world to an end in the present. She must act, not wait. She didn't have to be the passive agent. Had she not acted, demonstrating her freedom of will only the other day in the scullery with Elyahou Tsiblitz? Had she there not changed the world?

If old Dr Cartwright was correct and it was the juices in nature which brought about biological change, then they managed things in a very slow manner, unlike historical change which came about much more quickly. And the agency through which that change came about was knowledge. Second-hand, third-hand knowledge passed from father to son, mother to daughter. This was the asset which progressed the historical world. Knowledge and reason both. Learned as much from our contemporaries as our fathers. Her grandmother had been correct when at Sidall Junkin's funeral service she had said that God was an engineer. God was a contemporary progressing the world through man's knowledge and man's reason and a whole new world was coming

154

because of it, and she should act and be a part of it. So she decided she would be positive and brought the world to an end in that artificial present stretched and yawning between the walls of her strange laboratory.

But the idea of the end of history in the present is a nonsense, a lie, a fiction. The line which history travels doesn't stop, it just bends a little, loops perhaps, and the story becomes retold.

So Henrietta wrote in her journal for that day, 'My grand-mother, who was born on the day of the battle of Waterloo, slowly climbed the slope of Hunger Hill.' She then went on to recount how her grandmother had encountered Duncan D'Arcy and Lady Annabelle Kerr and the coming to our village of a strange foreigner called Elyahou Tsiblitz. She wrote of John Tregus and a rape and so many other things filling a whole volume. Thus did my great-aunt's history become a literary fiction and in her mind stones became real people. Many years later, discovering these volumes in an old chest of drawers, I rewrote her story, changing the relationships between herself and her characters for those between myself and those same persons, and adding a few words of comment here and there.

16

Introducing Count Schubert and Rosanne

The year after they brought the water they brought the gas to our village. They didn't in that year bring it directly to the houses, but only to the few straggled and dirty streets in the form of gas lamps which stood upon tall cast-iron standards and the light which shone brightly from their glass housings. We had one such lamp directly beyond our door, the full length of which we were able to see through the gap in Henrietta's wall. It was situated about half-way across the common and quickly became the meeting place for the lovelorn. Emily looking from the pale glow of rooms still lit by candles was able to keep a mental note of who was courting whom and by noting the sad and prolonged waiting of solitary figures, who had been jilted by whom.

It was under this light that one night a large wagon pulled by a massive shire horse came to rest. It was far too late an hour to attract the attention of any would be poker-user, for the whole terrace was wrapped in a warm and magical slumber. As the giant horse stopped so too did the two small liberty horses who were tethered by short leads to the back of the wagon.

The man who held the reins, and who was seated with his two companions at the front, looked back and said, 'I think we must have taken a wrong turning back there, in the last village. This is just a dead end.'

'No wait,' said his male companion. 'I know this place.' And peering about the common he jumped down. He banged his heels into the turf with his heavy boots. 'I know this place. I helped lay pipes under this grass.' He smiled a dazzling white smile from his ebony black face. The man on the seat put his arm about the second companion, a small fair woman with turquoise eyes, and said squeezing her to him, 'Rosanne, we shall sleep here the night. Prince Ndolo knows the place.'

She smiled back at the man, her turquoise eyes full of wonder, and crawled through into the wagon behind followed immediately by the man. Prince Ndolo tethered the big horse to the lamp standard, then climbed into the wagon by way of the high step at the rear situated between the two liberty horses.

When the terrace awoke it was to see a crimson red wagon with beautifully scripted gold lettering on its side informing all that housed inside were the full contents of Schubert's circus. The occupants were awakened by Albert who had climbed aboard and, peering into the wagon from the seat up front, was somewhat surprised to see the three occupants sleeping side by side all under one beautifully woven Mexican blanket, with Mr Ndolo in the middle, sandwiched between a man with long waxed moustaches and the most beautiful lady he had ever set his eyes upon.

Resting upon one elbow but otherwise in repose, the man introduced himself as Count Schubert and introduced the others as his wife Rosanne, the granddaughter of Madame Saqui, the famous rope walker, and Prince Ndolo of fire-eating fame. Albert offered breakfast in the laboratory and on the way back to the house pondered the marvellous dual role of flame-eater and water engineer. He decided that the prince should be the subject of a portrait.

The three visitors quickly arose, jumped down into the salmon-pink dawn and entered my great-aunt's walled enclave, there to receive bread and raspberry jam and cups of tea from the lady herself. Henrietta busily explained that her grandmother, who was almost one hundred years of age, would ordinarily have attended the visitors but that unfortunately she had been laid upon a bed of cotton wool for some time now and, at least according to her doctor, had temporarily lost her sanity. But why the blessed Lord should keep her in this state, hovering between life and death, she couldn't imagine, she told her visitors.

'I too have a grandmother whom the gods have condemned to wander,' said the woman with the turquoise eyes, 'Madame Saqui, the rope walker at the court of Napoleon. She died a long time ago, many years before I was born, but it seems her soul is condemned to walk a line between earth and sky. It is said that she is sometimes seen, a small figure in black, climbing at the rainbow's edge.'

'I've not seen her,' Albert blurted out, not taking his eyes from the beautiful Rosanne.

'Nor I,' she answered him, smiling and causing a blush to creep at his neck, 'but an old medium told me that I must perform one of her tricks before she would ever find her way into heaven.' She looked at her husband whose moustaches dripped copious amounts of tea, *'Pauvre grand'maman!'* she sighed. 'I must jump through a hoop of flames while balanced on the rope,' she explained directly to Albert whose face registered only a growing admiration for the woman and an agony for the plight of her grand'maman's soul.

'Do you?' asked Albert. 'I mean can you? Can you jump through a hoop of flame?'

'Yes, I can leap through the hoop on the ground, but not yet while balanced on the rope.' She pouted her lower lip. 'Someday, perhaps.' She sighed again.

'Are you to perform your acts here, on the common,' Lancaster asked excitedly and suddenly aware of the enormous potential of Schubert's circus.

Schubert pulled a quizzical face. 'I don't know,' he said. 'We are only here because we lost our way. We are on our way to Roundhay Park in Leeds.'

'But now you are here, you must perform at least once, Mr Ndolo.' Henrietta appealed musically to the one she had known before, hoping this familiarity might influence Schubert's decision.

'Yes, we could spread the word that you are here,' said Lancaster.

'Bring in the crowds from Castleford and Kippax,' added Albert, his eyes not leaving the face of the rope walker whose long hair now glistened gold in the weak morning sun. Such was his stare into her turquoise eye, that his artist's brain split her face asunder, and he saw her turn a fragmented joy and grief towards her husband. Like so many other artists of the day, working alone and unknown to each other, he committed her disassembled beauty to the canvas in his mind, struggling with notions of mass and space and the architecture of people.

'Chéri,' she pouted at her husband, 'perhaps just the once.'

Count Schubert, feeling now the intense pressure being exerted through both of his companions, agreed to a single

158

performance to commence that evening at seven o'clock. Much work was to be done, he told the small crowd which was beginning to assemble in the laboratory, and quickly led the way back to the wagon, squeezing the tea from his facial hair with a flourish at the ends of each moustache.

While Mr Ndolo instructed the helpers in the erection of the square tent, Rosanne strung a rope between the side arm of the gas lamp and the roof of our terrace, Charley Gill securing it to our chimney pot. Our roof of course was higher than the gas lamp's side arm but because of the distance, when pulled taut, the rope showed nothing more than a slight but steady incline. Meanwhile Schubert prepared leaflets, using a John Bull printing set, and gave them to my father and the twins, and asked for them to be distributed as Albert had suggested in Castleford and Kippax.

All that afternoon Rosanne, dressed in sequined tights and with ostrich plumes on her head walked, like her grandmother, between earth and sky, practising and preparing for the day when she would speed her antecedent's soul upon its journey to heaven. The square tent, striped like seaside rock, slowly unfurled then rose, a magic castle slap bang out of the middle of our common. By six o'clock the tent had been erected and people were pouring from far and near onto the green area beyond the terraced houses.

At a flap in the tent wall Count Schubert admitted the customers one at a time jangling their silvery sixpences in a cocoa tin. At seven o'clock with much embarrassment he had to explain to the many still outside that the tent was full, not another person could he admit to stand about the small ring inside. He had to concede that my father and his brothers had done an excellent job and promised there and then that there would be another performance at the same time the following evening. He then explained that as a consolation to the disappointed if they bought their tickets now he would only charge them half price. The offer satisfied most, the few complainants seemingly having just arrived the worse for drink, but Charley Gill who had assumed the role of policeman cracked a few heads together and quickly dispatched them noisily back to the pub.

The show began with Rosanne, still dressed in her sequined tights, riding around the ring astride the two liberty horses. She performed somersaults and various acrobatic tricks to thunderous applause and deafening whistles. Her husband then came into the ring and demonstrated his amazing teeth by using them to dismantle an orange box. Having pulled out the nails with his teeth, he then demonstrated his amazing feet by reassembling the box using his toes to hammer back in the nails.

The famous fire eater, Prince Ndolo, was then introduced. In a hushed silence the African doused flames, breathed flames, ate flames and then, quite accidentally, set himself alight. Rosanne standing by with a bucket of water had thrown the contents, within a second, over his head. The Prince, unharmed, then demanded to know where the water had come from before he could continue with his act. Schubert, uncertain of the relevance of his demands, accused the fire eater of time wasting and insisted that he continue to give the public their money's-worth. Before the argument could get too far out of hand, Mrs Henderson had shouted up from the audience that there was no need for Mr Ndolo to worry for she had drawn the water herself from the new tap in her scullery. The prince smiled at her and waved. Mrs Henderson smiled back. Emily glared at Mrs Henderson, then at the prince. Bill Pettit glanced even harder at Mr Ndolo. The act continued. Amid wild cheering the popular blackman eventually left the arena to be replaced by the husband and wife in Red Indian costume. Firstly he threw knives at her then, with the aid of a whiplash, he removed cigarettes from her mouth. Albert whinced each time the angry leather passed within an inch of her pretty mouth. While everyone else applauded, Albert quietly felt the pain. Albert was in love. But why did Mr Ndolo sleep in the middle, he asked himself. Why didn't she sleep next to her husband?

Count Schubert then introduced Princess Ndolo, the famous hermaphrodite, and Albert, because he didn't understand the word, still didn't know why. In fact it's doubtful if any of those present in the audience knew the meaning of the word hermaphrodite when Count Schubert introduced the princess, but they certainly knew when she removed her golden cloak, for Mr Ndolo had breasts. Tits as big as watermelons, yet from the great bulge in his pouch they all knew he had male parts as well. The ladies hid their eyes, the men hooted and whistled. Mr Pettit called him a black pervert. Albert now knew why Mr Ndolo slept

160

in the middle and his love became an angry love. He refused to clap the act from the arena.

Rosanne then walked a short rope in her ostrich plumes and danced back and forth ten feet from the ground. The entertainments ended with Schubert challenging for a fight. Any man who could last three minutes would be given a golden guinea. Albert, incensed by the way in which the Count treated his wife, stepped forward before anyone could stop him. The boy shaped up, southpaw, to the circus owner, received a single blow to the side of the head and was carried off unconscious amid laughter. Mr Pettit, who wished to demonstrate his anger against the employment of black perverts, then stepped forward but a right cross followed by a left uppercut sent him quickly to the same place as Albert. When Charlie Gill was floored and at the count of ten was still found to be wandering about on his knees, the audience knew that they were in the presence of a true champion and all volunteering ceased.

The wild applause which greeted the trio of performers when they came to take their final bows suggested to Count Schubert that this little backwater with its wide common might indeed be a place for future performances.

17

Tsiblitz cruising

Cissy Tsiblitz awakened her husband who was sleeping in the lower berth. She spoke in Italian softly tugging at his silk pyjama jacket.

'Wake up, darling. Wake up, the engines have stopped.'

Elyahou sat up in bed very slowly rubbing the sleep from his eyes and yawning deeply. He looked at his watch. They had retired to their cabin only forty minutes ago.

'What? What is it?' he asked.

'The engines.' She spoke softly but exaggerated each syllable as one does when speaking to a foreigner.

'What about them?' he asked scratching his head.

'They've stopped.'

Elyahou sat there concentrating his attention on his bottom. Sure enough the gentle throbbing which had accompanied them the four days since leaving Southampton was no longer pulsing through the sprung mattress. He swung his legs out of the bed and noted the lack of vibration on his long toes when they met the floor. He wiggled them a moment hoping that this might get the ship moving, but felt nothing either on the soles of his feet.

'What do you want me to do?' he asked.

'Go and see,' she said quietly in the same exaggerated way as before. Without expression he stood up, put on his dressing gown and slippers and left the cabin. At the end of the corridor by the stairs he found a steward.

'Why did we stop?' he asked.

'Dunno, sir. I expect it's nothing.'

Several people, warmly clad, hurried past them and up the stairs. Elyahou allowed his gaze to follow them until they had turned the corner and disappeared from his view.

'I'll go and see,' he said, nodding after them.

'Expect it's nothing much, sir,' the steward repeated.

He climbed three flights to the sun deck. Several people stood about quietly talking in small groups. The night air was cool, the sea dark. The sky dazzled with bright stars clearer than he could ever remember seeing them, but the strange lack of moon lent a darkness to the night. He looked again to the black sea. Without seeing it, but from the total lack of movement of the ship, he knew it to be very still. As a crew member scurried by, Elyahou grabbed the seaman's arm.

'What's happened' he asked.

'Nothing for concern, sir,' the sailor assured and pushed past continuing his urgent journey along the well-lighted deck. He then overheard an old man telling a lady wrapped in several furs how he was sure that the engines had started up again. Elyahou peered over the side of the ship and noted the tell-tale thin white line of foam which told him that the old man's statement was correct. The ship was moving again. He made his way back to the cabins to assure Cissy that all was well. She was already waiting for him, fully dressed and in the corridor.

'Get dressed,' she instructed, following him into the cabin.

'Now don't upset yourself, dear,' he said, 'it was probably some small mechanical fault. Everything's all right now. We're moving again.'

'Elyahou,' she said, braving herself to break bad news, 'Elyahou, the ship has hit an iceberg.' Her lower lip started to tremble.

'An iceberg?' he said, turning and taking her by the shoulders. Cissy nodded. 'A steward told me.'

'Oh, nonsense,' he said, hugging her to him. 'But even if it were true, this ship's unsinkable, remember.'

'Yes,' she smiled, pulling away and looking into his eyes. 'You and your stories. You'd tell me anything,' she added good-naturedly, and sniffed back the tears.

'That's because I'll believe anything myself,' he answered her laughing. Nevertheless, he was beginning to wish that he'd never agreed to the voyage. It had been his wife's idea. He'd been working too hard at the factory in Berlin, she said, and needed a holiday. Anyway she wished to see her family in Paterson, New Jersey. She'd not seen Mama in years. So when she'd learnt of the *Titanic*'s maiden voyage to New York she'd pressed him to buy tickets; after all they could afford it now, he being one of the

163

largest manufacturers of motor car tyres in the world. An Atlantic crossing with *hoi polloi* on the world's finest liner would be eminently suitable to solve both problems, she had said. He'd get away for a while and she'd see Mama. He wished now that he'd never agreed to it, but he kept reassuring his wife all the same.

'It is unsinkable, dear. It is, I assure you,' he said, as if he believed it, and started to dress. 'And even if we have scraped an iceberg little damage will have been done, I assure you. I've been on deck and there's no sign of damage. All is very quiet.'

Cissy helped him on with his jacket and overcoat and, when a steward knocked at their door and asked them to go up on deck with their lifebelts on, they'd joined a throng of passengers in the corridor. On the stairs he still insisted that it was only a precaution because the *Titanic* was unsinkable. And everyone about them agreed that the ship couldn't sink for it had been designed not to sink. Why, boats like that, with libraries aboard and salons and cocktail bars, lounges and grand bedrooms, tennis courts and swimming pools, they didn't sink. It was like imagining a grand hotel sinking. Impossible. And even when on deck for the second time Elyahou noted how the bows were now tilted downward ever so slightly he reasoned that Marconigrams would have been sent to every ship in the neighbourhood, and he told people how they'd be afloat all right when the rescue ships came to take them all off. So when an officer arrived and asked the women and children to go down to the deck below and there take to the boats while the men stayed where they were, Cissy said, 'No, I'll stay with my husband. I'll go in his boat.'

'No, madame,' said the officer, tugging her arm. 'Please go to the boats on the deck below.'

'No,' said Cissy, shaking her arm free, 'I'll be rescued together with my husband.'

'As you wish,' the officer consented and moved along the deck issuing his instruction.

Then curiously the band appeared on the upper deck and played waltzes and hymns, and Elyahou felt more cheerful and, while still wishing that he had not come, he told his neighbours that he wouldn't have missed the experience for all the world, and people about him laughed, and his wife told them how her husband was such a joker, and they roared all the more heartily, slapping his back for appearing such a good egg.

164

They were able to see the boatloads of women and children, each with a few crew members, being filled and lowered from the deck below into the dark sea. They saw each one rowed off into the night and clearly felt the continual slow slippage of the ship's front end into the water. They looked about continually but never could they see any evidence of the offending iceberg. Looking out from the deck beyond the small boats, the only visible thing was a continuous line at which the sky would meet the sea, slowly dumping its load of stars from one into the other as the earth turned, and somewhere out there the inevitable sun to greet tomorrow whatever might then be left of SS *Titanic*.

There was no panic. As the band continued to play and the crew worked non-stop to release the final few boats, the realization quickly spread that for the remaining male passengers, plus the few wives who like Cissy had insisted on staying with their men, there would be no place in the boats. The music stopped. Elyahou turned to see each of the bandsmen disappear into an icy sea, all upright, still attempting to produce music from their waterlogged instruments. Other passengers followed, walking off into the deep end. The last boat left, the ship tilted at an ever steeper angle and Cissy watched the ship's deck, miraculously still well-lit, as people swam about as if in a pool.

'Dive, Cissy, dive!' Elyahou shouted, grabbing his wife's hand and pulling her with him through the cold air to splash into the iciness seventy feet below. He hung on to her as they went down under the calm surface, held her hand as they swam like fish, then felt a short tug and she was gone, and he was rising upwards in the darkness. He broke the surface only two or three feet from a collapsible raft manned by crew members who, even before he could look about and shout for his wife, had hauled him aboard. 'My wife,' he protested. 'My wife is here somewhere.' But they were busy sailors and hauled another three men aboard. Then a stoker, dressed only in a singlet and shorts who had been appointed captain for the occasion, instructed his men to row like hell away from the black stern of the ship which now pointed like an accidentally hammered finger into the sky.

Elyahou remained both physically and mentally numbed until the dawn came, painting a line of hitherto invisible bergs a rosy hue, like pink champagne which had frozen in the chilled wind. There was excitement in the raft. They were to be rescued, he learned. Rowing around a large iceberg they came upon their rescue ship and joined the queue of boats waiting in the still, calm waters to be emptied of their cold and hungry loads.

Once aboard the rescue ship he found it to be a cruise ship, SS *Carpathia*, which had been bound for the Mediterranean. A passenger called McDevitt kindly lent him a spare set of clothing and he quickly sent a Marconigram to Berlin informing the factory of his own safety but of the fact that Mrs Tsiblitz had gone missing. The *Carpathia* changed its course for New York.

In New York Mama Bresci greeted him with wet kisses and wept like she'd not wept since the death of her Gaetano. At the factory they waved flags, German, Italian, American and British, and wore black armbands. He told Mr Meyer, his secretary, that it had been a cock-up. A typical English upper-class, fucking cock-up. Only enough lifeboat capacity for one-third of the persons on board, he said.

'For a few pennies more, sir,' said Meyer stiffly.

'It's not the pennies, Mr Meyer,' said Elyahou, 'it's the lack of foresight and that bloody certainly the English have. Certainty that no one's to blame, not on their side anyway. Even the bloody passengers left behind couldn't believe they'd been let down. It was all so good-natured, Mr Meyer, as if they were practising–teaching us all a bloody good lesson and practising for something.'

18

Albert learns of lies and truths
and Elyahou finds a partner

On the day of the second performance of Schubert's circus the village awoke to a grey dawn. A heavy cloud of steam hung about the winding-engine shed, disappearing it from view. The morning air, pregnant with its own moisture, fell in upon the white cloud rounding it, even kneading it a little but emphatically not allowing it to rise to reveal the hidden structures at the pit head. The villagers, who knew their weather only too well, told Count Schubert that the warm steamy object would probably remain most of the day but by nightfall would have dissipated as if it had never been. But, he was told, if he was in need of warmth during the day, there was no better place to be. It was the villagers very own Turkish bath he was informed.

'A *Schwitz*,' he said.

'Yes, a *Schwitz*,' Lancaster answered, setting down his kinematographic camera upon its tripod and not understanding a word of German.

So it was, with a large white ball settling about the pit like dough, circus perfomers emerging from their red and gold wagon and Lancaster preparing to film that strange troupe, that Elyahou Tsiblitz drove a white Rolls Royce onto the common, parked it alongside the Jam Sahib's motor car and asked Albert, seated at his easel in Henrietta's laboratory, if he may see my great-great-grandmother. Flustered by the rubber man's sudden appearance, my uncle asked him to wait and went selfconsciously into the house. Left alone in the walled enclave, the Transylvanian studied the work on the easel. What appeared to be two pierrots, one black-skinned, the other white with a single large turquoise eye, stared back at him. The whole composition was made up of simple geometric shapes, triangles, cubes and circles, each weighted differently with various colours. He slung his gaze to Hunger Hill and noted how in the grey light definition had gone.

The mountain's sombre face climbed bleakly to an angular peak. The dim-toned sky hemmed in the brooding rock. How clever, he thought, looking back to the canvas stretched on the easel. Clever and sad, for he saw how the turquoise eye shed what could only be a small white tear, as if the moon were tumbling from out of the sky.

'These are shattered worlds,' he told my uncle when he returned.' How come a boy like you can paint such a tableau of destruction?'

They both looked to Hunger Hill, hearing the whir of Lancaster's camera from beyond the wall.

'That camera can never capture what's behind the peak, Mr Tsiblitz. Lancaster films only what the camera sees, the reality of the circus in this instance.'

'And what about you, Albert, what do you paint?'

'The same thing, Mr Tsiblitz.'

'The reality of the circus?'

'Yes, but from a different perspective. I shall call it *The Water Engineer and the Lady with the Turquoise Eye.*'

'I see. You paint with much love, Albert, but you must learn to distinguish between what you see now and what you think will come. Don't confuse your tenses, Albert, not even on canvas.'

There was satisfaction in his voice, and assurance. The tones one hears from a man who has just learned a secret. A mystery solved although the suspicion had been held a long time.

Albert searched the foreigner's face for what seemed an age, then he said, 'I nearly died once, but it's the same me as here and now.'

'Yes, that's all very well. The past and the present are one, Albert; the sum total of you, Albert Brightside is your past right up to this very second. But it was the future I referred to, don't confuse what you now see with that which it will become.'

'But you stand there now, Mr Tsiblitz. You bring the future. I've heard you say it. I've heard you promise to bring the future. How can you do that if you are not confusing tenses?'

'Someone has to invent the future, Albert,' the rubber man shrugged.

'But aren't we all inventing a future, all of the time? What's so special about your future?'

'Yes, we all invent a kind of future; we all go about inventing the inevitable future. Like wars. It seems to be very easy to invent the destructive future. Dissipation is the way of the world, Albert. But someone has to invent the constructive and useful too. It's like extracting beautiful lies from a terrible matrix of truth. It's like taking one of these coloured stones from out of the black wall.'

Albert stared at his aunt's laboratory walls. He had never considered destruction as being an inevitable thing before, nor had he considered destruction as truth, but Elyahou Tsiblitz was making him see, by omission if by no other means, that there was nothing inevitable about the safekeeping of the world. It would have to be invented. It would have to come as a fiction, written out of the dark.

'And what lies did you bring with you today?' he asked of Elyahou, not in the least bit cynically.

'Come,' said the foreigner, casting his eyes to the gap in the wall. Albert followed him to the white Rolls Royce. Elyahou opened the rear door and motioned for the boy to step inside. Albert was immediately aware of a sharp drop in temperature, particularly about his feet and legs. A metal box, about a one and a half foot cube, stood in the middle of the floor in front of the rear seats on which they now sat.

'Do you see that?' said Elyahou.

'What is it?'

'It's a cold box. It works off the battery.'

'What's it for?'

'It refrigerates things, keeps them cold.' Elyahou opened the lid and put his hand into a smoking iciness. He withdrew a small glass container which appeared to be empty and handed it to my uncle. 'Do you know what that is?'

'Ice,' Albert said, turning the container in his fingers, and peering hard at the opaque fuzziness within.

'Good boy. Yes, ice. But it's a very special ice.' Albert looked at him questioning the speciality of the ice.

'It's from an iceberg,' Elyahou explained.

'An iceberg?'

'Yes, and not any old iceberg. It's from the iceberg which sank the *Titanic*.'

My uncle's eyes opened wide as saucers.

'You can have it,' Elyahou told him, dismissing those big hungry eyes with a wave of his hand. 'A present.' Albert was too thrilled to say anything but the saucers had indicated his appreciation of the gift.

As they left the motor and re-entered the laboratory through the hole in the wall, Elyahou said, 'I have also brought something to aid your manhood.'

'What's that about manhood?' It was Henrietta who spoke. She was standing by our door and the words caused Mr Tsiblitz to blush upwards from his neck to his forehead. Albert never would have believed it possible for anybody to turn so red. 'I believe you wish to see my grandmother,' she said, ignoring her visitor's rubrication but inwardly congratulating herself on being able to bring about such changes in his blood supply. She had embarrassed him; that gave her a power she had not felt before. 'My grandmother is unwell,' she went on before he could answer. 'She has lost her memory, but as you must be counted a special friend of hers I can hardly deny your request. Please come in,' she invited, ignoring his smile. Henrietta led him through the empty parlour and up the rickety stairs to the bedroom. Her grandmother was still lying upon a bed of cotton wool and the Transylvanian was shocked to see how green and wizened was his elderly friend.

'Emily and I bathe her daily, but we don't seem able to rid her of the black lines on her face. No sooner do we wipe off the soot than it returns. It's like it were coming from within; a hundred years of coal dust oozing out.' Henrietta then bent close to the old woman.

'Wake up, grandmother, there's someone to see you,' she said, ruffling the sleeve of her nightdress. The old eyelids flicked upwards, like shades at the windows, to reveal eyes as mischievous as he would ever remember them.

'It's Mr Tsiblitz, grandmother' Henrietta shouted.

'I can see that, girl,' said the old woman, startling her granddaughter for a moment. Henrietta looked to Elyahou a second in panic, then composing herself said, 'It's the first time she's recognized anyone for months. Please don't tire her with bothersome questions.'

'Hold tha' tongue, lass, and get downstairs,' ordered the old woman and, with her newfound confidence fully recovered, my great-aunt descended to the parlour below. Elyahou sat upon the

170

bed and told the old woman that a war was coming and he felt powerless to prevent it.

'This country and Germany too – they are both full of hate for one another. Filled with people like your Mr Pettit, it will be impossible to avert a war. They call themselves socialists but they're not. They're working class, they're trade unionists but they're not socialists.'

'What are they then?'

'I don't know. They're not liberals either. They have an almost pathological hatred of everything that's not of themselves.'

'They're called nationals, luv. They believe in their country and their king, right or wrong.'

'But they're nothing more than cannon fodder for the capitalist wars.'

'What do you expect? If the state has a cannon, it's got to have an army.'

'And if it's got an army it has to have an enemy,' he suggested to her.

'That's right, luv. It's the way of the world.'

Elyahou suddenly saw that the small square window had been filled with massive sequined thighs which disappeared as abruptly as they had arisen. He noted too that they took themselves off heavenward. The strange noises from the roof suggested that they had been safely there received.

'Pigeons,' the old woman muttered. 'Ernest should do summat about them pigeons.' She seemed to turn more green as the bile rose in her blood. 'Did tha' steal the Ascot Gold Cup?' she suddenly asked him. Elyahou stood and watched expectantly, then the small window filled with soft sequined buttocks rubbing worlds together. He watched them recede from view as the taut wire which supported them sprang to life in a strange twangy harmony.

'No, but I know who did,' he said, turning from his view of the common to the old woman. 'He was an over-exuberant lieutenant to the cause. The cause needed money but some things are beyond destruction. It was senseless to steal a think like that.'

'And the hat?'

'My brother-in-law. It was his hat. I found it among my things. I had to be rid of it, but I was too sentimental. You saved it for me.'

'Giaconda?'

171

'I returned it to Paris,' he said, turning again just in time to see the window filling once more with the sequined thighs. My great-great-grandmother started to laugh loud enough to bring Henrietta up the stairs. By the time she had reached the top step her grandmother was rambling on about being glad, and then complained of feeling unwell and of not knowing who she was. Henrietta asked Elyahou to leave as she tucked up the wizened old woman with the olive green skin. He went, but not before he had seen the small square window fill again with sequined buttocks, bringing worlds into being and shattering others in hopeless collision.

By the time Elyahou had returned to his motor, word had spread that the rubber man had come again to the village. Despite the counter-attraction of the circus performers at practice, the enthusiastic greetings of the gathering crowd of women and children showed that the Transylvanian had lost none of his magical attraction. They wanted to touch him. They wanted to touch his motor. And more than anything else they wished for the inflatable suits. And the sale of course – what had he got for them this time? What wonders from an inventive world would he cast among them today?

'But first, the suits, ladies and gentlemen' – his eyes twinkled at the children – 'and I have a real surprise. At my factory I have perfected the flying suits. There will be no more bouncing around, no more earthbound children; today you shall all fly. Eagle, osprey, bee and bat, gulls and tits, parrot, pig and pterodon – dozens of them. Here, you shall all fly today.'

'Pig?' shouted Bill Pettit from out of the crowd. 'Pigs can't fly.'

'Today, my friend, pigs shall have wings,' the foreigner called back. 'You'll see.'

'Stuff you, Tsiblitz,' Bill bawled back. 'Stuff you and your kind.' He spoke a clear king's English, lapsing out of his regional accent.

'My kind, Mr Pettit. Whatever is my kind, please tell,' the Transylvanian answered elevated now on the running board of his motor.

'Jews, anarchists, blackies, Germans. I dunno but damn you, Tsiblitz, and all like you.'

'Don't be such a killjoy, Mr Pettit,' Mrs Henderson called out as the collier pushed his way rudely out of the crowd and towards the house in which he lodged.

'Come' – Elyahou jovially coaxed the audience – 'forget the interruption. Here, there are even large size suits for those adults who wish to savour the wonder of flight.' Then, taking up in his hands a suit of green rubber, he pushed his way out of the throng to where Lancaster stood alone filming the proceedings. Looking directly into the lens he confronted my uncle.

'Come, Lancaster, show them. Show them that there is no need to be afraid.'

'Yes,' said Lancaster in a muffled voice from out of the black box and still turning the film, 'I'll show them.' Elyahou disappeared from my uncle's view but he could soon feel the familiar hands dextrously dressing him from behind. The bitter smell of the rubber product came again to his nostrils and then with a greater inrush of air than ever before, Lancaster inflated and sailed majestically into the air still clutching the camera to his eye. The tripod fell away landing harmlessly but with a clatter on the ground, and all the while Lancaster committed the expressions on the receding upturned faces to the recording eye of his machine. It was the very first aerial photography attempted with a hand-held camera, and it worked.

With more great inrushes of air others sailed into the grey skies until the air in our village was filled with floating people – perhaps twenty children and maybe a dozen adults, including Mrs Henderson and Charlie Gill who took off from earth like rockets holding hands all the way. Unfortunately, as they approached the rooftops they accidentally nudged Rosanne's rope where the walker was still at practice. The lady held her balance awhile, almost fell, regained her balance momentarily then, unable any longer to connect feet with line, tumbled into space all the while watched from immediately beneath by my uncle Albert. The twin, attentive, indeed expectant of the exotic lady's soft flesh about to pour itself into his clutching fingers, was somewhat surprised to receive a heavy blow which flattened him much as a falling tree might have done. For the second time in only two days Rosanne was to be the cause of my uncle's loss of consciousness. He was unable to hear therefore the many apologies shouted from above as both adults, still with hands held, probably more out of fear than affection, flew off towards the steam cloud and the pit head. Meanwhile Albert, amid heady perfumes, came to be tucked under the Mexican blanket in Schubert's wagon. His hand was held and patted by the rope walker who, as she leaned over him repeating *'Pauvre garçon, pauvre garçon'* many times, almost poured her burgeoning bosoms over him in much the same way as she so recently had cast her whole self upon him. Realizing with sudden alarm that he was occupying the approximate position that Mr Ndolo had so recently taken up, the boy quickly made his apologies and ran from the makeshift bed, still only semi-conscious.

It was with the memory of Rosanne's breasts falling to meet him that Albert stumbled back to the crowd to see Elyahou Tsiblitz stretching a rubber object about six or seven inches long between his fingers and thumbs.

'It's called a sheath,' he heard him say. 'It stretches over the penis and enables one to have sexual intercourse without fear of babies.' Albert sensed the embarrassment of the audience, but probably because the recent accident had played havoc with the zone of inhibition in his own brain, found himself asking if the sheath was washable.

'Yes, young man, quite washable, and you can peg it up with your underpants and shirts to dry on the line.'

'I'll have one then,' Albert said, amid a mixture of gasps and laughter from the onlookers.

Well, if Albert Brightside could have one so too could anybody else, thought the crowd, and within minutes practically everybody in the village was equipped with a washable, reusable condom. Only just in time, thought Henrietta, who was one of the few not to purchase a sheath, for she knew that the blue bottle on the scullery shelf revealed how near to extinction was her grandmother's female mixture. It was down to the last quarter inch and with the old woman in her present state there looked to be no hope of replenishment. Looking to Elyahou, she thought what a madman he really was and, looking to the sky, thought what a mad world he was bringing them. Mrs Henderson and Charlie Gill seemed to be mighty close to the ball of steam at the pit head, she observed.

All afternoon, Count Schubert practised alone in the tent. He put his rocklike body through crushing pain but as always emerged

174

intact. His muscles rippling with sweat, he poked his nose outside the tent, immediately felt the chill and decided to partake of the *Schwitz* as Lancaster had advised. A quick look told him that the steam hadn't budged from its original location, so with head bowed (he was the shy, retiring sort) he made his way to the pit head. Once within the hot mass of vapour he realized how variable its temperature was, but nonetheless removed his leopard skin leotard. Some pockets were more dense than others, in fact certain areas were free of steam altogether. The lack of uniformity surprised him and he was grateful too to stumble across a small patch which appeared ideally suited in which to both relax and to bathe. The only problem was that it was already occupied by two small boys who were quite unsuccessfully trying to inflate a rubber object. He watched their pathetic attempts a while then offered his services. The boys smiled as whispy trails drifted before their faces. Although the sheaths had thick rubber walls it was no problem for the strongman to inflate them, the inspiration coming from deep within his soma in short bursts. The more of the objects he blew into white balloons, the more the children seemed to produce. He let them rise into what seemed to be a chimney of clear air cleaving upward within the steam ball.

Meanwhile, on the common, fears were growing for the safety of Mrs Henderson and Charlie Gill. They were now dangerously near to the steam cloud at the pit head. If they were to fly into it there was no telling what might happen; a fearful accident with the winding wheel perhaps or landing amongst the belting machinery seemed favourite conjectures. Others thought they might be scalded alive in the hotter upper reaches of the ball. The temperature was unknown; nobody had ever entered from that end before. The crowd hushed as the two ballooning adults', hands locked more firmly than before, tried to fight back the approaching cloud, but the more they struggled the more perilous their situation became. With one last sad kick of their legs the two neighbours disappeared completely into the hot white steam, leaving the many onlookers both on earth and above to pray that nothing untoward should befall them. Lancaster, filming the whole sorry episode, was probably the first to see what happened next and certainly it is there preserved on film. The unfortunate pair came shooting out of the centre of the steam ball with a great whoosh at about a hundred miles an hour, supported and pushed by dozens of inflated white balloons. They were directed so far and so straight that Lancaster had to learn quickly to float upon his back to be able to film the ascent. Viewed from ground level it seemed that they almost disappeared altogether, showing in the sky as two blackbirds might on any old grey day. Then the terrifying plummeting as the two blackbirds grew bigger and the crowd realized that they had long since lost their supports. Vertically down they fell straight into the white steam ball – this bit of course is not on film – to land by the side of the now naked bather with the waxed moustaches. Now this is the truly incredible part of the story and perhaps, as Ernest later pointed out, gives credence to the power of prayer, for as all those villagers prayed for their safe landing it appears that on their way down through the steamball Mrs Henderson and Charlie Gill came across several inflated contraceptives rising to meet them, thus periodically breaking their fall finally to land on a cushion of the things which littered the ground three or four deep, these having failed to rise at all. There was, as they struck base, an almighty explosion of contraceptives, the energy from which caused the cloud to move from the centre outwards. As the steam lifted in whisps and drapes it was eventually revealed how close Count Schubert had come to being totally flattened. Charlie Gill, with Mrs Henderson on his knee and travelling in excess of one hundred miles per hour, would have been resisted by nobody, not even Charlie's conqueror of the last evening. Charlie, however, didn't hang around to find out what was happening. Believing as he did that there had been an explosion at the pit face, he tucked Mrs Henderson under his arm as if she were a rugby ball and hared off to the common as fast as he could. The count, dazed and covering his modesty with a condom, a fully blown one that is, walked back to his wagon with as much dignity as he could muster for the occasion. It was then that the shy man – looking at the ground under such circumstances no longer helped one's dignity – saw the open sky for the first time since the rubber man's arrival in the village and realized that people were actually sailing about the air above our terraced houses. Being first and foremost a man of business, the Count dressed quickly and then sought out the person who was able to affect such a wondrous trick. Elyahou Tsiblitz was introduced to him as the owner of the manufactory where the flying suits had

176

been produced. No, Elyahou would not sell his suits to Schubert's Circus. Nor would he rent them, nor make others even for £1000 each. What need had he of money? What he needed was a new life. A life which would provide him with a few comforts and an access to ordinary people whom he could entertain and service with his own peculiar brand of magic. He was still distributing condoms like seed corn to chickens when Schubert offered him partnership, a life in the circus, Rosanne, Ndolo. It would be a hard life teeming with joy and service. Would he take it? More condoms, more seed corn. Yes, he would take up the offer. He shook the hand of his new partner.

'Good. We are leaving tonight. We pack up straight after the show,' said Schubert.

The flying villagers came to land one at a time. The suits were deflated and stored away in the white Rolls Royce. The first condoms were pegged onto washing lines in those houses where occupants had been quick off the mark and by seven o'clock the steam had dispersed from around the winding-engine shed. The circus performers went through their acts as they had done the previous evening to applause as thunderous as any to be heard at the scoring of a try by the home team at the rugby ground. By the early hours of the next day, the loaded wagon pulled away, the big shire horse at last having something to do. The liberty horses trotted after it and between them the white Rolls Royce idled along, driven by Elyahou and with Rosanne and Mr Ndolo sitting in the back one at either side of the cold box.

Albert looked again at the bottle containing the iceberg but saw only water and marvelled at the sadness in science. Dissipation would be forever the way of the world.

'It were only a bit of ice, lad. 'Ow could it 'ave been from the *Titanic*? 'Ow could 'e 'ave brung it all this way, all this time. It 'd've melted lad. 'E were lyin' to thee, like 'e allus does,' said Bill Pettit.

Albert thought about the coloured bricks in the laboratory wall – inventing things from out of the darkness, like a cold box. He thought of Rosanne and grand'maman's tormented soul. Henrietta thought of Elyahou and wondered sadly if she'd driven him out forever. When the terrace awoke the next morning it was to find that the laboratory wall had been painted yellow. Outside and inside all the bricks were painted yellow. Albert would admit

177

to nothing and swore that he'd been asleep the whole night. Some folk said that it was the work of a boy from Castleford, Henry Moore, who had visited the circus that evening. Meanwhile the flakes of paint beneath Henrietta's nails wore slowly away.

19

Revelation in the dark

The cinema at which Lancaster worked the projector was a poky fleapit of a place called the Royal. There was nothing regal about it, however, and the regular patrons, a hard-nosed bunch of realists, preferred to call it the Pigsty after the name of the owner of the establishment, Mr Pinkofsky. It was a small building tucked between a public wash-house and the smithy. The former was responsible for the building's distinctive odour, it being carried on the clothes of the washerwomen who, in the afternoon certainly, formed about half the audience. The second neighbour ensured that the afternoon performances were accompanied by the continual clanking of metal as the farrier brayed and brayed again the objects upon his anvil.

Although it was a filthy place in which to operate, and even though Lancaster knew that he could have got a similar job at one of the many picture palaces which were mushrooming in the area, my uncle stayed at the Pigsty. For one reason Mr Pinkofsky shared his enthusiasm for film and often developed free of charge the celluloid products of Lancaster's fingers turning usually with great appreciation for the results. Of course, these short, experimental films were not shown to the fee-paying audience but Mr Pinkofsky would at odd hours make the cinema available for private showings and here was a very good second reason for staying on. Lancaster was able to view the fruits of his labour and even allowed to use the projection room for the editing of his film. Mr Pinkofsky hoped that one day they would be able to produce a commercial film together.

My uncle worked six days a week, operating the projector for two and sometimes three performances each day. Since the onset of my great-great-grandmother's illness Emily had assumed the responsibility of accompanying the family on their weekly cinema treats. It was only natural once her son had landed the job at the Royal (she never could bring herself to call it anything else) that support for the establishment should be seen to come from the family. It was a loyalty which Mr Pinkofsky could appreciate and prompted him to allow them in without payment. So it was that every Saturday afternoon the family would accompany Lancaster to work, take up their seats in an audience composed roughly half of washerwomen smelling deeply of chlorine and half of urchins who scratched and passed their fleas, and wait, with breath held to conceal their rising excitement, for their family member to load the spools and get the show underway.

One Saturday, due to a mix-up with the spools, Lancaster accidentally loaded the projector with the film he had himself made during the time in which he had been flying in a rubber suit. The audience, unsure of what they were viewing, (Lancaster too was unsure, for Mr Pinkofsky had only just handed him the recently developed spool), patiently waited for the action to commence. The opening unsteady shots of a crowd receding and filmed from above was novelty enough to keep them quiet. Then a short sequence in which a dumpy lady in tights and with ostrich plumes on her head fell upon a frail youth brought whoops of laughter from the washerwomen and a deep unseen blush from Albert. People dressed in animal costumes and floating in space caused uncomfortable speculation about the nature of trick photography. The sequence was met by a stony silence. There are some things that an audience would not accept even in the make-believe world of cinema. After a short interlude in which the camera seemed unable to decide where to deliver itself, the lens finally homed in on my family's earth closets and the surrounding ash-pits. A man was seen to walk along the path leading to the toilet, enter and, because the closets were devoid of roofs, was seen to drop his trousers and to sit upon our toilet seat. Why on earth Lancaster should have wished to film a man upon the toilet God alone knows, but there the camera lingered for a full five minutes amid howls of sheer pleasure from the cinema audience. It wasn't rude, don't get me wrong now, for the film was taken from almost directly above and the man's shirt tails adequately hid those bits which otherwise should have been censored out. But the audience rolled about clutching their sides and laughed at the little things people do when sitting upon a toilet. The man scratched his head right on the bald spot at the back. People fell out of their seats as he leaned forward to read the scraps of newspaper, probably the *Mercury*, strung behind the wooden door. Then as the man cricked his neck to view the sky and the unseen camera caught a face of desolate boredom the audience shrieked uncontrollably. As always when laughter becomes uncontrollable the pain came too. Oh, it hurts – it hurts, they shouted, seeking to fill their collapsed lungs with good air, most of which was outside the cinema. The man scratched his nose and twizzled his feet in the folds of trouser leg which hid them. From behind the screen the farrier rang his empty metallic sounds, braying the metal, and with tears streaming down their dirty faces they shouted stop, oh stop. Some just doubled up and keeled right over, but the film didn't stop; it kept right on running, and the farrier kept on banging. The man continued to sit and scratch and twizzle and read, then he suddenly stood up, a fragment of *Leeds Mercury* in his hand, lifted his long grey shirt tails and wiped his bottom.

'Cut, cut!' shouted Mr Pinkofsky, waving his arms frantically to the projection room, for he took seriously his duty to protect the public from such sights, but on this occasion the projectionist was unable to help. The public would have to suffer the crudity of the flickering images on the screen. Either that or hide its eyes; Lancaster was asleep. Hysteria mounted as the bottom on the screen wriggled. And what a dirty bottom it was too, a black bottom. The ghost of the closets came back to haunt William, and he thought what a dirty bottom Mr Tsiblitz has.

The urchin audience gesticulated, the washerwomen rolled in their seats and cried, and Henrietta, her heart leaden, her head stilled amidst all that simple joy, knew the cause of that bottom's blackness. Nobody could possibly read it but she knew her name was there, repeated many times. She beamed into the dark, hearing the torrents of hidden laughter then, carried on the bier of pointing fingers, she too began to howl until the stitch in her side pulled tight and thankfully at last sewed up the organ of mirth.

20

Thwaite, and how I came to possess a strange birthright

It's time now that I told you something of Thwaite. Thwaite circles the time of my family compressing the volumes of their history like grotesque bookends. At one end, in the beginning, sat Thwaite the family friend. For it was Thwaite, the mate of John Brightside who, at the very outset of my great-aunt Henrietta's chronicle, would tease my youthful forebear about his love for Jane Moore. Swallow him up boots and all, he'd said, and he was right. She did. It was Thwaite, the young mate who entered the darkness of the pit for the first time on the exact same day as John Brightside. Novices with only candles to relieve their gloom, they trapped the ventilation doors huddled together with rats for company. Eight years old, alone for ten hours at a stretch, they learned to amuse one another, learned to laugh together in an eerie darkness. Then as youths on to the tubs, chasing the lasses in their grubby skirts, chasing them and catching them in a torrid blackness that only those who'd been to hell could describe. And the two mates grew and learned to love. To love the women, to love one another as only best mates can. Then into their twenties and manhood, the one married, the other single but still in that stinking hole, the best of friends, trusting, trusting. For a hewer on his side, working an eighteen-inch seam, had to learn trust, and as the coal chipped away the trust grew and entwined them like trails of stonecrop growing from the crevices in search of the sun. The sun had to be there somewhere; even under the rotten earth they had to believe they'd find the sun. Trust in each other's ability to find the sun.

So, how come Thwaite ends up a coal owner and succeeding generations of Brightside finish up digging coal? I'll tell you, I'll tell you. The land all around both in our village and miles away in the village where Thwaite and John Brightside lived and worked was owned by one family. The Phillips had owned the land for centuries and there were good Phillips and bad Phillips, but at about the time of John Brightside's marriage Snotnose Phillips took up his inheritance and moved into the manor house. It was Thwaite who christened him Snotnose on account of the fact that, unlike his father, he could never demean himself to speak with anybody who lived on his land. It seemed that they were only to dig out his coal, fatten his cows and sheep and pay him rent for the privilege of doing so.

But Snotnose had a weakness; he liked a gamble. He was particularly keen on the cards and would spend weeks on end at his London club dissipating his fortune. So it shouldn't have come as a surprise to find that one day he'd suffered too heavy a loss and as part payment of his debt he had to sign over the deeds of some of his land to Viscount Fitzroy somebody or other, a man who had never travelled north of Grantham and frankly never had any wish to do so. The land which had changed hands wasn't worth much; it was poor land, and extended to a total of less than fifty acres. It didn't include the pit or the village where Thwaite and Brightside lived, but it did include an old disused pit and a few small farms and it was a shock to those people to find that the landowner was quite prepared to gamble away their houses and their stock at the turn of a card. But it must have been even more of a shock for them to learn that the Viscount didn't want the land or the stock, or their rents for that matter. To him, Yorkshire might have been as distant and as inhospitable as the North Pole for he immediately issued an offer (probably to rub old Snotnose's face in it a little harder, for he wasn't liked at his club either) to all tenants on the Phillips' estates. He offered to give to the first person who could provide him with four winners in a day's racing at an Ascot meeting title to the land which he'd recently won. Notices were posted on the farms which he then rightfully owned and soon the news had reached the ears of all who dwelt on the Phillips' estates.

Thwaite at first suggested that he and John Brightside should offer a combined entry choosing two possible winners apiece, but my great-great-grandfather protested that because his wife disapproved of gambling he could not lend his name in entry to such a competition. Thwaite thought about it carefully but his tendril was already trailing far ahead of that of John Brightside in search of the sun. He put forward an entry in his own name for the final day's racing at the summer meeting and his four choices came in. It was rumoured that another collier had provided the Viscount with four winners on the first day of the same meeting, but as the gentleman hadn't taken advantage of the tips given, choosing a different entry for that day, the form was declared void. I have no idea if there ever was truth in that rumour but the Viscount certainly used the Thwaite entry and accumulated a small fortune on the day, for all four horses were rank outsiders, and being the gentleman that he was he coughed up the title deeds.

On taking possession of the title (he was made to receive the documents at the London Club), Thwaite suggested that the Viscount should give him a percentage of his winnings from the final day's racing; after all, he told him, his winnings surely were much in excess of the value of the land. The Viscount was so taken with the cheek of the collier that he gave him £1000 on the spot. So Thwaite was learning the rudiments of capitalism even before he'd come into his property. Then on returning to Yorkshire, he sold the livestock, sacked the tenants and moved into the big house. He sank a pit on the land and built our village of terrace houses, then he invited the labour in, and one of the first to come up from the village where until so recently Thwaite himself had been living was the youthful James Brightside with his new wife Aggie. And they moved into our quiet house that first day to watch the teeming rain.

Then at the other end of our history, much older and fatter and with his top hat and cane, sits Thwaite the relative, my other great-grandfather. About nine months after Elyahou Tsiblitz's last visit our village experienced a baby boom; his condoms developed holes, I'm afraid. They appeared to be excellent on first using but reuse wore the fabric thin; eventually they burst, every single one of them. And there was no more of great-great-grandmother's female mixture to see the lasses all right. Well, as I say, there was Thwaite the bookend holding back the final volume for all he was worth and there was me bursting at his granddaughter's belly. And with John and James and Ernest and William right behind me, Thwaite couldn't hold it any more and I came tumbling into the world with waters and words and all ready to write more volumes. Old Dr Cartwright said I had eyes like my mother who in turn had inherited hers from the coal owner. A lively blue and forever searching he said they were, and told us all that it was a Thwaite characteristic and carried in the genes. He'd at last identified his vital spirits and his language had moved smoothly from one jargon to another. To Henrietta he confidently expounded a scientific explanation, a genetic explanation for the Brightside melancholia, but she turned away from the old doctor telling him that the stones no longer spoke to her. Then she explained that she didn't mourn the loss of what had been a very special ability.

'I'm pleased to hear of it,' he told her long and elegant back, and quietly to Emily and out of Henrietta's hearing he advised that the best thing for her would be to find herself a husband and settle down to child-rearing.

On first hearing of the pregnancy, Thwaite refused to speak to his granddaughter and threatened to cut her off without a penny but she said that she didn't care, for she loved William Brightside and he loved her too, and to prove it they were soon married at the church in the next village. But Thwaite stayed away from the wedding. Then came the birth and Thwaite stubbornly refused to have anything to do with my mother. On hearing that the child looked like himself, however, his attitude softened, and then when he learned that I should be given his name, Donald, he at last decided to pay me a visit. (I think, too, the name Westminster must have aroused curiosity.) When he saw me he cried, blubbered like a child on his granddaughter's shoulder and called my father Willie.

It was an extraordinary thing for the hardened coal owner to have done and Emily said that it was all the bad coming out of the man brought on by the sight of the angel in the cot. Then he took some documents from his inside breast pocket, signed them with Henrietta's pen which still resided with the rent book on the mantelshelf, and handed them to my mother. It was my birthright he told her. I had become the owner simultaneously of a coalmine, a cemetery and a museum, for he had assigned me the title to the disused pit at the bottom of Hunger Hill. We didn't see a lot of him after that, but Ernest still paid him three shillings and five pence rent each week, certainly until the week Thwaite died.

Epilogue

After the departure of Schubert's circus, Albert fell into a morose silence. It lasted until well after my christening and nobody in the family was sure whether it might have been because he had not had opportunity to use his condom (considering the population explosion, if it were so, then he must have been the only one not to), but Albert knew the reason for his mood only too well. For it was in his heart. Within its slowed beatings there was a pining for the woman he loved. Rosanne the rope walker, she of the sequined thighs and the falling breasts, she with a grandmother crawling towards God along the outer edge of the rainbow (what colour lane would that be) who had first quickened and then, on leaving, slowed his heart to a drawl. Lub! Lub! Worst of all, was the uncertainty. Who was her lover? Schubert? Ndolo? Tsiblitz? All three perhaps? Albert had to find out. But to find out would take money and they were probably somewhere on the continent by now. Who knows, France, Germany, Spain? He decided to sell his few possessions. He received four guineas for *The Blue Boy* (an inferior copy) and three guineas for the *Mona Lisa* (an even more inferior copy). An assortment of other paintings brought him another twelve pounds ten shillings. Less than twenty pounds was hardly enough with which to be planning a trip to Europe. Albert's dejection worsened.

One day he found some undeveloped photographic plates. They were the ones he had used years ago when photographing his great-grandmother the morning of his illness. An idle curiosity caused him to have them developed and when he received them back he saw that he had been filming his great-grandmother at the Roman Wall. On her head she wore a cap and she held an old suitcase in both hands, cuddling it beneath her ugly grin as she would a small child. Now Albert of course had heard stories of the old woman's fortune and so set off immediately for Hunger

Hill using his shovel as a walking stick. Albert dug earth from around the base of at least half the circumference of the wall but found nothing. He went back to the house and complained to the old woman that he couldn't find her money. He asked her where she'd hidden it, but she only reflected back his solitude by failing even to open her eyes. She breathed quick shallow breaths waiting for him to depart and he knew she wished him to leave her to whatever it was which she did when alone.

He dug more holes and found nothing. He sank holes on my land which that winter quickly filled when it rained and when Aggie came to visit towards the end of 1913 she commented how the village was beginning to revert to what it had been when she and James had first come there. Puddles were everywhere, and soft mud oozed through the very best leather squelching into the socks, but Albert found nothing and remained silent.

Then one summer night when the moon and stars were lined up, it seemed queueing above the pit head waiting to be cycled into the earth and shown the blackness of the mine below, and the dark stinking galleries would in magical turn accept the shining heavenly bodies and be cleansed for ever by their radiance, a big horse pulled a red wagon onto the common jolting the occupants over the uneven ground and caused them to wake from their slumbers beneath a comforting Mexican blanket. Schubert's circus came to rest once more beneath the gas lamp beyond our door. Mr Ndolo jumped from the small steps at the rear of the wagon and tethered the horse to the lamp standard. My great-aunt Henrietta on seeing that the circus had returned ran immediately from the house enquiring if Mr Tsiblitz was well and still with them.

'He's in the wagon,' Ndolo answered her.

She thrust her face between the canvas drapes at the rear to see Elyahou sitting up between the prone figures of Rosanne and Count Schubert who were still snuggled in the warmth of the blanket. A hurricane lamp hung above their heads.

'Mr Tsiblitz, I know what you have on your bottom,' she declared. The Transylvanian who had shaved all hair completely from his face and head coloured significantly, all but a healing scar on his crown that is, which remained stubbornly white. He had recently been fired from a cannon.

'I have a headache, Miss Brightside. Can it not wait until some other time?' he said.

'It certainly may not, Mr Tsiblitz. I have seen your bottom on kinematographic film and I know it has my name on it,' she insisted.

Count Schubert leaned across and tapped Rosanne 'This must be Henrietta Brightside,' he advised. His wife opened one eye, sat up in bed clutching the blanket to her beautiful neck. 'Not the Henrietta Brightside, child of charm, poetry and love,' she said with a snigger.

'What is it that you want?' moaned Elyahou, still nursing his head.

'I want what's mine, that which I stamped.'

'My bottom? You want my bottom?' He stood up in the wagon revealing himself completely to my great-aunt – and to my uncle Albert who had now joined her. Her initial reaction was to recoil, withdraw from the sight of the naked man, but she stood her ground.

'Yes. That and the other bits,' she said.

The Count and Rosanne started to laugh and playfully rolled about in the makeshift bed.

'Leave her be,' shouted Albert angrily from beside his aunt.

The count looked up, an expression of concern clouding his normally happy countenance. As Mr Ndolo somersaulted into the bed from the front end of the wagon, Schubert spoke: 'There's an awful lot of instruction being passed here, but I can't see any generals,' he said.

'I want what's mine,' my great-aunt repeated.

'And so do I,' sang Albert in the chorus of her conviction.

'Now look here,' Schubert said, allowing the blanket to fall from his shoulders and revealing his massive chest and rippling biceps, 'there's nothing that belongs to either of you in here, so please leave before I throw you out.'

'Chéri, chéri,' Rosanne said sulkily. She blew Albert a kiss and settled herself back into the bed.

My two relatives climbed down from the steps and walked back in that punctured night to our house, where smoke as always curled from the chimney.

Hours later war was declared on Germany. The news came hurtling from the other side of Hunger Hill and Albert went to the police station in Castleford. He told them that there were enemy aliens camped outside his house. An inspector and a platoon of infantry men were dispatched back with him and Schubert was arrested immediately. The inspector didn't like Austrians and Bill Pettit cheered the news from the window. After the inspector had consulted his map and found Transylvania to be a part of the Austro-Hungarian empire Elyahou too was arrested. When Bill Pettit told him that Transylvania was the place where Dracula came from, the inspector declared his aversion to vampires and decided that he didn't like Transylvanians either. He instructed the sergeant in charge to see that they were put on a train to France and then sent on to Vienna. Henrietta said that she would go too, for she was to marry Mr Tsiblitz. The inspector looked doubtful until she told him that he could take down the Transylvanian's trousers if he wished and would find her name imprinted on the man's bottom. The inspector allowed her to go, reasoning that there was no place for a woman of such doubtful moral worth in Britain at such a time of crisis anyway. Rosanne, however, was allowed to stay for she had such a lovely smile and the French too were our allies.

Bill Pettit argued that Mr Ndolo too should be arrested, but the inspector pointed out that the man was a citizen of the colonies. Mr Ndolo agreed and informed the inspector that he would like to join the British army, but on learning that he was hermaphrodite the inspector couldn't decide where to send him, so he put him in jail instead.

Albert moved in with Rosanne and lived in the wagon on the common for the duration of the war. He got a job in the pit but still had to pay my great-grandfather three shillings and five-pence rent each week for the space the wagon occupied under the gas lamp. Nonetheless by the time war had ended Rosanne could leap through a hoop of flame while on the aerial wire and her grandmother was never seen again in anybody's rainbow.

My great-aunt and Mr Tsiblitz were married in Vienna and Count Schubert was their best man. Henrietta was settled with some friends of Schubert in a classy Viennese suburb and the two men went off to war. They both joined the Austrian army as privates and quickly fell in with another soldier Ludwig Wittgenstein, the philosopher. They became an inseparable threesome, at least until Schubert bought one at Cettinje. It was soon after the death of Schubert that Tsiblitz confided to Wittgenstein the passion which his new wife had for thinking while immersing her hands and arms in water.

Meanwhile at home, Lancaster joined the Royal Flying Corps and Bill Pettit became an infantryman. Army life agreed with Bill; the regimentation of men was no different to the regimentation of the stacks in his head. He'd be a socialist when the bloody war was over, he told everybody; it was the death of anarchy. He hated bloody anarchy, he told them. He'd even been won over to the cinema. Watching a good story, with a beginning, a middle and an end from the rows and rows of seats in a darkened theatre; it was ordered. He'd learned to love the cinema, the death of anarchy. Bill died with a metal filing cabinet. It was painted battledress green and had louvred doors. The company was retreating, not very far; nobody went very far in that war – just to get there was a long way – but after that nobody went any distance. They were retreating only a few yards – from one hole to another. He and another man had been detailed to carry the filing cabinet. It was bitterly cold. He'd got his greatcoat buttoned to the neck and he'd been advised to wear his respirator; there was a possibility of gas attack. A bullet struck him and another hit the metal filing cabinet. He heard the ping as the bullet smacked into the metal. His tin helmet was still on his head and his respirator was in place as he fell back into the hole. He and the filing cabinet fell into the hole. Bill fell on top of the filing cabinet with its louvred doors. His greatcoat caught on some wire so he didn't fall all the way into the hole, just part way down the slope, and the filing cabinet which lay on its back looking up at the bleached sky prevented him falling any further too. It started to rain but it didn't prevent the gas from wafting across from one muddy hole to the next. Bill cursed everybody as he lay dying. Nobody came. Just the rain. It rusted the filing cabinet. Bill's flesh soon rotted. Even beneath the respirator the flesh disappeared. Bill became a skeleton with its feet resting on the rusted metal. The slats in the louvred door looked like rows of sandwiches, their brown crusts exposed. The pipe from the charcoal box to the mouth remained intact, like a short cable connecting nothing to nothing. Charcoal had spilled from the box, though. It was as if things had all poured out of his head, just like when he lived, but there was nobody there to rearrange the stacks. It was the kind of confusion Bill hated and he would have been glad not to be there.

GENEALOGY

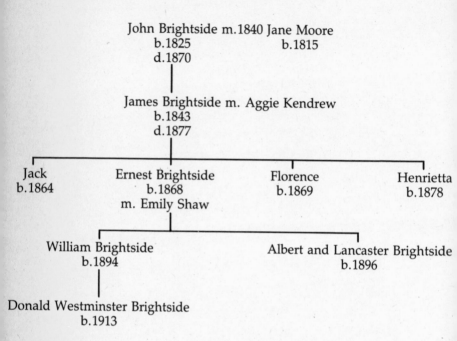

John Brightside m.1840 Jane Moore
b.1825   b.1815
d.1870

James Brightside m. Aggie Kendrew
b.1843
d.1877

Jack
b.1864

Ernest Brightside
b.1868
m. Emily Shaw

Florence
b.1869

Henrietta
b.1878

William Brightside
b.1894

Albert and Lancaster Brightside
b.1896

Donald Westminster Brightside
b.1913